"Lottie's Freedom allows readers to finish a beloved trilogy with a sigh, grateful for Tucker's skillful wordsmithing and the joy of escaping into hospitable Midwestern life."

—RJ Thesman, author of Life at Cove Creek Series

"A drop of mystery, a sprinkle of sadness and a splash or romance."

—Cindy Regnier, author of *Mail Order Refuge*

Lottie's Freedom

JANE M. TUCKER

CrossRiver
BREWSTER, KANSAS USA

One

*I*t must be here somewhere."

Lottie Braun ran an agitated hand through her fluffy white hair and looked around. Maybe it was under the pile of mail on her desk. She grabbed a letter, stared at it for a distracted moment, and dropped it back on the pile.

"Aunt Lottie?" Her niece Patti appeared in the doorway with little Sarah in her arms. "What are you doing?"

"I'm looking for that old photo of the Neverland Orchestra. After all my talk at dinner, I wanted to show you what the boys looked like."

Patti shrugged. "Don't worry about it. You've told me so many stories I already feel like I know them."

"But you really have to see how they looked in their suits, with their hair all slicked back. They were so young." She yanked open the top drawer of a metal cabinet and thumbed through the files. Neatly typed labels in alphabetical order helped to speed her search. Thank goodness for Miranda's orderly mind. "Personal Correspondence...Professional Photos..." Lottie yanked each one in turn and flipped the contents. "Where would she file an old photograph?"

Patti shifted her sleepy daughter to her other hip. "It's all right. You'll find it later. I washed the dinner dishes."

Lottie glanced up. "Thanks...Maybe she put it in the desk." She leaned down and opened a random drawer. More tidy files fanned out in front of her eyes. "That assistant of mine is an organizational genius."

Patti sighed. "Okay. It's bedtime for Sarah. I'll put her down for the night and come help you search."

"Thank you." Lottie planted an absentminded kiss on her great-niece's smooth cheek and resumed her search. As she checked each file in turn, the muffled sounds of Sarah's good-night routine drifted in from down the hall. First pajamas and brushing teeth, then snuggles and a picture book. Last of all, Patti tucked the eighteen-month-old into bed and turned out the light.

Lottie raised her head to listen as her niece began to sing. Patti's voice, light and sweet like her mother Helen, brought on a flood of memories. Long before Helen had a daughter of her own, she had raised her baby sister when their mama died too soon. She'd sung that very lullaby to Lottie many times when the wind blew or the storm raged around their snug farmhouse. Now, as Patti sang the comforting words to her own daughter, Lottie's eyes welled with tears. Helen would have loved the connection of mother to daughter to granddaughter—with one maiden aunt thrown in for good measure.

She was still lost in thought when Patti spoke at her elbow. "Have you looked through that mess on the desk?"

Lottie jumped. "Mess? What mess?" She followed her niece's pointing finger to the pile of mail. "Oh. That."

"The picture might be lost in there." Patti's eyebrows lifted. "A lot of things might be lost in there."

Lottie shrugged. "That's the mail I've gotten since Miranda left."

Patti shot her a quizzical look. "You haven't opened your mail for a full week?"

"She doesn't want me messing with her filing system." A defensive note crept into Lottie's voice. "I do open my own mail, you know." When I have to, she added silently.

Patti reached for an envelope. "I could organize the pile, if you want."

"Would you mind? It has gotten a little out of control." Lottie bent her head over the file drawer. "I'm just not good at office work. I've always had an assistant to take care of it."

"Lucky you." Patti dropped an ad for cosmetics in the trash and picked up an envelope. "I'll put the bills in one pile and the letters in another. Do you throw away all your junk mail?"

"I don't know. Is that what most people do?"

Patti's voice quivered with amusement. "I'll throw it away."

Relieved, Lottie pulled another file from the drawer. "You're a dear to help out. Miranda does take care of so much. Which reminds me." She looked up. "I've got a dress that needs to go to the dry cleaner."

"And?"

"I don't know where Miranda takes them."

Patti stopped sorting and stared at her in astonishment. "Do you mean to tell me you don't drop off your own dry cleaning?"

Lottie shook her head, feeling sheepish. "Not usually."

"Mom always went to Pelham's on Second Street." Patti held up a cream-colored envelope with fancy writing on the front. "This looks urgent. Maybe you'd better open it."

Lottie glanced at the return address. "No thanks. I don't need anything the Los Angeles Philharmonic is selling."

"What have you got against them?"

"It's nothing personal. I just don't go to L.A."

Patti turned the letter over. "Mind if I open it?"

"Go ahead. You won't change my answer."

Patti slid her finger under the flap and withdrew a typewritten letter. "Dear Ms. Braun," she began.

"There's a form of address I really don't like," Lottie said with a smile. "'Miz Braun'. There's nothing wrong with an old-fashioned 'Miss.' All the Mizzing in the world won't change the fact that I'm not married, and I'm not ashamed to own it."

Patti looked up. "Would you rather I read this to myself?"

Lottie shrugged. "Makes no difference to me."

"All right, then." Patti resumed her reading. "Your secretary has made it clear that you are not interested in receiving the Los Angeles Philharmonic Orchestra's first annual Lifetime Musical Achievement award. Still, I wish to make one last appeal. You have distinguished yourself during your long and accomplished career. Not only have you redefined the standards of piano performance, you have also generously paved the way for all who came after you. For these reasons we desire to honor you. We hope you will see fit to grace the city of Los Angeles with your music for the first time ever at our upcoming awards concert.

"I hope you will give our offer your thoughtful consideration. We believe giving you the Lifetime Achievement Award offers a rare opportunity for mutual benefit. Please call my assistant, Richard Morgan, if you wish to pursue this matter.

"Sincerely, Ernest Fleischmann, Executive Director."

Patti smoothed a crease in the paper. "A lifetime achievement award? That sounds exciting."

"Yes, and a 'rare opportunity for mutual benefit.' That's a nice bit of double talk." Lottie pushed a file folder back into the desk drawer. "It means they'll plaster my face on billboards all over southern California and raise the ticket prices to extortionate levels."

"You don't know that for sure."

She shuddered. "I'm not interested in finding out."

"Do you avoid L.A. because of what happened all those years ago?" Patti waved a dismissive hand. "Nobody blames you for that, Aunt Lottie."

"That doesn't mean I want to return to the scene of the crime." Lottie's voice was sharp. Until recently she believed everyone blamed her for the death of her nephew, Billy. Certainly, the toddler would not have choked if thirteen-year-old Lottie had stayed home with him that night. The guilt had defined her entire life and caused her to live in frozen isolation despite her success as a pianist. Only last fall, because of Helen's forgiveness, had she begun to understand she could be free from the events of her past. Helen didn't hold her responsible for the boy's death, and neither did God.

Still, a shiver of fear went through her at the thought of seeing that city again. She wouldn't willingly go back to Los Angeles.

"I don't understand why it's such a big deal." Patti glanced at Lottie's face and set the letter on the pile. "Never mind. It's none of my business." She picked up the junk mail pile and dumped it in the trash. "Why don't you call Miranda about the missing photo? You have her phone number, don't you?"

Lottie glanced at her watch. "It's a little late to call tonight."

"California is two hours behind us." Patti shrugged. "It's only seven o'clock there."

Lottie brightened. "I'll get the number."

A minute later she dialed and twisted the telephone cord around her index finger.

"Hello?" The woman who answered had a slight accent.

"Miranda Charles, please. This is Lottie Braun."

The woman hesitated slightly. "One moment."

"Lottie? Is everything all right?" Miranda sounded concerned.

"I've been looking for that photo of the Neverland Orchestra. I've searched all your files, and I can't find it anywhere."

"All my files?" A note of worry stole into Miranda's voice. "Did you put them all back?"

Lottie glanced around the paper strewn office. "I will when I'm done. You'll never know I was here." She avoided Patti's ironic gaze.

"Check the storage boxes in the closet for your photo. That's where I store all your personal mementos."

"Hold on a moment." Lottie set the receiver on the desk and opened the closet door. Sure enough, she found the photo in the first box she picked up.

She emerged triumphant from the closet just as Patti picked up the receiver. "Hey, Miranda? Tell your boss she should go to L.A. and pick up this lifetime achievement award. …Yeah, that's what she said, too, but I think she should go."

Shaking her head, Lottie reached for the phone. "I found the photo."

"Oh, good." Miranda sounded cautious. "Did I do the right thing to refuse the invitation from the L.A. Phil?"

"Of course. How is your father?"

"Still unconscious." Miranda hesitated. "Since it's a head injury, the doctor can't predict when he'll wake up. I need to stay another week or two, if possible."

Lottie closed her eyes. Could she go without an assistant for another two weeks? "That's fine. You need to be there for your family."

"Oh, thank you, Lottie." Relief filled Miranda's voice. "I don't deserve this. Oh, and by the way, your Mercedes is due for an oil change next week."

Lottie smiled. "I know, dear. That is the one thing I can keep track of."

She hung up and looked around. "I'd better clean this place up. Miranda deserves to come back to a tidy office."

Patti scooped an armful of files off the floor. "She sounds pretty caught up in her family's life. Are you sure she's coming back?"

"Of course, she is." The very idea gave Lottie chills. "What would I do without her?"

Her niece chuckled. "Pick up your own dry cleaning?"

She let the pointed comment slide, her attention on the photo in her hand. "Can you believe how young they all were?"

Patti glanced at the group in the picture. "There's something about black-and-white pictures that makes everyone seem old."

Lottie pointed to a tall, solid-looking young man at the end of a row. "Do you know who that is?"

"Is it my dad? Those little wire-rim glasses were awful on him."

"I thought he looked nice."

"Nope. Too serious." Patti stretched and yawned. "I've got a big day tomorrow. I guess I'll get some sleep."

Lottie glanced at her niece. "What time is Mitchell picking you up?"

"It depends how late his study session goes tonight." Patti's fiancé, Mitchell Harms, was temporarily living in Iowa City while he studied for his long-delayed bar exam. The February exam was only two weeks off, with their wedding to follow soon after. "He's hoping to be here bright and early, though. We have a nine o'clock appointment at the bakery."

"That sounds like fun."

The bride-to-be wrinkled her nose. "It would be, if Mitch didn't have so many opinions about things."

Lottie chuckled. "You two are well-matched in that area."

"What about you?" Patti said. "Isn't Sam picking you up at nine?"

Lottie groaned. "I guess all the Harms men are early risers. To be fair, though, auctions are an early business. The bidding starts at noon."

"We'd both better get to bed, then. Good night." Patti gave her aunt a hug and went on her way.

Left alone, Lottie set the picture on Miranda's desk and gave it a fond pat. "I guess I'll tell her more about you boys some other time."

The clock above the sink ticked loudly in the silent kitchen. Miranda took one last half-hearted bite of sambal and rice and set down her spoon. "Lottie didn't know she was calling at dinner time."

"It was rude all the same." Her mother's amber eyes sparkled with irritation. "You should be grateful. If your father were here, he would not even have let us answer the phone."

"Thank you, Mother." Miranda gave her a look of irony. "I needed to take that call. I would like to have a job to go back to once Dad is on his feet again."

Sonia Charles bristled. "She doesn't sound like a good employer if she would fire you for not answering a phone call."

Heat rose in Miranda's face. She'd come home to help out in a crisis, not to be treated like a ten-year-old again. She had forgotten what it was like to have every decision questioned by her parents.

Across the table, her brother Zac caught her eye and gave an imperceptible shake of the head. She took a steadying breath. "Are you going back to the hospital tonight?"

"Yes, of course." Her mother pushed her chair back. "We need to be there when your father wakes up."

"I wish you'd stay home and get a decent night's sleep." Miranda touched her mother's arm. "The doctors said Dad's recovery is going to take time. You'll need your strength to help him."

Sonia turned away. "We will take turns sleeping in the waiting room."

"I'm not going back," Miranda said as gently as she could manage. "I'll stay here and do some cleaning tonight. Tomorrow morning I'll take your place so you can come home and sleep."

Miranda steeled herself for a fight that didn't materialize. Instead

Sonia turned to her son. "Zac, get your coat. We will leave in five minutes."

"I'll be ready." Zac waited for her to leave, then turned on his sister. "You're just staying home so you can call your boyfriend."

"What's wrong with that? I'm going back to him once Dad is on his feet again."

He glared at her. "What if he never gets better? What then?"

Yes, what then? Would she go back to Iowa then? She pushed the thought away. "Now is not the time to talk about that. He's going to be fine."

Sonia returned, her purse on her arm. "Zac, aren't you ready yet?"

He jumped up. "Sure, Mom. Let's go."

The apartment door closed behind them, and Miranda gave a sigh of relief. After seven solid days of family togetherness, she needed some time alone.

A week ago, she'd been shocked to hear Zac's panicked voice on the phone. Their father had been hit in the head by a wooden beam that fell from a shelf in his warehouse. He was in a coma. They needed Miranda to come home.

She hadn't heard from her family in five years. She'd nearly wept with relief to think they hadn't forgotten her. But any rosy visions of reconciliation had died in her first few days here. Her mother ignored Miranda's absence and treated her like she'd never left—like she was still a rebellious schoolgirl who needed to comply. Her father lay unconscious in that sterile hospital bed, unable to respond to anything they said or did. And Zac, who had sounded so desperate on the phone, seemed to resent her presence.

Jason Harms called while she was scouring the kitchen sink. His voice sent a thrill through her. "How is your dad today?" he asked.

She sat on one kitchen chair and propped her feet on another. "No change. He's still unconscious."

"What do the doctors say about his condition?"

"They're not encouraging. There's no guarantee he'll survive. If he does recover, they say he'll always need a wheelchair."

As she related the medical details of her father's case, she felt the tension inside her begin to unwind. Jason listened carefully, stopping her once in a while to ask a question. His steady sympathy calmed her fears. "So, you won't be coming home any time soon," he said when she finished.

"Not for a few weeks."

His voice deepened. "You do know how much I want you back, right?"

"That's the only thing getting me through right now."

"What does your mother think of your Iowa boyfriend?" When she didn't answer, he added, "You have told her about me, haven't you?"

"I haven't had a chance. All of Mom's attention has been taken up by my dad."

"That's understandable, I guess." He sounded uncertain.

"I will tell her, though. When the time is right." She squeezed her eyes shut, imagining his dear face. "Jase, I love you. I'm coming back to you as soon as I can."

Two

Mitchell Harms arrived early Saturday morning and kicked the snow off his boots before stepping into Lottie's warm kitchen. His smile lit the room as he kissed his fiancé and lifted Sarah into his arms. "How's our girl today? Are you ready to taste some wedding cake?"

Sarah patted her new daddy's cheeks with small hands and repeated the operative word. "Cake."

Lottie gave the little family a fond smile. "How goes the studying, Mitchell? Are you ready to pass the bar exam?"

Mitch flashed a grin. "I'd better be. I've got a job offer riding on it."

Patti gasped. "You got the job with Milton and Milton? When did you find out?"

"They called last night."

"On a Friday night?" Lottie said with admiration in her voice. "You must be someone special."

"He's the smartest man I know." Patti tucked her hand into the crook of his arm. "We'd better not be late. The bakery's doing us a favor working us in on short notice."

Mitchell raised his eyebrows. "Short notice? The wedding is still a month away."

Patti threw her aunt a laughing glance. "Like I said. Short notice."

They left hand-in-hand, their exuberant laughter perfectly audible from inside the kitchen. Lottie watched as they hurried down the walk,

15

Sarah toddling along between them, and met Mitchell's dad Sam, who was just arriving. Mitch conveyed his news about the job offer, and after a stunned moment Sam enveloped his younger son in a big bear hug.

When they parted, Sam squatted in the snow to greet the little girl and pack a snowball for her to carry to the car. Sarah gazed at him with trusting eyes; she and her future grandpa had developed a promising friendship.

"Milton and Milton, huh?" Lottie said when Sam reached the house. His face shone with pride. "How about that?"

"So he won't be going into partnership with Ed Williams?"

"No. All that boy can talk about is moving to Chicago."

"Too bad." Lottie adjusted the collar of her red wool coat with a gloved hand. "I hate to think of them raising Sarah so far from family."

"Agreed." He held open the door for her. "We'd best get going or we'll miss the auction."

She stepped past him and down the porch steps, with Sam following close behind. "How far away is Columbus Junction?"

"About an hour. That's why we're getting an early start."

"It's a pretty day for a drive." Lottie turned to wave at the bow window of the house next door. Nathan Bartholomew waved back as usual. The wheelchair-bound professor had become Lottie's neighbor last fall, once he'd gotten the rundown little bungalow modified to meet his needs.

Sam caught the exchange and rolled his eyes. "I see he's watching your house again."

"Not just my house. He keeps an eye on the whole neighborhood."

"And you don't find that strange?"

"Not really. When you live alone for years and years, you develop a few quirks." She smiled up at him. "I should know."

He gave her a sidelong glance. "There's a difference between quirky and creepy. I think he rides the line."

She chuckled. "If I didn't know better, I'd say you sound a little jealous." She knew it wasn't true. Lottie and Sam were simply good friends.

His face relaxed in a rueful smile. "Not jealous. Concerned."

Lottie pulled up short at the sight of the faded blue Plymouth Fury parked in front of her garage. "We're taking Bessie? I figured you'd have the work truck, in case you buy something big."

Sam opened the driver's side door. "The truck's in the shop. If I buy a large item, I'll have Jason pick it up on Monday."

She hesitated. "We could take my car. We'd make better time."

He slid behind the wheel. "Bessie does just fine."

Suppressing a sigh, Lottie climbed in beside Sam and settled back against the vinyl-covered bench seat. She sympathized with Sam's attachment to the car, a relic of the happy years before his wife died. But old dependable Bessie depressed her. She'd much rather ride smoothly along in her cherry red Mercedes with its soft leather upholstery and V-8 engine.

"Speaking of Jason," she said as Sam drove down the alley, "I talked to Miranda last night. She asked for another two weeks' leave."

His eyebrows drew together in a slight frown. "That's not good news. Jase is driving me nuts with his absentmindedness. If his girl stays away much longer, I'll have a crazy man on my hands."

"Sounds like she's gotten pretty bogged down in her family's problems. He may have to go out to San Francisco and bring her back." She looked out the window at the passing farm fields. "Tell me about this auction. Is it a big one?"

"I'd say so. It includes all the household goods and a barn full of tools. Another case where the family farm has no one to take it over. Sad."

An hour later they drove up a dirt lane, parked Bessie in a makeshift lot and waded down the slushy lane toward the sale. "I want to start in the barn," Sam said. "Why don't I meet you when the bidding starts?"

He strode away and she headed for the house to see what wonders it might hold. At the door she signed the auctioneer's list, took a number, and joined the line of strangers straggling through the first floor.

She made short work of the front room, where boxes of books vied for space with an old stereo console and a dusty record collection. Lots of Elvis and Bing. Nothing substantial.

She moved on to the cramped dining room where a long table stood against one wall, crammed with odds and ends. People stood two-deep around it, craning their necks to see. She waded to the front and spied a cast-iron train engine, painted green, with the Lionel brand name printed on one side. It brought back memories of her cousins at Christmas, playing trains after dinner in Aunt Cora's attic. Turning it over, she frowned. In neat letters on the bottom, a long-ago owner had painted his name: Johnny Higginbottom.

She stared at the toy, chasing a wisp of a memory. The name rang a bell deep in her mind, but she couldn't quite make the connection.

Someone poked her in the back. "Hey, lady."

Eyebrows raised, she glanced over her shoulder. "Yes?"

A barrel-chested man with a walrus mustache pointed at the train. "You can't take that with you."

She looked down her nose at him. "I'll be finished in a minute." Setting it back on the table, she walked away, her mind on the puzzle she'd discovered.

In the kitchen she picked up a casserole dish and found a return address label glued to the bottom. Mrs. James Higginbottom, Route 12, Columbus Junction, Iowa. "Higginbottom," Lottie muttered under her breath. Columbus... "Excuse me." She turned and pushed her way back through the crowd to the registration table. "Can you tell me the name of the family that lived here?"

The girl glanced sideways at her coworker. "I'm not supposed to."

Lottie tried to look appealing. "Not even their last name?"

"Sorry."

A square-jawed woman in a blue parka stepped up to the table. "I'm the daughter of the family. I can tell you what you need to know."

The sun was just beginning to peek through the windows of Oakland General Hospital when Miranda reached her father's floor Saturday morning. She found Zac asleep in the waiting room, his lanky body stretched out across a row of chairs. He looked young and defenseless, without the guarded expression he usually wore, and she was surprised by a wave of love for the little brother she'd grown up with.

"Zac."

He opened his eyes and sat up in one fluid motion. "How's Dad?"

"I haven't gone in yet. Why? Did something change during the night?"

He rubbed his eyes and yawned. "The nurses were worried about his blood pressure, but I think they got it stabilized."

"You should go home and get some real sleep. I'll stay here." She reached out to smooth his hair, but he ducked.

"I'll go if Mom doesn't need me." The defensive note was back in his voice. "I gotta go to the bathroom."

She watched him cross the waiting room, hands stuffed in his sweatshirt pockets, tufts of black hair sticking up at odd angles. Before he pushed open the bathroom door, he pulled his Walkman headphones off his neck and settled them on his ears.

At twenty-one, Zac was an odd mix of boy and man. Unlike Miranda, he had never lived away from home. Instead he'd done everything his parents asked, graduating from the local community college and working for his dad's construction company. Ever since she'd come home, her mother had lost no opportunity to remind her: Zac was the compliant one, Miranda the rebel. He had gained his parents' favor. She had lost it.

Zac's attitude was harder to read. One minute he was the man of the house, protective of his mom while his dad was sick. The next, he blazed with resentment because she still ordered him around.

He emerged from the bathroom with his hair slicked into place, and she joined him in the hall. They walked in silence to the room where Dad lay in semi-darkness, his body swathed in sterile white sheets.

Sonia looked up from her seat by the bed, lines of exhaustion etched around her eyes. "No change."

The defeat in her tone went straight to Miranda's heart. "It's going to take time."

"So they tell me." Sonia stood and swayed wearily. "I need breakfast."

Miranda reached out a steadying hand. "Go home and sleep, Mom. I'll stay."

Sonia stepped away from her. "I am all right."

Miranda threw her brother a pleading look.

He put an arm around their mom. "She's right." His voice was gruff. "Let me take you home for a few hours. Miranda can call you if anything happens."

To Miranda's relief, she gave in. "All right, Zac. If you say so."

As he herded her out of the room, he looked back with a grin that was half-apology, half-triumph.

She shrugged and turned away. It was only natural that her mother would depend on Zac in a crisis. He was the son of the family. Even though he had no blessed idea what to do in these circumstances, he was still the one in charge.

I don't mind, she told herself firmly. In a week or two I'll go back to my life, where I answer to no one.

The thought didn't comfort her as much as she would have liked.

Before she settled in for the day, she opened the shades. Sunshine poured in, illuminating the figure in the bed. Her dad was not tall, but his compact frame was sturdy. He was a capable craftsman who commanded the respect of his workers. With his reputation for hard work and fair wages he never lacked for good employees.

Many of those men had dropped by to pay their respects this week. Sonia treated them like family and took great comfort in their warm wishes. But their presence made Miranda vaguely anxious. These men had been thrown out of work by Dad's injury. They couldn't afford to be idle for long. Their visits would inevitably taper off as they found jobs with other companies.

One visitor stood out from the others. Balan Prakash, the son of her father's second cousin, had arrived in San Francisco after Miranda left for college. A slender, clean-shaven man in his late twenties, he had greeted Miranda with quiet friendliness the first time they met. "Uncle Suresh will be happy you have returned, cousin Miranda. He has always spoken well of you."

His comment surprised her very much.

Every time he stopped to check on Dad, her mother glowed with pride. "Balan lived with us when he first came," she told Miranda after they met for the first time. "Your father gave him a job in the office, and he's done wonders for the business. He is very good with numbers."

Her meaningful glance seemed to suggest he was also a matrimonial catch, but maybe Miranda was reading too much into it.

She wasn't sure what to think of this new member of their family. He seemed like a decent man, but something about him rubbed her the wrong way. Maybe it was the way he could carry on a conversation without saying anything important. Maybe it was simply jealousy that in her absence he had somehow become Sonia and Suresh's oldest child.

She settled into the chair by the bed and pulled today's newspaper out of her bag. The headline read, "Reagan Prepares for Second Inauguration," but she couldn't muster any interest in Nancy Reagan's new beaded gown.

She wondered again about Dad's business. He probably had jobs scheduled months in advance. Was everything running smoothly in his absence? What would happen when the scheduled jobs ran out? She had tried to bring up the subject with her mother, who refused to discuss it. "This community knows your father," she'd said firmly. "They will take care of us. Besides, we have Balan. He will keep things running until your father is on his feet again."

Miranda hoped she was right.

Lottie watched Sam pack his purchases into the trunk of the old sedan. "Do you think it will all fit?"

"Yep." He stacked a mint-condition electric drill on top of a box of brass hardware. "Would you hand me that hose?"

She passed him the green coil. "What are you going to do about the rocking horse?"

"It'll go in the back seat."

"And this crate of motor oil?"

He straightened and looked at her. "Mind if I put it on your side? You can set your feet on it like a footstool."

They finished loading the car and started for home. Lottie propped her long legs accordion-style on the oil as they chatted about the auction. The crowd had been in a bidding mood, and several items had gone for more than Sam thought they were worth. "People go crazy at auctions," he said.

She chuckled at his pitying tone. "I notice you paid extra for this oil I'm sitting on."

He shrugged. "It's the kind I use for Bessie. Besides, I like the crate it comes in. People are always looking for stuff like that to put in their living rooms."

She wrinkled her nose. "Do you think you can get the motor oil smell out of the wood?"

"I've done it before." He jerked his chin toward the back seat. "The real treasure was that rocking horse. I haven't seen one of those in a long time."

Lottie turned to look at the item in question. The big wooden horse was in rough shape, with unattached runners and ears chewed off by some unauthorized barn resident. "You paid an awful lot for that heap of kindling. Can you really restore it?"

"Sure."

"And then what? Will you sell it?"

He glanced at her. "I want to give it to Sarah. Do you think she'll like it?"

Lottie gazed at her friend with warm admiration. "She'll love it."

He nodded at the cast-iron train in her lap. "I'm not the only one who got auction fever. You seemed pretty set on having that train, even when the other guy pushed the price up."

She patted her new toy. "I took exception to his mustache."

"I didn't know you liked trains."

"They make me feel nostalgic." She ran a finger over the name painted on the bottom of the toy. "Did you know that farm belonged to Johnny's family?"

He glanced at her. "I figured. There aren't too many Higginbottoms in the world."

She chuckled. "That name is a mouthful. No wonder he changed it to Johnny Columbus." Johnny was the co-founder of the Neverland Orchestra, the swing band where Sam and Lottie first met as kids. She turned to look at his profile. "I talked to his sister for a while. She said Johnny settled in California after the war. He wanted to be a studio musician for one of the big movie companies. She couldn't remember which one."

"Is that right?" Sam's tone was neutral. "What's he doing now?"

Lottie shrugged. "She doesn't know. They lost touch a long time ago."

"Too bad." He pointed down the road at a tidy farmstead. "We put a new kitchen in that house last year. Nice folks."

"I like their red barn." Lottie smiled at her friend. "Sam, why does every drive in the country become a tour of your old remodeling jobs?"

He gave her a startled glance. "Am I that bad?"

She chuckled. "I don't mind. You have every right to be proud of your handiwork."

His face relaxed. "I'll try not to bore you."

"You don't." But she didn't always appreciate his lectures on the finer points of home construction. "What kind of wedding cake do you want those kids to pick?"

"Chocolate cake, white frosting. There's no other option."

She raised her eyebrows. "I beg to differ. White cake with raspberry filling is nice. Or what about spice cake and espresso flavored icing?"

"You're kidding." He gave her a disgusted look. "No fancy coffee for me."

For the rest of the drive home they kept up a lively debate about the right way to throw a wedding. They disagreed about most of the details, which only made the arguing more fun. As they reached Lottie's neighborhood, she sighed. "I guess there's one thing we can agree on. Patti and Mitch belong together."

"Right you are." Sam pulled up next to Lottie's garage and frowned. "That sycamore outside your living room is dying. You need to have it removed before it falls over."

She looked in the direction of his pointing finger. The tree seemed fine to her. "I'll get someone to look at it come spring."

"I can cut it down if you want."

She patted his arm. "You're a busy man. I don't want to add to your workload."

Lottie felt a pang of sympathy for Sam's kids as she hurried up the walk. He really liked to give advice.

"Hello, neighbor." Nathan was rolling down the ramp that led from his house to the garage. "How's that big orange cat of yours? I haven't seen him around lately."

"He's been hiding in the house during this cold snap." She smiled fondly at the thought of Marmalade. "He's a lazy old thing at heart."

Nathan grunted. "I'd sooner call him a stone killer. The mice aren't safe in this neighborhood, thank God." He put his wheelchair in motion again. "Give him my regards."

Sam watched until Lottie was safely inside before he headed down the alley. He had one more stop to make before he went home, and he needed to get there before sunset.

The cemetery lay cold and still beneath its blanket of snow. Sam parked in the lane and unearthed a beat-up broom from Bessie's overstuffed trunk. He hadn't brought flowers. Nancy never had much use for hothouse bouquets. Too expensive for her taste, especially in January.

Snow crunched beneath his boots as he made his way to her grave. Once he'd swept off the stone he stood and looked at it, his gloved hands stuffed in his coat pockets for warmth. "Hullo, Nance."

She didn't answer of course. He'd gotten used to that. She'd talked his ear off every day when she was alive. Now it was up to him to keep the conversation going.

"Patti and Mitch are here this weekend. They're picking out the wedding cake today." The crisp winter air seemed to amplify his voice. He looked around to see if anyone had heard, but he was alone in the cemetery. All the same he stopped speaking out loud.

Those two were good together, Mitch and Patti, just like Nancy always said they would be. If she'd lived, she would have been overjoyed to dance at their wedding. He smiled at the thought. Come to think of it, he was pretty proud of his younger son. It did the heart good to watch him with little Sarah, treating her like she was his flesh-and-blood daughter. Ready-made fatherhood was not a job every man could stomach, no matter how sweet the child was.

On the other hand, Jason was driving him nuts. Seemed like he was missing half of himself with Miranda gone.

Sam was struck by that idea. The boy really had found his other half in the dark-haired beauty from California. If he had any sense, he'd carry her back to Iowa and propose sooner rather than later. Not that he'd take his dad's advice. Nobody did anymore.

Nancy would have loved that auction today. She'd have approved of the motor oil. She was thrifty that way. More than once she'd bought half-empty bottles of cleaner from a sale just to stretch the budget.

Lottie wouldn't dream of doing something like that. She probably didn't even clean her own house. Didn't have to. What she'd spent on that toy train would have kept Nancy in groceries for a week.

Not that you'd know it to talk to her. Lottie didn't put on airs. People knew she had class just by being around her. He admired her for that.

They'd had a good time today. Even when she started talking about Johnny, he'd been able to change the subject. She talked about the Neverland boys too much for his liking. It wasn't good the way she romanticized those years. She seemed to have forgotten all the drinking and gambling the band members did, and all the in-fighting about who carried the biggest workload.

Sam had been thirteen when his older brother pushed him into playing the drums, and sixteen when Eva Reed and her police detective husband gave him a permanent home in New York City. The years in between had been the roughest time of his life. Unlike Lottie's fiercely protective sister, Sam's older brother had expected him to fend for himself among the other band members. At best they'd ignored the half-grown boy. At worst they'd taken out their frustrations on him. He couldn't count the number of times he'd been casually tripped or kicked or shoved out of the way by one of those "great guys" Lottie remembered so fondly.

Things had improved when Lottie showed up. The band finally had an audience draw: A cute little kid who could really play that keyboard. Lottie was their meal ticket, a kind of side show act who ensured a good box office take. Everyone knew they were riding her coattails, from old Mr. Schultz right down to young Sam. The only person who didn't seem to understand was Lottie herself.

Sam had treated her pretty rough at first. At fourteen he'd thought of Lottie only as a dumb little show-off, but her sweet temper and lack of vanity had gradually won him over. In the end they'd become friends.

She was as sweet now as she'd been back then. Maybe that was why her cockeyed memories of her Neverland days made him so mad. Her stories about Johnny were his least favorite. Sam had no respect for that guy, and Lottie's attitude bordered on hero worship. He just didn't get it.

He knew what Nancy would say. She'd say Johnny needed Jesus and Sam had a responsibility to tell him so. That was the same thing she'd said about his brother Walt. She was right, too. But Sam wasn't any good at sharing his faith. He'd left that stuff up to his wife.

He scuffed a hole in the snow with the toe of his boot. And what would Nancy say about Lottie? Would she understand the warmth that existed between Lottie and Sam?

That was a question he'd rather not answer.

Sam shivered and looked around. Streetlights glowed in the gathering dusk. "I'm keeping Bessie in good condition, Nance. She still runs like she did the day I bought her for you." He picked up the broom and turned to go. "Happy birthday, sweetheart."

Three

By three o'clock, Miranda had reached her limit of television. She'd finished with the newspaper, including the puzzle page. The latest issue of *Architectural Digest* lay on the floor by her feet. She told herself she was glad Zac had managed to get Mom to rest for so long, but that wasn't strictly true. She was sick and tired of her own company.

Her father lay unmoving in the bed, as he had all day, serenely unconscious of his daughter's restlessness. Never a talker, Dad was eerily silent now.

His beard, now flecked with unfamiliar gray, had grown in the week he'd lain unconscious. In her memories it was clipped close to his chin and soft to the touch. As a little girl she had idolized her father and followed him everywhere with wide trusting eyes. Her mother had been the disciplinarian, the one who made her eat her vegetables. Dad was always coming home from work with some new delight: a plywood box for her doll clothes, a tiny bird he'd carved from scrap lumber.

Those simple gifts had given Miranda concrete evidence of her father's love, but they'd given her something else as well: the desire to make things with her own two hands. On the rare days when he had taken her to work with him, she'd played happily in the sawdust on the floor of his workshop. When she grew a little older, he'd given her two boards, some nails, and a hammer, and she'd been the happiest child on earth. Zac had whined and begged to go home, but not Miranda. She could have stayed at her father's workshop for days on end.

If she'd only been a boy, she might have gotten her wish. But her father wanted his son, not his daughter, to follow him into business. The older Miranda got, the less welcome she was in her father's workshop. Eventually he forbade her to come to work with him at all. "Construction is a man's world," he told her. Her beloved father had become her unyielding opponent.

Her last memory of him was the fight they'd had the night she left home. "It's a full-ride scholarship to a great school, where I can study architecture." she'd said for the fiftieth time. "Why are you against it?"

He had repeated his stand. "Your place is here with your family. Go to a local college. Find a man from our community. What good will that professional degree be to you when it's time to marry and raise children?"

"You'll never understand!"

Miranda wiped a stray tear from her cheek. She'd give anything for one more chance to reconcile with him. "Get well," she whispered to the man in the bed. "Oh, please get well."

When she reached her limit of silence, she wandered down the hall to the nurses' station. A nurse about Miranda's age sat at the desk, writing notes in a patient's chart. As she worked, she sang along to the radio behind her. She looked up when Miranda approached. "Can I help you?"

"Not really." Miranda gave her a tentative smile. "I'm just taking a break from sitting with my dad."

The nurse nodded. "You have to do that sometimes." She leaned across as the song ended and turned up the volume on the radio. "I've been waiting for this new DJ to come on. He calls himself Vindaloo Z. He's really fun."

Miranda wasn't sure how to respond to this. The DJ's name implied he was Indian—or he could be making fun of the Indian community. Cautiously she said, "What kind of music does he play."

"Anything, really." The nurse shrugged. "Some New Wave, a little hard rock. And something he calls Indi Pop."

Miranda was only half-listening. Down the hall, a stranger was knocking at the door to her father's room, and his boots and cowboy hat told her he was not a doctor. "Excuse me," she said to the nurse, and hurried down the hall to see what he wanted.

"Are you looking for Suresh Charles?" she asked the stranger.

"Yes, I am." The man removed his hat, revealing a full head of gray hair underneath. "I heard about his accident. Real sorry. I'm Dan Hollis, by the way."

She shook the hand he offered. "Miranda Charles. My father has more friends than I ever suspected. Do you want to see him?"

He darted a glance toward the room, and back at her. "As long as I'm not imposing."

She ushered him into the room and took a seat in the visitor's chair. Dan Hollis stood next to her father's bed, his expression sober. "Your dad's a good man. He's built a strong business."

"Yes, he has," she murmured.

He cleared his throat. "Suresh and I have worked on a lot of jobs over the years. When he was starting out, he was my go-to man for electrical work."

Miranda smiled. Her father had started out as a one-man business, with his wife keeping the books.

"These days he's my competition, but sometimes we help each other out." He shook his head. "He's careful to a fault. Drives me nuts, the measures he takes to keep a job site safe."

"That sounds like him."

He rotated the cowboy hat in his hands. "I was surprised that your dad of all people would be hurt on the job like that."

She blinked. "It was a freak accident. A wooden beam slid off a shelf in his warehouse. It hit him before he had time to react."

"Yeah, I heard." His bushy eyebrows drew together in a frown. "If it can happen to him it can happen to anyone, I guess. Makes a man think." He glanced at her. "Listen, your dad's recovery is probably going to take a while. If there's anything I can do to help in the meantime, just say the word."

She took the card he offered and studied the black lettering: Hollis Construction. Daniel P. Hollis, CEO.

"Well, I'll be seeing you." He left before she could think of a response.

When Mom and Zac arrived, she showed the card to them. "A man named Dan Hollis dropped by. He offered to help out while Dad is sick."

"Dan Hollis? Pah!" Mom took the card from her and tore it in half. "We have plenty of help from our friends."

Miranda looked at Zac, who shrugged. "We hate Hollis."

"Why?"

"Dunno. We just do."

Sonia threw him an exasperated look. "Hollis Construction is the competition. Balan helped your father see that Dan Hollis always tries to undercut his business."

Miranda drew her brows together. "Mr. Hollis respects Dad, though. He said Dad has high safety standards."

"He probably made it sound like a fault instead of a virtue."

Miranda couldn't argue with that.

Sonia raised her chin. "Your father is very careful, and for good reason. The first time he didn't wear his hard hat, look what happened. It's a good thing Balan hadn't gone home yet, or nobody would have found him until morning." She walked around the bed and picked up Dad's hand. "Hello, Suresh. You are looking better today."

Miranda looked at her father. His face had not changed.

Sonia continued. "Zac and Miranda are here with me. We all want you to wake up and join us." She looked up. "He needs to know he can't stay asleep forever."

Lottie put the toy train on the kitchen windowsill and set down her purse. Static crackled in the air as she peeled her wool coat from the sweater underneath. She hung it in the front closet and returned just in time to see her purse tip over and spill its contents on the floor.

"Oh, mercy!"

She picked up all the odds and ends and stuffed them back into her bag—all except a yellowed bundle of letters, which she carried to the music room.

The letters had occupied a corner of her thoughts ever since Johnny's sister handed them to her that morning. "I don't know what else to do with these," Maria Wheeler had said. "Mother kept them in case Johnny came back to Iowa, but he never did. Seems like fate, you asking about him today. Since your sister is the person they're addressed to, I wish you'd take them home."

Lottie had protested that Helen was gone, but it made no difference to Maria. "I want you to have them. Mother was heartbroken when Johnny left. I feel like I'd be breaking faith with her if I threw them out."

"Why didn't he ever come back?" Lottie asked.

Maria shrugged. "Dad was always real hard on Johnny. When he came home that summer during the war, at first Dad was pleased. He thought Johnny had finally gotten music out of his system and would settle down and help him on the farm. But my brother had some other reason for coming home." She nodded at the letters. "I guess it had something to do with your sister. Anyway, he and Dad finally had a big blow-up fight, and Dad pretty much disowned him. The letters were returned after Johnny left."

Lottie lowered her gaze to the packet in her hand. "What do you expect me to do with these?"

"Throw them away if you want. I don't care." Maria had turned away. "Just take them off my hands."

Lottie settled on the love seat in the music room and slipped the rubber band off the packet. Four letters, all addressed to Helen Turner, all postmarked Columbus Junction in July 1944. Each yellowed envelope bore the message, "RETURN TO SENDER" printed in block letters. The one with the earliest postmark had been neatly slit open.

She ran her finger across the fuzzy edge of the open envelope. Had Helen read this one before sending it back? Probably not. Helen had been deeply depressed after Billy died. She'd hardly left her room at Aunt Cora's for months on end. More likely Aunt Cora or Uncle Otto had taken one look at the first letter and rejected the rest.

Helen would probably say she was glad she hadn't gotten those letters. Her life had turned out better without Johnny than it ever could have with him. Still, Lottie felt a pang of sympathy for the lovesick young man who had followed her sister home to Iowa.

What would Sam say? She'd meant to talk it over with him before the conversation veered off in another direction.

It almost felt deliberate, him changing the subject like that. He often did it when she brought up the Neverland. Well, maybe she did talk about those days a lot. After forty years of silence, it felt good to remember happier times. She'd been genuinely delighted to meet Maria Wheeler this morning and to learn something more about Johnny's life.

Until last spring she'd thought of Johnny as a great friend of her childhood. She'd admired his brash good looks and constant high spirits, which had carried the Neverland along in their wake. Sure, she'd been angry with him for a while after she read Helen's letter. His actions in Santa Monica had been irresponsible in the extreme. But to Lottie's mind the time for blame was past. They'd all been young and stupid. Surely the intervening years had brought wisdom, even to Johnny Columbus.

So the question remained: What should she do with his letters?

Setting aside the envelopes, she crossed the room to her magnificent Steinway and played a few preliminary chords. She focused her gaze on the wall opposite, where a child's purple dress hung in its shadowbox between the French doors. Helen had made that dress for Lottie's eleventh birthday when they first joined the band. She treasured it as tangible evidence of her sister's love, a now-fading reminder of her odd and wonderful childhood.

If she could, she'd gladly turn back the clock to the year she wore that dress.

Simple chords took shape beneath her hands, filling the room with a sacred melody from centuries past. The ancient Bach hymn turned her thoughts to prayers as she sifted through the matter of Johnny's letters.

Reverend Summers taught that everything happened for a purpose. Maybe God had a plan for this, too. Maybe He wanted Lottie to track Johnny down and return the letters. Or perhaps He simply wanted her to take them off Maria's hands and throw them away. It was hard to tell with God.

When the final chords faded, she reached a decision. The letters were none of her affair. To Maria, they symbolized her mother's love for a prodigal son, and for that reason Lottie was glad she'd accepted them. But the time had come to get rid of the past. When the final chords of the hymn faded, she picked up the bundle and started for the kitchen.

Marmalade met her in the hall, meowing loudly. She knelt to scratch him between the ears. "What's the matter, fella? Is it supper time already?" He rubbed his head against her knee to reward her correct guess. "We'd better get that taken care of."

Setting the packet on the counter, she reached into the cupboard for a can of cat food. She was dumping it into the dish when she heard the crunch of tires on gravel. As the car door slammed, she reached for the letters and tossed them in a drawer, safely out of sight.

"Did you order a cake?" she asked when Patti and Sarah walked in.

"Yes, and we checked on the tuxes and added boutonnieres to the flower order." Patti looked at her aunt with a puzzled smile. "What are you still doing here? I thought you were having dinner with Cal and Teresa tonight."

"Oh, my goodness, you're right." Lottie ran agitated fingers through her hair. "I'm late. Do I look all right?"

Patti looked her over critically. "You might want to change your sweater. Otherwise, you look wonderful as always."

Cal Jefferson had been Lottie's first ally in the Collison College music department. He and his wife Teresa, an English professor, lived in a small house on the south edge of campus. Its demure white exterior contrasted wildly with the colorful interior, where Cal's collection of jazz concert posters made bright splashes on the living room walls, and a big abstract oil painting took pride of place in the dining room. Lottie enjoyed the young couple's company. Their wide range of interests always made for lively and unpredictable conversation.

"So the new performing arts building has finally reached the planning stages," Cal said as he passed the potatoes. "I wish I knew who donated enough money to get the ball rolling. I'd like to shake his hand."

"Me too." Lottie knew quite well who had made the donation. She'd cashed in a couple of CDs to make it happen. She didn't plan to broadcast that fact, however. "I understand the college will need to do some fundraising to raise the rest. Any idea how they'll go about it?"

"I'm guessing they'll hit up the alumni. Why?"

She shrugged. "We're a performing arts department. Shouldn't we get up a show of some sort?"

Teresa laughed. "A benefit concert. That's perfect!"

Cal looked less excited. "Where are we supposed to have it? Our auditorium is falling down around our ears. It's the main reason for the new building."

"So, we invite the public to a great show in a lousy space. Let them get a first-hand look at the reason for the building fund. They're more likely to give if they understand the need." Lottie sliced a bite of pork chop. "Any idea who'll be on the committee to choose an architect?"

"All the usual suspects," Cal said. "A trustee, a member of each department, and one or two people from the community. Do you want to be on it?"

Lottie chuckled. "Me? I know nothing about architecture."

"And everything about a good performance space," Cal said. "You're the perfect candidate."

She shook her head. "I'm sure whoever they choose will be just as well-versed as I am in the needs of a music department."

Teresa gave her a teasing smile. "You don't want the chance to design your next office from scratch?"

"My little office suits me just fine." Lottie waved her fork in the air for emphasis. "It has charm and function, and thanks to Elaine and all the excitement last fall, it even has a certain amount of lurid history."

Teresa shuddered at the mention of Elaine Woodson, the mentally unbalanced woman who had harassed Lottie when she first arrived. "Why would you want to remember that?"

Lottie smiled. "I made a lot of friends while that was going on.

Nothing cements the bonds of friendship like a crisis."

"Speaking of friendship...." Cal looked at his wife, who nodded. "We have an idea to run past you, but we're not sure how you'll take it."

Lottie set down her fork and sat back, suddenly wary. "Let's hear it."

"We'd like to write a book about the Big Band era," Cal said. "A thorough, scholarly treatment of traveling orchestras like the one you were in. I'll do the research, and Teresa can write the book. She does a great job with this kind of subject."

"There are already plenty of books about that period," Lottie said. "How would this project add to the subject?"

Teresa took up the argument. "Sure, people have covered Benny Goodman and Glenn Miller. The famous bands were few and far between, yet they get all the attention. We want to study the rest of the crowd, the small players who toiled on the dance hall circuit. For instance, your time as a child performer is fascinating. If you'll trust us, we can write it down for posterity."

Cal leaned forward, his face alight with excitement. "I want to tell how you won that talent contest and went on to land a job with a regional dance band. Lots of people remember those years when they spent Saturday night at the local dance hall. They should know the real story of that life."

Lottie frowned. "You won't find much information about the Neverland. It's not like they kept any records."

"Give me a chance. I'm a very good researcher."

Teresa caught Lottie's gaze, her eyes soft. "Look, you don't have to tell every detail of your story. We understand there are things you don't want to make public. But your fans would love to know more about you. How about giving them a glimpse of your real childhood?"

Lottie sighed. "It's worth exploring, I suppose. What kinds of things do you want to know?"

Cal's face lit with triumph. "For one thing, how did the Neverland Orchestra get started?"

A memory flashed into her mind. "It all started when an unemployed baritone named Walter Harms met Johnny Columbus playing his trumpet on a Chicago street corner."

Teresa leaned in. "Walter was Sam's brother, wasn't he?"

She nodded. "Their parents had died in an accident the previous year, so Walt was responsible for his little brother's welfare. That's how Sam ended up in the band."

Cal and Teresa were born academics, Lottie thought as she pulled the Mercedes into the garage. Imagine being excited to write about an obscure subject like regional dance bands of the Big Band era. They had their work cut out for themselves.

Young Thomas Allen was walking up the alley when she emerged from the garage. "How is the music going, Thomas?" she called out in greeting. "I haven't heard you play in a while."

He looked glum. "We practice in Kyle's basement when it's cold like this."

"It's a cold night for a walk, isn't it?"

He kicked at a loose piece of ice with the toe of one sneaker. "I don't have a car."

She gave up. "Well, take care. Say hello to Faye for me."

His frown deepened. "We broke up."

With that he turned and trudged away.

Lottie watched him go with a pitying smile. Poor boy. Seventeen could be a lonely age. It certainly had been for her. That was the year Madame D'Abri had arranged for her to study in Vienna, a lone American girl in a country where she didn't speak the language. And while she was gone, Madame had died. Lonely indeed.

She was getting ready for bed when she remembered Johnny's letters. Could Cal and Teresa use them for research?

She retrieved the packet from the kitchen and curled up in the middle of the bed to examine it. Maybe she should read that first letter to see if it would be useful to Cal. Since the envelope was open, no one would ever know. If it wasn't historically significant, she'd throw them all away.

With careful fingers she removed the brittle stationery from its envelope and spread it before her on the bedspread. Bold black hand-writing scrawled across the page.

Dear Helen,

I'm here at my father's farm, missing you like crazy. Yesterday I hitched a ride to Westmont and asked around til I found out where they're keeping you. I knocked at the door, but your aunt answered warned me off like a prison gard. Said you didn't want to see me but I know she was lying. They better be treating you o.k. or else!

Meet me at the station in Collison on Thursday at 3 and we'll take the flier back to CA. The kids are safe with your family now. You've taken care of everyone for so long you deserve to have someone take care of you for a change.

I hope to God this reaches you somehow. I'll see you at the station.

Love forever,

Johnny

The letter was all Johnny: Ardent, sweet and badly spelled. Lottie might as well be looking at a photo of the carefree young man with a thing for her lovely sister. It sounded like he didn't know about Billy's death. Somehow it made him seem like less of a jerk for following her married sister back to Iowa.

She slipped the letter back into its envelope and placed it on the stack. On the other hand, he'd taken it for granted that Helen would turn her back on the child and hop on a train with her new love. It hurt to see his lack of character laid out so clearly in black and white.

Lottie put the letters in the top drawer of her nightstand and turned out the light. She couldn't show them to Cal and Teresa.

She climbed into bed and lay back, her mind on the proposed research project. She'd be happy to help out any way she could. No doubt Sam would, too. But a successful treatment of the subject would require many primary sources. If only she could find some of the musicians she'd worked with back then. Their memories would be a gold mine. But where could she look for them now?

The thought crystallized as she dropped off to sleep: Maybe Johnny wasn't the only Neverlander who followed a music career to California.

Four

Lately Sam looked forward to Sunday morning more than any other day of the week. Sharing a pew with Lottie on one side and Jason on the other brought him the greatest contentment he'd known since Nancy passed. He didn't ask himself why that might be. He just wanted to bask in the moment.

He knew people were beginning to talk about all the time he spent with Lottie. Well, let them. Anyone who seriously thought a small-town contractor and a world-famous pianist could be anything more than old friends was touched in the head.

The sermon wound to a close and Reverend Bob Summers gave the benediction. Sam followed Lottie down the center aisle and stopped with her to greet the minister at the door. "You're looking pretty tan for January, Bob. How was Florida?"

"It was beautiful." The minister gave him a hearty handshake. "The reunion with my seminary class was a lot of fun. It felt good to spend time with people who knew me way back when."

Lottie beamed at the minister. "I know what you mean. I've been thinking about old friends quite a lot lately."

The lilt in her voice caught Sam's attention and made him smile.

"You always take interesting trips," Bob Summers said to her. "What do you have planned for this year?"

She looked mysterious. "I have a chance to go somewhere exciting. I'm thinking it over right now."

"You seem pretty happy about this new opportunity," Sam said on the way home. "Want to talk about it?"

Her eyes lit up. "The L.A. Philharmonic Orchestra wants to give me a lifetime achievement award. I'm considering going to Los Angeles to accept it in person."

He thought this over with his customary caution. "Are you sure you want to do that? Your fans might not like it."

She flashed him a quick smile. "I think my fans would love it. I can't count the number of times someone from southern California has written to ask when I'll play nearby."

"But you don't play L.A. It's part of your story."

She shrugged. "Stories can change. This would simply be a new chapter. Anyway, that's not my only good news."

He was beginning to feel a little out of his depth. "Oh?"

"Cal and Teresa want to write a book about regional bands of the early '40s." She was talking fast, her voice full of excitement. "They're especially interested in the Neverland Orchestra."

Sam's world tilted a little on its axis. "You mean they'll write about Walt and Johnny and all the rest? Is that a good idea?"

Confusion flitted across her face. "Yes. Why wouldn't it be?"

A trickle of sweat formed under Sam's collar as he searched for something positive to say. "It'll be a hard subject to research, won't it? There's nothing written down about those little dance bands."

"I know," she said. "They'll probably have to rely on oral histories from the band members. That's the other reason I want to go to L.A."

His heart sank. "To find Johnny?"

She glanced away. "Not just him. I think some of the other guys settled there, too. I ran into Bobby Richards in Santa Monica once."

He frowned. "When were you in…?" The truth dawned. "You mean when you were a kid? You saw Bobby in Santa Monica way back then, and you think he's still there?"

He felt her recoil before the words had fully left his mouth. "I guess it does sound like a dumb idea," she said after a moment. "Never mind."

Sam glared out the windshield at the road ahead. He shouldn't have taken the wind out of Lottie's sails like that. Now she looked like a whipped puppy and he had no idea what to do. "There must be other ways to track down some of the guys," he said finally. "If you still want to, I mean."

The return of her smile was his reward. "Cal and Teresa can start by interviewing me and you."

The idea didn't thrill him, but Sam held his peace. He couldn't risk chasing away that smile again.

They passed Thomas Allen trudging down the sidewalk about a block from Lottie's house. "That boy walks all over town these days," she said.

He caught the note of sympathy in her voice. "Good for him. Walking builds character."

"I feel sorry for him," she said. "There's a limit to how much band equipment you can haul on your back."

This made him smile. "You always take the musician's angle."

"Not only that," she said. "I think his girlfriend left him for a guy with a car."

Sam rolled his eyes. "She sounds pretty shallow. He's probably better off without her."

She shook her head at him. "You try telling that to a seventeen-year-old boy."

Miranda walked briskly up the block from the parking lot to the hospital, stopping just long enough to adjust her collar in the window of a card store. The place was closed, which surprised her until she remembered it was Sunday. The days were beginning to run together.

Mom and Zac had stayed the night with Dad again, with the understanding that Miranda would relieve them this morning. She was glad they'd come up with a plan that allowed Mom to take a break. She'd been more energetic last night, more like the feisty mother she remembered.

She crossed the hospital lobby and paused at the bank of pay phones against the far wall. By the time she'd gotten home last night, it had been too late to call Jason. Maybe she could sneak downstairs sometime today to talk with him.

Balan was with her mother when she reached the room. He leaned against the windowsill in a striped dress shirt and gray trousers, his leather shoes scuffed at the toe. He greeted Miranda with a friendly smile. "I was just telling Aunt Sonia how much better Uncle Suresh looks today. I truly think he is beginning to recover."

Sonia turned to her daughter. "Balan was telling me about a story he read in the newspaper. Recently a man was hit in the head, like your father, and his coma lasted only two weeks. Balan thinks he could wake up any time now."

Miranda nodded, her mind on other matters. "Balan, I've been wondering. Does the company have any jobs scheduled for this week?"

Mom's smile disappeared. "Miranda, there is no need…"

Balan shrugged. "I don't mind." His open gaze didn't quite meet her eyes. "As a matter of fact, we do."

"And for next week?"

He nodded. "And for next week, too."

"Good." Her thoughts sped on to another subject. "Are you able to make bank deposits? Or did only Dad do that?"

"I have authority to do the banking in your father's absence."

"Good." She ignored his slightly sarcastic tone. "So, you've been able to issue paychecks to Dad's employees. Now, what about the work crew? Do you oversee them?"

"No. Each crew has a supervisor who reported—reports"—with an apologetic nod to Sonia—"to your father." He stood up. "I can see we're upsetting your mother with all this business talk. Why don't you stop by the office sometime this week? I will show you around and give you a better feel for things."

She jumped at the suggestion. "I can come tomorrow."

Faint frown lines appeared between his eyebrows. "I apologize, but Mondays are always very busy. Call me at the office, where I can look at my calendar. We'll schedule something for later in the week." He leaned down and kissed Sonia's cheek. "Time for me to go."

"Oh no, Balan." Sonia stretched her hand toward him. "Stay as long as you like."

He looked into her face, his smile warm. "I have to leave now to get to church on time." At the door, he looked back at Miranda. "Don't worry. I'm doing my best to keep the business going."

As his footsteps receded from earshot, Sonia rounded on her. "How dare you question Balan like that? He is doing his best in a bad situation. We should fall at his feet with gratitude, not question his competence."

Miranda shrugged. "I just want to know how Dad operates his business. I have a little experience with businesses like his."

"What experience?" Sonia scoffed. "You're too young to know much."

"It's obvious Balan is competent," Miranda said quietly. "I'm sure he doesn't mind my questions."

"Of course he minds. He's not accountable to you."

"Well, I hope he's accountable to someone. Otherwise he might feel free to"—she searched for a nonthreatening example—"skim from the coffee fund, say."

"But we know Balan. He is family." Mom's hands were on her hips now. "I would sooner accuse you of that. You are more of a stranger to me."

Miranda had no answer for this.

Sonia turned to Zac, who lounged against the wall beside Dad's bed. "Give me my purse. It's time to go home."

"Coming." He picked up the leather bag and handed it to her. Sonia settled it in the crook of her arm and swept out of the room, Zac following in her wake. At the door he looked back with an odd, almost approving smile, but he said nothing.

As the hospital room fell quiet around her, Miranda realized she was trembling. A stranger. Her mother's words had pierced her protective armor. She was a stranger here.

She settled into the chair by the bed and stretched out her legs. Might as well get comfortable. Stranger or no, she was the family member on duty. She leaned her head back and closed her eyes. Why had she felt the need to stir up trouble like that? Mom knew the young accountant better than she did. If she said he was a trustworthy friend, who was she to doubt it?

She opened her eyes when the nurse came in to tend to Dad. The woman gave Miranda a friendly smile. "The waiting is hard, isn't it?"

Miranda nodded, grateful for a friendly face. "Do you think we'll see any change in him today?"

"Hard to say. We're going to give him a bath now, to prevent bedsores. Would you like to stay or step out for a few minutes?"

Watch her father take a bath? "I'll wait outside."

She stood in the hall for a moment, then headed for the elevator. With any luck, Jase would be home from church by now.

He picked up on the first ring, the delight in his voice unmistakable.

"You don't mind the reversed charges?" she asked.

"I'm a single guy with an AWOL girlfriend. What else would I spend my money on?"

She leaned her forehead against the wall and smiled. "I'm coming back, you know."

"I know." He sounded serious now. "How's it going out there?"

She pinched the bridge of her nose. "I managed to get my mom all riled up."

"How'd you do that?"

As she poured her tale into his sympathetic ear, she began to feel a bit better. It always helped to talk to Jase.

"Let me get this straight," he said when she finished. "This Prakash guy is good-looking, educated, and he's a shirttail relative of your Dad? Your mom is probably hoping you'll marry him."

Miranda laughed. "Stop joking."

"Think about it. If the two of you got hitched, she could keep her daughter nearby and make him a true son of the family."

"That's not going to happen."

"There's one sure way to get her to stop thinking about it."

She smiled. "Tell her about you?" His silence confirmed her guess. "I will, when the time is right. And today is not that day."

"I'm sorry you're having a rough time," he said. "You were trying to look out for your family, and you got slapped for it."

"That's it exactly. I've always loved the company Dad built. I just want to make sure it runs smoothly while he's sick."

He was quiet a moment. "It's possible your Mom would have blown up no matter what you said. People under pressure sometimes let it out that way."

She smiled a little at his serious tone. "In that case, it makes perfect sense that she'd yell at me. She seems bent on making Zac out to be the perfect son."

"You mean he's not?"

"No." The word exploded out of her. "He's—I don't know, absent, somehow. Like this whole thing with Dad is keeping him from important business elsewhere." As soon as she said it, she knew it was true. Zac wanted to be somewhere else.

"Where?" Jase said, interrupting her thoughts.

Where indeed? Five years' absence had robbed her of an answer.

She closed her eyes. Suddenly she was finished with Zac and his mysteries. "What about you? How's your dad?"

"He's fine. I saw him at church this morning. With Lottie, of course."

"Of course." Her employer's odd friendship with Sam always made her smile. "Has anything changed?"

"Nope." Jase sounded amused. "Dad's moving pretty slow."

She laughed. "Like father like son. You moved pretty slowly at first, too."

"Well, he'd better wake up. A woman like Lottie must know a lot of interesting men."

"And yet she's only interested in your dad."

"You think so?" He sounded pleased.

"I do."

Monday morning Lottie practically skipped up the stairs at the Performing Arts Building. Today was the day to begin some new adventures.

Her first stop was Cal's office on the second floor. "I've got some source material for you," she said, pulling the old studio photo of the Neverland out of her bag. "Here's the group in 1942."

Cal examined the picture closely. "Can you tell me who's who? It won't be much use without names."

"I made some notes." She pulled a piece of notebook paper out of her bag and handed it to him. "I wrote down everything I remember. Names, hometowns, that kind of thing. If I had any hunches about where they are now, I wrote that down as well."

"That's great." Cal glanced at his watch. "We'll have to take this up later. I've got a meeting downstairs in five minutes."

They walked together to the main staircase, passing Nathan's office on the way. "Did you hear?" Cal said. "Nathan's going to represent the music department on the PAB building committee."

"Better him than me," Lottie said, and meant it. Committees were not her strong suit, especially without Miranda to help keep the paperwork straight. Nathan would be a strong advocate for the department.

Her sense of anticipation returned as she headed for her office. One adventure begun. One to go.

After she taught her morning class, Lottie called the L.A. Phil and asked for Richard Morgan. "Mr. Morgan no longer works here," said a nasal female voice. "I am Amelia, Mr. Fleischmann's new assistant. How may I help you?"

Lottie cleared her throat, surprised to find she was nervous. "This is Lottie Braun. I wanted to speak to Mr. Morgan regarding a lifetime achievement award. I have a letter here from Mr. Fleischmann."

"You must have received that letter a while ago." Amelia sounded anxious. "Richard Morgan left this job three weeks ago."

Lottie glanced at the date at the top of the page. "You're right. It's taken me a while to respond to the offer."

"This is rather awkward. Mr. Fleischmann took your silence as a refusal. A week ago he offered the award to Vladimir Horowitz."

Lottie swallowed around a lump in her throat. "Did Mr. Horowitz give you a commitment yet?"

"He accepted right away."

Disappointment drained the warmth from her cheeks as she hung up the phone. After all the times she'd rejected the L.A. Philharmonic, of course they'd taken no for an answer. How could she have thought they'd wait forever?

She gave herself a mental shake. Three days ago she hadn't known this opportunity existed. She still felt ambivalent about it. The whole thing might have been a terrible idea. And yet she couldn't shake this sense of loss.

"Knock, knock." Katherine Snelling, the head of the music department, stuck her head around Lottie's door. "Are you going to lunch soon? Whoa." She pulled up short at the sight of Lottie's face. "What's wrong?"

Lottie shrugged. "I just got rejected by the L.A. Philharmonic."

Katherine frowned. "What are you talking about?"

Lottie told her about the award. "But they're giving it to Vladimir Horowitz instead." She attempted a smile. "Apparently we're interchangeable. Like cogs in a machine."

Katherine patted her shoulder. "I'm pleasantly surprised you talked to them at all. It takes courage to change your ways, especially in this case. Think of the publicity."

This brought a smile to Lottie's lips. "I'm pretty sure that's why they wanted me. 'Lottie Braun Plays L.A.'. They could sell a few tickets to that spectacle."

"By the way," Katherine said as they started down the hall, "Cal says you want us to stage a benefit concert for the PAB."

Lottie rolled her eyes. "Word gets around fast in this place."

Katherine smiled. "I think it's a good idea. Scheduling will be the biggest problem."

"What if we combine it with the March recital? We can feature a mix of students and professors." Lottie smiled. "Maybe we'll catch the interest of both the parents and the alumni that way."

Katherine nodded. "It can't miss as long as you're the last act of the evening."

After lunch, Lottie took her dress to the dry cleaner.

The woman behind the counter looked at her curiously. "I've seen this dress before, but you're not the one who brought it in."

Lottie smiled. "You met my assistant, Miranda Charles. It is my dress, though."

The woman's eyes widened. "You're Lottie Braun? Well, this is a thrill. I'm Doris." She wrote up the slip and handed it over. "Your dress will be ready Thursday after two o'clock."

"Be careful of the beading," Lottie said.

"We always are." Doris set the ticket on the counter and looked past her. "Next?"

Out in the parking lot she ran into Sam. "This is a surprise," she said.

"I'm dropping off my good suit," he said, pointing at the bundle under his arm. "I have to be sure it's ready for the wedding."

She chuckled. "Sounds like Patti's been giving orders again."

The lines around his eyes crinkled when he laughed. "You guessed it. Say, what did you decide about Los Angeles? Will your trip interfere with the wedding?"

Her smile faded. "I'm not going out there. They decided to give the award to someone else."

For a moment she could have sworn he looked relieved. "Sounds like it worked out for the best. No sense digging up painful memories." He nodded toward the shop. "Well, I'd better get my errand run."

She watched him cross the parking lot, tall and lean, his shoulders slightly bowed by a life of responsibility. When he looked back and smiled, she caught a glimpse of the boy she'd known so long ago.

Cal set his tray down next to Lottie in the faculty dining room on Tuesday. "Teresa and I spent last night examining that photo of the band. It's very interesting."

She looked up from her salad. "You don't think it's a dead end?"

"Of course not." His enthusiasm made her smile. "You gave us several names we can follow up on."

"How will you go about it?"

"For starters, a lot of those men served in the military." He waved his fork in the air as he talked. "We can look for their names in various service records. The trombone player who lost part of his hand. What was his name again?"

"Bobby Richards."

"He probably won a medal, so we'll check those lists for his name. You remembered the home state of most of them, too, so that helps." He pointed the fork at Lottie. "But the first thing we're going to do is interview Sam Harms. He'll be able to fill in more details about his brother."

She nodded. "Give him a call. I'm sure he'd be happy to help."

Nathan rolled up to the table and set his brake. "What's this I hear about a benefit concert in March? That's pretty short notice."

Lottie shrugged. "Not if we showcase music the students have already mastered."

He glared at her. "Do you really think people will pay to see student performances? Most of the time they can go to those for free."

Cal jumped in to defend the idea. "The department heads have really gotten behind this idea. We'll showcase the very best of our music, theater, and dance students, with a few professors thrown in for good measure." He nodded toward Lottie. "With the great Lottie Braun as our last act, we can't miss. When was the last time you saw a world class concert pianist for just ten dollars?"

"That's all you're charging?" Nathan stared at them, unsmiling. "So you sell cheap tickets to wealthy alumni, give a good concert in a terrible space, and pass the hat at the end?" He shrugged. "That could work."

"You left out the townspeople," Lottie said. "They'll support this project too, if they're given a chance."

Nathan grunted. "Fat lot you know. The town and the college are cordial enemies."

"And on that note." Lottie scooted back her chair and picked up her tray. "I'll see you both later. I've got class in a few minutes."

She was halfway across the quad when the president of the college caught up with her. Norman Isley was short and rotund, with a booming voice. "I wanted to talk to you about the PAB building committee. I know you said you didn't want to be on it, but I thought you'd like to have a say in who is appointed."

She glanced at him. "I don't understand."

Dr. Isley chuckled. "You own a controlling interest in the proceedings, if you will."

"No, I don't."

The man's eyes protruded a little farther from his round face. "Because of your donation, I mean."

She stopped in her tracks and faced him head-on. "Look, Norm. I told you before. The donation is anonymous. I don't want recognition. No name on the building, no ribbon-cutting ceremonies, nothing. Choosing the committee is your job."

He nodded along with her words, a man accustomed to agreeing with big donors. "I respect your point of view," he said when she finished, "but it seems wrong to let your donation pass unnoticed. Isn't there anything we can do to acknowledge your generosity?"

"There is one thing," she said. "The performing arts departments want to stage a benefit concert this spring, to demonstrate the need for a new PAB. If you choose to throw your influence behind the idea, I'll consider myself thanked."

A puzzled look crossed his ingratiating face. "That's not at all what I had in mind."

"Take it or leave it." She set off again at a brisk pace in hopes he wouldn't follow.

Dr. Isley hurried after her. "You can count on me." He was panting a little. "A concert is a marvelous idea. Gee, I'm glad we've had this talk."

They continued together in silence, though Lottie's thoughts were roaring. Why couldn't anyone understand what anonymous meant? She'd run into the same problem with her donations to hospitals. No matter how much she protested, they assumed she gave money in order to receive recognition. Nothing could be further from the truth.

As they approached the PAB, she was pulled from her thoughts by the crowd of students at the bottom of the steps, many of them without their coats. The obnoxious blat-blat-blat of the fire alarm blared from the open doors. Lottie turned to Dr. Isley. "Yet another reason to build that new building, the sooner the better. Fire alarms interrupt my classes every other week at least. I don't care who you name to that blasted committee, just get it going."

Five

hanks to Nancy, Sam kept his house in good repair. Blown fuses and burned out light bulbs had driven her crazy, so he'd always taken care of them right away. He didn't mind a good 'honey-do' list, especially because it kept him in his wife's good graces.

It didn't matter that she'd been gone three years. Old habits die hard.

When the bathroom faucet started its telltale drip, he set aside Wednesday evening to replace it. He wanted the chore out of the way so he wouldn't miss his Thursday pie night at Annie's.

Lottie called Wednesday morning as he was blowing the steam off his coffee. He took the call at his desk with his back to the room. The office wasn't the place for private conversations.

"Cal Jefferson wants to interview you for the book," Lottie said. "He'll probably call you this evening."

He drew a momentary blank. "Book?"

"The one about the Neverland Orchestra." She sounded hesitant. "I told you about it on Sunday?"

"Oh." That book. "I don't think I'll be much help." He fiddled with the zipper on his jacket. "I don't remember as much as you do."

"I'll bet you know more than you think," Lottie said. "Anyway, that's not why I'm calling. There's an Alfred Hitchcock double feature at the Orpheum tonight."

Her enthusiasm made him smile. "Which two movies?"

"*Rear Window* and *North by Northwest*. Want to go?"

"Tonight?" He frowned. "I can't. I've got some things to do."

She paused for a split second. "Never mind. It was a long shot. I've got things to do tonight, too."

Her bright, impersonal tone made his heart sink. It was the voice she used to keep people at arm's length. "We're still on for tomorrow, right?" he asked.

"Of course." She sounded like herself again. "Pie at Annie's at seven."

He hung up with a sigh of relief. Disappointing Lottie was the last thing he wanted to do. Still, that faucet wouldn't fix itself.

The day crawled past. January was always slow for construction, but Sam had never had time on his hands like this. Ever since he turned the business over to Jason, he'd felt this growing restlessness. He wanted Jase to do the meaty stuff, but he hadn't realized what that would mean for himself.

Around two o'clock he grabbed a clipboard and headed out to take inventory of the warehouse. This was the advantage of his new situation. All the boring jobs were up to date.

He was counting boxes of screws when Jase walked in, his work boots echoing across the concrete floor. "Dad? It's quitting time. What are you doing?"

Sam waved the clipboard under his nose. "What does it look like?"

Jase laughed. "Why didn't you go home if you were this bored?"

Sam gave him a tolerant look. "I taught you better than that. Something always needs doing in a place like this. How is it going on that kitchen remodel?"

"It's a pretty standard job. I could use your opinion on the dishwasher hookup, though. I left the drawing in my truck."

As they walked to the parking lot, the tightness in Sam's chest eased. His boy still needed him.

Sam approached home repairs with the same methodical precision he brought to any job. Tonight, he opened the box from the hardware store and laid out the faucet parts on the bathroom floor. Turning off the water valve, he reached for his crescent wrench. Off with the old. On with the new.

The pipes came apart easily and freed the inevitable sludgy buildup in the old plumbing. As he reached for a clean rag to wipe his hands, the phone rang.

He glanced toward the kitchen. "All right. Hold your horses." He stuck a bucket under the pipe stub and caught the call on its fifth ring.

"Sam? Norman Isley here. We met at a Lion's Club meeting last winter."

"Yes, Dr. Isley." Sam caught sight of himself in the reflection from the kitchen window and frowned. "What can I do for you?"

"We've started a steering committee for the new performing arts building on the college campus. The committee is required to have a representative from the community. I wondered if you'd be interested."

"I'd be willing to consider it. What's involved?"

While Dr. Isley launched into a description of the project, Sam exchanged a look of disbelief with his reflection in the window. Collison College had never taken any notice of him before. He was a little surprised Norman Isley even remembered his name.

"That's about it," the college president said finally. "Do you have any questions for me?"

Sam cleared his throat. "What put me on your radar for this?"

Dr. Isley sounded surprised. "You're a respected member of the community. And your experience in the building trades would make you invaluable. I know your time is precious, but I hope you'll think about it."

"Will do, sir." Sam hung up and caught his window reflection grinning back at him. He had to admit he felt a little flattered. Still, he couldn't quite picture himself turning up at committee meetings in his dungarees and work boots. Those high-minded professor types would eat him for lunch.

Turning out the light on the fool in the window, he headed to work.

The new faucet went in like a pat of butter on a pancake. He was getting ready to tighten the P-trap when the phone rang again. This time it was Jason. "What did you say about that dishwasher hook-up, Dad? I got home and couldn't remember."

Sam repeated his advice, but couldn't help adding, "Next time you should try listening."

He could picture Jason's apologetic shrug. "Sorry. My mind must have been elsewhere."

"Humph. Have you talked to Miranda lately?"

"Yeah, that's another reason I called. She's trying to figure out if her dad's business is in good hands. I don't think she quite trusts the guy who's in charge while he's in the hospital."

Sam leaned against the counter and listened as Jase outlined Miranda's concerns. "Sounds like she's on the right track," he said when the boy finished. "Here are some other things to think about."

When they'd finished discussing the ins and outs of Miranda's situation, Sam mentioned Dr. Isley's request. "What do you think, son?"

Jason thought it over. "It would do them good to have someone as knowledgeable as you on board. Wouldn't hurt our business, either." Trust Jase to see the marketing angle. "I think you should pray about it, anyway."

This brought a smile to Sam's face. "Good idea."

Jason's tone changed. "Hey, I've got to go. *North by Northwest* is the nine o'clock show at the Orpheum."

Sam frowned. "Don't you have to work tomorrow?"

Jase laughed. "I can handle one late night. Besides, if I'm tired it'll be your fault. You taught me to love Hitchcock."

Sam hung up and scowled at his reflection. "What are you looking at? I've seen that movie twice."

He stomped back to the bathroom to pick up his mess. When all his tools were back in the box, he reached over and turned on the faucet. Water sprayed out from below, catching him at knee level.

He'd never finished tightening the P-trap.

Thursday morning, Miranda found Zac alone with Dad. He slipped off his headphones when she came in. "It's about time you showed up."

She glanced at her watch. "It's not even nine o'clock yet. What's eating you?"

He shrugged. "Nothing."

She let this pass. "Do you think Balan will stop in today?" She hadn't been able to visit him at the office yet this week. Each time she called to set up a time, he had a scheduling conflict. He'd been at the hospital on Tuesday, but as luck would have it, Miranda had already gone home.

Zac yawned and stretched. "You just missed him. He stopped here on his way to work."

She frowned. "I'm beginning to think he's avoiding me."

"Why do you want to see him so much? You have a boyfriend, don't you?"

"This is strictly business. Don't you want to know how things are going without Dad?"

"Not really."

"I thought so. That's why I want to see Balan. Where's Mom?"

"She went downstairs to get breakfast."

Miranda caught up with her mother in the hospital cafeteria. As usual, Sonia looked calm and collected, her salt-and-pepper hair smoothed back in a bun at the base of her neck. Deep shadows under her eyes were the only hint of the exhaustion she must feel.

"How's Dad today?" Miranda asked.

"No better, no worse."

The defeat in her mother's expression went straight to Miranda's heart. She reached out and took her hand. "This is so hard on you."

Sonia closed her eyes, and for a moment Miranda thought she was going to cry. When she opened them, she had her emotions under control. "It is hard on all of us." She slipped her hand out of Miranda's. "Zac is so restless he can hardly sit still."

"Why not send us home for today?" Miranda said. "Zac and I can take care of the things that need to get done. I'll buy groceries, if you like. And I can go to Dad's office and talk with Balan."

"Again with the business." Sonia wadded up her napkin and set it on the tray. "Where did you learn to be so suspicious?"

From you, she wanted to say, but refrained. "I told you I'm not suspicious. I just think someone should show an interest in the family business."

Sonia tipped her head to one side, her eyes bright. "What good will it do for you to learn the business? Soon you will return to your job with that Lottie woman and forget about us."

Miranda gave a frustrated shrug. "Zac certainly doesn't seem interested."

Her mother didn't deny this. "Balan is family, too, Miranda. I trust him to steer the business until your father is well again, no matter how long that takes."

Miranda gave her mother's arm a squeeze. "I'm sure he'll wake up any day now. Maybe even today. And you're the first face he'll want to see when he opens his eyes."

Sonia sighed. "All right. It will be as you wish. The two of you can go home and put our life in order." She gave her daughter a meaningful look. "You can call that Ohio man you think I don't know about."

This surprised a smile from Miranda. "It's Iowa."

"Huh." She picked up her tray and walked away, her round curves swaying beneath a lightweight yellow dress. Miranda watched her with a mix of pride and exasperation. Behind her carefully bland expression, Sonia Charles was a force to be reckoned with.

They rode upstairs in rare harmony, the tension that normally crackled between them gone. When they reached Dad's room, Sonia opened the door with a flourish. "Zac, you and Miranda are going home."

But Zac was not there.

A flash of irritation crossed Sonia's face. "Zac?"

"Maybe he's in the bathroom," Miranda said. "Or at the vending machine."

Sonia looked at her watch. "Don't wait for him. Go home. I will deal with him if he comes back."

She was halfway down the hall before she registered her mother's words: "If he comes back."

Almost as if she knew he wouldn't.

She wasted no time leaving the hospital. The day was sunny and mild, blue sky stretching overhead. She started down the sidewalk to the parking lot. At the corner she turned—and there was the family car, leaving the lot with Zac at the wheel. He never looked in her direction but turned right and drove away.

Seething with anger, she waited for the cross-town bus. Who did he think he was, sneaking away like that without at least talking to them first? She entertained herself with visions of beating the answer out of him.

She reached home an hour later, after walking the final few blocks from the stop. "Zac?" she called as she opened the door. "Zac."

Silence answered her call. The apartment lay still and silent in the late morning sunshine, everything just as she'd left it this morning. Her brother was nowhere to be found.

She made a quick check of the rooms, then stood in the living room, grinding her teeth with frustration. "Okay, little brother. If you didn't go home, where did you go?" What was he up to?

A knock sounded on the front door. Relieved, she went to open it. "I swear to you, Zac—"

But it wasn't him. Instead the building manager stood there, looking put out. "The rent check bounced. Again."

Miranda frowned. "There must be some kind of mistake."

"See for yourself."

She took the check from his outstretched hand. It was stamped, "Insufficient Funds".

The manager crossed his arms. "I need rent. Preferably in cash."

She came to a quick decision. Pulling her checkbook from her purse, she wrote a check and handed it to him. "It's not cash, but I swear I have the funds to back it."

He raised his eyebrows. "I can't take this. It's out-of-state."

"I'm good for it," she repeated firmly. "If it bounces, you can evict us."

Shaking his head, he turned to leave. "You can count on that."

Miranda reached the hospital room an hour later. In a few short sentences she updated her mother.

"It bounced?" Sonia looked bewildered. "I don't understand. There's always enough money."

"Really? The guy said this has happened more than once." Miranda knelt beside her mom on the hospital linoleum. "Did Dad have any financial setbacks lately?"

"Not that I know of." Mom gripped the visitor's chair with one tense hand. "I never look at the books. He takes care of the household budget."

"I went to the bank, but they wouldn't let me see your accounts. You need to go talk to them."

Her mother frowned. "I will need you to drive. You know I do not drive the highways."

She shrugged. "You'll have to take the bus anyway. Zac has the car. I got to the parking lot this morning just as he was pulling away."

"Did he say where he was going?"

"He didn't see me."

Sonia accepted this news without further comment. "Well then, we must carry on without him." She rose, swayed on her feet, and sank back into the chair. "I think you'd better come with me, Miranda. Your father will be all right for an hour or two."

The money was all gone.

Miranda stared in disbelief at the apologetic bank manager. "There must be some mistake. Perhaps a bank error?"

"No error, I'm afraid." The man handed her the canceled checks and withdrawal slips for the current month. "It's all very cut and dried. There is no money left in your accounts. Not in checking. Not in savings."

Miranda picked up each check in turn. All were written in her father's bold hand. Most were for common needs: the electric bill, new clothes. One or two for cash. The checks he'd written to himself increased in amount over time. She glanced at her mom. "Does Dad do a lot of business in cash?"

"Not really." Her mother frowned. "He gives me cash for the grocery budget, but every Saturday he writes checks for the bills that have come in during the week."

Miranda nodded. "Do you use the checkbook?"

"I never need to." Sonia's eyes were suspiciously bright. "I only wrote the rent check because he could not."

She looked at the bank manager. "There are no deposit slips here. Are they stored separately?"

The manager shook his head. "No deposits were made this month."

Miranda tried to recall her conversations with Jason about how Harms and Sons operated. "Mom, do you know what method Dad uses to pay himself? Does he give himself a salary? Or does he only deposit money when the business gets paid for a contract?"

Her mother shrugged. "I do not know the first thing about it, Miranda."

"Balan would know, wouldn't he?"

At the mention of his name, Sonia's brow cleared. "Why didn't I think of that?" She turned to the bank manager. "May I use your phone?"

Sonia dialed the office and waited, but nobody answered. From her seat beside her mom, Miranda heard her father's voice on the answering machine before she hung up. "He might be in the warehouse. They can't hear the phone out there." She gave the man a nervous smile. "Come, Miranda. We can catch him at the office if we hurry."

The bank manager cleared his throat. "We have a few matters to finish up before you go." He pushed a printed form across the desk. "Your signature at the X will close your accounts."

Sonia pushed the form away. "I do not wish to close them. This is only a temporary situation."

"You're accruing penalties and fees as long as the accounts are empty."

Miranda drew her checkbook out of her purse. "How much do we need in each account to avoid service fees?"

"One hundred dollars," the man said.

"Done." She wrote a personal check and handed it across the desk. "We'll be back tomorrow with a bigger deposit."

Once they knew what to do next, Sonia's spirits made a visible recovery. She marched out of the bank with purpose in her step, only to stop short when they reached the street. "Is it that late already?"

Miranda followed her gaze to the bank's digital time and temperature sign. "Four forty-five? That's what my watch says."

"We're too late, then. Balan closes the office at five." Sonia started down the sidewalk. "We may as well go back to the hospital."

Miranda hurried to catch up. "So we have to wait until tomorrow to clear this thing up?"

"Not at all." Her mother picked up the pace. "We will give him an hour to get home, and I will call him there."

Miranda caught her mother's elbow. "If we're not trying to get to the office, why are you in such a hurry?"

Sonia shot her a sideways glance. "Because that is our bus."

The bus was packed, so they stood in the aisle and clung to the overhead bar for balance. At the next stop a man stood up and offered his seat to Sonia, but she refused it. "Do I look that old today?" she murmured to Miranda.

Miranda hid a smile. Her mother looked...timeless, if that made any sense. Classic. "He was being polite," she murmured back.

They got off at the hospital as raindrops began to fall. Sonia resumed her brisk pace, not slowing down until they reached the lobby. While they waited for the elevator, Miranda braced herself against the wall to catch her breath. "Where'd you learn to move like that?" she asked between gasps.

"I walk everywhere."

"But I'm a runner."

Sonia raised an eyebrow. "Does Idaho have hills like ours?"

"I'm pretty sure Idaho has mountains." Miranda smiled in spite of herself. "I live in Iowa, Mom."

They were almost to Dad's floor when Miranda remembered her brother. "I wonder where Zac has been all day," she said.

Sonia's eyes widened. "I really couldn't say."

Which was not the same as saying she didn't know. Miranda was about to follow up with more questions when the elevator door opened, and Zac himself stood in front of them.

His hair stood on end, his shirt was untucked, and there was a wild look in his eyes Miranda had never seen before. "Where on earth have you guys been? I've been waiting forever." His voice broke on that last syllable.

Mom's face went slack. "What happened?"

"I came back a little bit ago." The words came with an effort. "The nurse was waiting in the room. Dad had a seizure this afternoon. He's gone."

Six

am poured another cup of coffee and trudged back to his
desk. His head had been in a fog ever since he got up this
morning. He might have done all right if he'd been on a job site. Physical work tended to get his blood flowing. But today he'd gone over accounts with the bookkeeper, checking them for accuracy before they went to his tax accountant. He'd nearly fallen asleep several times over.

The slam of the truck door outside brought him to attention. Jason walked in, bringing a gust of cold air with him.

Sam wrapped both hands around the warm mug. "Shut the door. It's cold in here."

Jase shot him a tolerant smile. "Hello to you too, Dad. Tough day with the books?"

He opted not to answer.

Jase unzipped his jacket. "You missed a good movie last night."

Something in the boy's tone, a note of suppressed glee, caught Sam on the raw. "I've seen it." The words came out more forcefully than he intended. "Ends the same way every time."

Jase nodded wisely. "That's what Lottie said, too. I sat behind her and Nathan Bartholomew." This time he didn't try to hide his grin. "They're a lot of fun at the movies."

Sam's first sip of coffee burned his tongue but did nothing to stop his shivering.

The ringing phone saved him from having to reply. Jase leaned over and grabbed it from the desk nearest the door. "Hello? Oh, hey."

Sam knew by his tone it was Miranda. He turned away and feigned interest in the ledger before him.

Jase's voice abruptly changed. "He did? When? Are you okay?" He paused. "Do you need me to come?"

Sam glanced over his shoulder. Jason's head was bent. "Call me later, okay? You're sure you don't need me to fly out there? Okay. Bye, honey."

The boy hung up and paused a moment, his hand on the receiver. "Miranda's dad passed away this afternoon. They say he had a massive stroke."

"That's a real shame. How's she doing?"

Jase glanced at him. "She says she's fine."

"But you're not sure?"

He shrugged. "I wouldn't be 'fine' if I were in her shoes."

Sam took another tentative sip of coffee. The boy had a point. "Do you need to take a week and go out there? I can hold the fort here."

Jase shot him a grateful smile. "I think I'd better wait till I'm invited. I might be more of a shock than her mother can take."

"She doesn't know about you?"

"Not yet." Jase frowned. "Hey, Dad. Are you all right?"

"I'm fine. Why?"

"You seem—I don't know. Out of it, I guess."

The blood pounding in Sam's ears made it hard to think. "I'm a little tired, I guess."

"Go home and get some rest."

"I'll do that." Right after he had dinner with Lottie.

"I don't blame Jason for not going out there. I gather Miranda's family is difficult at best." Lottie scooped bite of banana cream pie into her mouth and closed her eyes in bliss. "What does Annie put in this stuff?"

"That's all the more reason for him to get on a plane," Sam said, sticking to the main point. "She's going to need some support."

She opened her eyes. "They're both adults, Sam. You have to trust them to know what's best."

"Humph."

Lottie resisted an urge to laugh out loud. She'd never seen him so out-of-sorts. Ever since they sat down, he'd been like a cat with a sore paw. Worrying about one thing and griping about another. She didn't know what to make of him.

"I heard you went to the movie last night," he said abruptly.

"I sure did." She smiled at the memory. She was glad she'd asked Katherine to go with her, and even more glad they'd run into Nathan at the theater. He and Katherine both knew a lot about Hitchcock. She enjoyed watching them outdo each other with bits of trivia. She was lucky she'd sat between them. If she'd been on Katherine's other side, she might have been ignored altogether by the two combatants. "Did Jason tell you we saw him there?"

He glared at his plate. "Yep."

"You should have come. We had a good time."

"I had chores to do. Old houses don't maintain themselves you know."

She set down her fork, eyes wide. "What is wrong with you tonight? Honestly, you're like a fussy old woman."

His head came up. "I am not."

For the first time she noticed how red his cheeks were. Come to think of it, his eyes were awfully bright, too. "Why, Sam, are you shivering?"

She reached across the table to feel his forehead, but he flinched away. "Leave me alone," he mumbled. "I'm fine."

"You're running a fever." Lottie reached for her purse and looked around for the waitress. "Could we have the check?"

A minute later she steered Sam by the elbow through the wet parking lot to the Mercedes, where she opened the passenger door. "Get in. I'm taking you home. "

For a moment she thought he was going to be difficult. Then he collapsed into the bucket seat and sighed. "I can't leave my car here," he said without conviction.

Lottie turned the ignition key and the engine roared to life. "Don't you worry about Bessie. I'll get someone to pick her up. And I'll call Jason and tell him you won't be in tomorrow."

He raised his head. "You'll do no such thing." The last word ended in a cough.

"You've got the flu," she said firmly. "If you get Jason sick, he won't be able to fly to California even if he wants to."

He massaged his throat with one hand. "Come to think of it, my throat hurts like a son of a gun."

She drove through downtown as quickly as she dared, then up the hill to Sam's home on the river bluff. He was out of the car before she could reach him, trudging up the walk with his collar turned against the cold.

At the door he glanced at her. "Thanks for the ride. I'll be okay from here."

Lottie wavered, wanting to believe him. She didn't know how to nurse a sick person. Then he swayed and had to catch the handrail for balance, and she followed him into the house. "I'll make you some tea while you get yourself to bed."

She thought she heard him say, "I don't like tea," but he was mumbling, so she might have been mistaken.

She found a kettle in the kitchen and filled it with water. When tea bags eluded her, she settled for a rather wrinkled packet of instant cocoa. Hot liquid was important. That's what she'd always heard. While the water heated, she checked out the bathroom cabinet for cold medicine and came up with two or three different types. She placed them on the tray, along with a couple of aspirin. Sam would know what worked for him.

When the kettle whistled, she poured water over the cocoa mix and stirred it up. Then, armed with mug, pill bottles, and a couple of cough drops from her purse, she climbed the stairs.

She reached the second floor and flipped the hall light with her elbow. Sam's room was obvious from the snores that reverberated within. Pushing open the door she found him asleep on his back atop the covers, still in his coat and boots, snoring like a freight train.

She set her supplies on the nightstand and shook his shoulder. "Sam."

He didn't respond.

She shook him harder without success.

"Well, this is a fine how-do-you-do," she muttered. Hands on hips she stared at the man, slack-jawed in sleep, with that horrible noise coming from his nose and mouth. His tanned profile contrasted with the white pillowcase, the iron-gray crew cut slightly fuzzy in the dim light.

Without warning, her heart flooded with tenderness. This was Sam, without his usual careful defenses. His weathered face, with its fan of lines around his eyes, was as familiar as her own reflection. He was sick, he was snoring, and—mercy!—if she didn't move quickly, he might also drool.

And she loved him. She gasped at the realization. Somehow, she'd lowered her practiced defenses and lost her heart to her oldest friend.

Without warning he opened his eyes and struggled to sit up. "I'm all right. You can go."

"Take your coat off," she said, ignoring his feeble protest. "I'll help you with your boots."

She untied his brown leather work boots and tugged them off his feet while he shrugged out of his coat. With those chores finished, he burrowed under the covers and soon was snoring again.

Lottie leaned over and dropped a kiss on his flushed cheek. "Get some sleep, my friend."

He smiled and sank deeper into his pillow. "Thanks, Nance."

The mumbled words washed over Lottie's heart like a bucket of cold water. She stood up, eyes wide, suddenly aware of her surroundings. This was Sam's bedroom—Sam and Nancy's bedroom—and she did not belong there.

She grabbed the tray and whisked it back to the kitchen. While she dumped the untouched cocoa and rinsed the mug, she gave herself a stern talking-to. "Sam Harms is a one-woman man," she announced to her reflection in the window. "You've always admired his loyalty to his wife. You've got no business wanting something he can't give. You're Lottie Braun, for goodness sake. Austere and eccentric. Now, act like it."

She drew a deep breath as sanity returned. Sam was simply a friend who needed her help right now.

She reached for the phone. "Jason? This is Lottie. I'm calling from your dad's house. I brought him home from Annie's with a fever and a cough, and he went right to bed." She wrapped the phone cord tight around her finger. "He really doesn't sound good. I'd feel much better if someone were keeping an eye on him." She bit her lip. "I'd stay, but..." but I'm not Nancy.

"You don't have to stay. You don't want to give the gossips something to talk about." Jason sounded reassuring. "I'll be right over."

She hung up and took a deep breath. Gossip? She didn't care what people said, so long as Sam was taken care of. But Jason was probably right. He'd lived in the fishbowl that was Collison all his life.

Jason walked in a few minutes later, raised his eyes to the ceiling, and grinned. "He's really sawing logs up there. I sure hope that's not what I sound like when I'm asleep."

Lottie gave him a reluctant smile. "I'm probably being overly cautious about this."

He shook his head. "When Dad gets sick, he gets really sick. Last winter, he ignored a bad cold and ended up with pneumonia. The amazing thing is that he let you take care of him."

Her heart sank. It wasn't that amazing. He'd mistaken her for Nancy. She forced herself to sound cheerful as she reached for her coat. "Well, now that you're here, I'll be on my way. Call me if I can help out."

Jase walked her to the door. "Mitch is staying with Dad this weekend, so you don't need to worry. We'll take care of him from here."

She left feeling noble, and sharply disappointed. The Harms family had closed ranks to take care of their own. And she was on the outside looking in.

Once the news spread that Suresh Charles was gone, friends surrounded the family with love, support, and food. Mom and Dad's minister guided them through the process of planning the funeral. Their neighbor, Mrs. Menon, organized the church ladies, who cooked vast quantities of sambal and rice to feed the sympathetic visitors. And there were plenty of visitors, despite the torrents of rain that set in Thursday night and didn't let up. The Indian Christian community was small and tight knit.

Many of Dad's employees stopped by to offer help. Miranda had known some of them, like Karthav Singh, the head electrician, since childhood. He held her hand in a comforting grip while he offered his condolences. "Try not to worry about the business for now," he said. "Max, Jose, and I—" here he nodded to the lead carpenter and plumber, "will keep things going. We can wait to be paid."

Her eyes filled with tears as she thanked them, humbled by their loyalty to her father.

Younger employees peered curiously at the family over their plates of free food. Few of them spoke to her, preferring to offer their sympathies to Zac.

Balan Prakash was conspicuous by his absence. Thursday evening, when Sonia had called to tell him about Suresh's death, Balan had more sad news. His mother was dying, and he'd booked a flight to India to be with her.

Sonia had hung up shaking her head. "Poor Balan. He's had two shocks today. First his mother, and now Suresh."

Miranda had listened to the emotional conversation from her seat at the kitchen table. Balan's sobs were audible through the receiver. "He sounds distraught. Maybe he should come over, so he isn't alone."

"He's packing to leave," Sonia said. "His flight leaves early tomorrow morning."

Miranda would have thought this strange if she hadn't heard the man wailing on the other end of her mother's phone. His grief was unmistakable.

Other people didn't know that, though. Mrs. Menon brought the matter up with Zac and Miranda on Sunday afternoon while their mother was speaking with other visitors. "Is it not strange that Balan has had two tragic deaths at once?" she said with a mournful sigh.

Miranda nodded politely. "These things happen, I guess."

Mrs. Menon quirked an eyebrow. "The timing does seem unusually tragic."

Zac shrugged. "Our cousin wouldn't leave right now without a really good reason. He thought of Dad as a second father, and Dad treated him like the son he never had."

Miranda's heart sank at the bitterness in his tone. So, she wasn't the only one who felt usurped by Balan Prakash.

Mrs. Menon took their hands in her warm grasp. "Your father loved his children very much, you know. He did not always know how to show it."

Sam woke up and checked his alarm clock. Eight o'clock? He'd overslept. He'd have to call Jase and let him know he was running late.

He made an effort to jump out of bed and make up for lost time, but his arms and legs wouldn't obey. He collapsed against his pillow and stared at the ceiling, trying to muster the strength to sit up, but nothing happened.

His memories of last night were fuzzy. One minute he was at Annie's with Lottie, the next he was home in bed with no idea how he'd gotten here. Sometime in the night Jase had propped him up and made him take pills and drink water.

He closed his eyes. No, that couldn't be right. That part must have been a dream.

A painful cough tore from his throat. Come to think of it, he could use another glass of water.

Before he could figure out how to sit up, Mitchell appeared in the doorway. "It's about time you woke up."

Sam tried to clear his thoughts. "What are you doing here? I thought you weren't coming till tonight."

Mitch chuckled. "Dad, it's Sunday. You've been asleep for two days."

"Cut it out, Mitch. You're too old for this stuff." He hated it when his kids played practical jokes.

"I'm serious. You've got the flu." Mitch walked over to the bed. "You won't be getting up today, doctor's orders. Can I get you anything?"

"A glass of water." Sam's voice came out in a raspy whisper.

"Sure thing."

The next time Sam woke up, long shadows lay across the bedspread. Somewhere nearby, Jason was talking.

"He's always this way when he's sick. Last winter he ended up in the hospital, so when Lottie called, I knew we needed to pay attention." He paused. "You're still coming to the wedding, aren't you?"

Sam sat up. "Hey, Jase?"

His son appeared in the doorway, the receiver to his ear. "Yeah, Dad?"

"Is it still Sunday?"

Jason smiled. "Yep."

"I'm starving."

The boy pointed to the phone. "I'll be off in a minute, okay?"

Sam pushed away the covers. "Don't bother. I'll get up."

Jase's eyes widened with concern. "I've got to go," he said into the phone. "Call me after the funeral."

Sam put his feet on the cold floor and stood up. Granted, his legs were a little shaky, but they held. Pushing away his son's offer of help, he shuffled around the bed to get his bathrobe from the closet. "I don't need a babysitter, son. I'll be downstairs in a minute."

"All right."

The boy left the room, and Sam leaned against the wall to catch his breath. A cough wracked his body, and he closed his eyes. This was going to be harder than he thought.

Voices floated up through the stairwell as he started down the hall. Jason and—Lottie? Sam blinked. What was she doing here?

All at once his memory returned. Lottie had driven him home from the café. She'd helped him off with his boots and pulled the covers up around his chin. That was where things got fuzzy. He'd surely dreamt the swift kiss on his cheek just before the hall light went out.

In the bathroom he splashed his face and peered into the mirror. Gaunt, unshaven, and red-eyed, he wasn't an inspiring sight. What would she think if she saw him like this? For a split second he thought about shaving, but he didn't have the strength to lift a razor to his face.

When he reached the kitchen, Jason was alone. A pot of soup bubbled on the stove, and the scents of chicken and Lysol mingled in the air. "I thought I heard voices a minute ago," Sam said.

Jase looked up from the soup he was stirring. "Lottie just left. She's been in and out all weekend." His lips turned up in a half-smile. "Did you know she's a compulsive cleaner when she's worried?"

"Huh." So, Lottie was worried about him. This bit of news pleased him more than he wanted it to. He sniffed the air. "Where'd you get the soup?"

"Annie sent it over. Said it was the least she could do."

Jason filled a bowl and handed it to him. "Bessie is back in the garage. Lottie and I handled that on Friday."

He couldn't muster any interest in the fate of the car. "The soup's good. You should have some."

"I already ate."

"Right." Sam gobbled the rest of his soup and handed back the bowl for more. "When is she coming back?"

Jase shot him a quizzical look. "Who, Lottie? I don't know. She had to get ready for work tomorrow."

That made sense. His pleasure in the soup dimmed a little bit. "I might take a half-day tomorrow." He coughed.

"You're not working this week," Jase said firmly. "Mitchell's getting married on Saturday. You've got to get your strength back."

Seven

fter constant rain all weekend, Monday morning the sun
shone in a cloudless blue sky. Miranda closed the kitchen
shades against the offending light while she heated a pan to make dosa,
the rice and lentil pancakes of her childhood. She could not imagine
burying her father on such a heartlessly beautiful morning.

Sonia joined her in the kitchen, fully dressed. "Why are you working
in the dark? If the sun shines, it shines, Miranda. We cannot change that."

Her matter-of-fact tone flicked Miranda on the raw. Today of all
days she could not stand a lecture. She bent her head over the stove
and concentrated on flipping the dosa in the pan.

Sonia adjusted the shade, and light poured across the scarred coun-
tertop. "Your father was a realist. He would want us to face the day we
were given, bravely and honestly." Her voice cracked on the last word.

Tears burned Miranda's eyes, blurring her vision. Her mother's
courage was more than she could bear. Dropping the spatula, she
turned and reached for her.

For once, her mother returned the hug. They clung together in the
middle of the kitchen, tears running down their faces and onto one another's shoulder. After a moment, Sonia loosened her grip and stepped
back. "I am glad you came home," she whispered.

Miranda gazed at her mother in amazement. "You are?"

"All the time you were away, I prayed you would come back. So did
your father. I'm so sorry you did not feel that you could."

Miranda blinked away more tears. "But Dad told me if I left, he'd disown me."

"That was an empty threat. He said that to make you stay, but you left anyway." Sonia's eyes were filled with sorrow. "When you didn't come back, he knew he'd lost the fight. But he was too proud to go find you and ask you to come home."

"Oh, Mom." She closed her eyes against a fresh wave of grief. "What a waste."

Zac walked into the kitchen, rubbing sleep from his eyes, and grabbed two dosas off the stack beside the stove.

Sonia turned on him. "Why aren't you dressed yet? We must get going."

Her brisk tone galvanized the whole family into action. As she spread chutney on her first dosa, Miranda put her grief on the back burner. Later, she would sort out her tangled thoughts. First, she must get through the day.

Miranda's mother and father had lived in the San Francisco Bay Area for twenty-five years, so the funeral visitation took a long time. The family gathered near Suresh's body as one by one the good man's friends paid their respects.

Mixed in with their friends and neighbors were her father's business associates, broad-shouldered men who looked uncomfortable in suits and ties. They spoke of Suresh Charles as a fair-minded and dependable contractor who they respected deeply.

Dan Hollis was one of those men. He murmured words of condolence to Miranda, then continued in a quiet tone. "Your dad did me a favor once, and I owe him. If there's anything I can do to help you folks out, don't hesitate to ask."

Miranda made a snap decision. "As a matter of fact, Mr. Hollis, there is something. I've been trying to understand the state of Dad's business affairs, and I have questions about the general state of the industry, and how well Dad was doing. Would you be willing to talk with me about that?"

Frown lines appeared between his eyes. "I was under the impression your dad had a second-in-command who'd be taking over. Can't he answer your questions?"

She shrugged. "Unfortunately, he was called away this week on personal business. We don't know when he will return."

He nodded. "So you're taking over for a while. Are you sure you're up to the job?"

She hid her irritation behind a smile. "I'm stronger than I look."

He gave her a searching look. "Yes, maybe you are at that. If you've got half the grit your dad did, I'd be happy to help you." He gave her another of his business cards. "Give my office a call this week to set something up."

Dad's workers came forward together. Most of them expressed only sorrow at the passing of a great man, but a few let slip their worry about where they would find work now. "We are still in business," Miranda told them. "We will still have jobs for you."

Their downcast eyes and doubtful nods told her they didn't believe it.

The funeral service passed in a blur. Forever afterward Miranda could only remember snatches of hymns about heaven, the slow drive to the cemetery, and the surprising warmth of the damp earth she dropped onto her father's coffin at the end.

After lunch in the church hall, Mrs. Menon put her arm around Miranda's mom. "You must go home and rest, Sonia. Your job here is done."

Sonia bridled. "I'll do no such thing. There is a kitchen to clean."

"That is not your job this time." Mrs. Menon snapped her fingers at Zac. "Take your mother home. She needs to put her feet up for a while." She looked around for Miranda. "Go on. You need time alone."

Sonia gave her friend a brief hug and gathered her children. Shoulder to shoulder they made the short trek down the main commercial street of their neighborhood. They walked in silence, absorbed in their private thoughts, but the warmth of her mother's arm brushing against hers gave Miranda quiet comfort.

Nobody knew quite what to do when they reached home. For a time, they stood together in the front hall, each waiting for someone else to make a move.

Zac was the first to break away. "I need a nap," he said, and started for his room.

"Good idea." Sonia stepped out of her shoes and stretched out on the burnt-orange couch in the living room. "I could sleep for days."

Miranda could see no other option but to retire to her room and leave her mother alone, but she didn't feel like sleeping. She changed into jeans and polo shirt and flopped onto the bed, her mind abuzz with questions.

Before long, she heard her brother moving around his bedroom. A few minutes later he walked down the hall, spoke to his mother, and left.

She padded into the living room and found her mother mending a shirt. "Where did Zac go?"

Sonia looked up, her face calm. "A boy Zac's age doesn't always tell his mother where he's going."

"What is he into, Mom? Is it legal?"

"Legal?" A ghost of a smile flitted across Sonia's face. "Don't be ridiculous."

"He should have asked if we needed the car, at least."

"Is there someplace you want to go?"

A knock at the door cut the discussion short. Two of Dad's framers stood in the corridor, looking anxious. One of them, a young man named Arun, spoke up. "I left my toolbox in the warehouse on Thursday, and Friday the place was closed." He nodded toward Sonia. "Out of respect, we thought. So we stopped over there just now to get it back." He twisted his baseball cap between his hands. "The place was locked up, so we went around to the side to look in the window, and it was broken—glass everywhere."

"Did you call the police?" Miranda asked.

Arun glanced uneasily at his friend. "We didn't want any trouble."

She accepted this. Young men who worked construction didn't always have the cleanest records. "Will you take me back there?"

"That's why we came by. We thought your mom might need a lift. But if you want to come instead...." Arun gave her an admiring look.

Sonia set the shirt aside and stood. "Let me get my purse."

Miranda put out a hand. "You don't have to, Mom. I'll let you know what's going on."

"Nonsense." Sonia raised her chin. "I want to see this with my own eyes." She hurried to her room and returned with her handbag.

The two young framers exchanged a questioning glance. "We've got my pickup truck," Arun said. "Sajeev can ride in the back, but the cab is pretty small for three people."

Sonia clutched her purse more firmly. "We shall have to make do."

The truck in question was a turquoise Dodge from the early 1960s, with whitewall tires and polished chrome fenders. Miranda started to slide to the middle of the bench seat, but her mother elbowed her out of the way. Sonia settled her ample rear end between the two young people, while Arun sat behind the wheel. He turned the key, and the cab filled with the driving beat of a pop song.

He tipped his head so he could speak to Miranda. "You mind if I play some music? Vindaloo Z comes on this time of day."

She shrugged. "Sure."

Between them, Sonia gave an involuntary start. "Oh, no," she murmured.

Arun glanced at her. "Are you okay, Mrs. Charles?"

Sonia was staring at the radio as if it might bite. "Change the station, please."

Miranda nudged her mother. "What's wrong?" she whispered.

Sonia glanced at her. "I do not like this kind of music. I would rather hear the news. Is that all right with you?"

Arun changed the station with a tolerant smile. "My parents are the same way," he said. "They're too traditional." He hit the gas as they entered the highway, and they leaped forward to the staccato sound of the stock market report.

Miranda could feel her mother trembling. "It's been a terrible day," she said with quick compassion. "You're exhausted."

Sonia sat up straighter. "I'll get through this. What choice do I have?"

They reached the office building, and Arun led them around to the side with the broken window. Jagged pieces of glass clung to the frame, but the middle was gone.

The office beyond lay in chaos. Desk drawers hung half-open, their contents jumbled and spilled. Splinters of glass covered the desktop. The drafting table lay on its side, architectural drawings strewn around the floor. In the corner a metal box sat at a crazy angle, its lid torn off the hinges.

Sonia unlocked the office door and they filed inside, glass crunching beneath their feet.

"Don't touch anything," Miranda said. "I'm calling the police."

Arun shifted his weight. "Can I check the warehouse for my tools?"

"Only if you take my mother with you." She held up a hand to stop his protest. "I'm not in a position to trust anyone today."

Sonia took the warehouse key from its hook by the door and led the two men out of the office, while Miranda reached for the phone.

The three returned with encouraging news. "Looks like the robber stayed out of the warehouse." Arun said. "It's still full of inventory."

"Good. The police are on their way." Miranda nodded toward the corner. "Mom, what's that metal box?"

Sonia looked surprised. "How should I know?"

Arun cleared his throat. "I think it's where they kept the petty cash."

Both women turned to look at him. "Why do you say that?" Miranda asked, her voice sharp.

The young man shrugged. "One time, Balan asked me to pick up some supplies on my way to the office, and he reimbursed me with cash out of that box."

Two police officers arrived and took charge. They questioned Arun and Sajeev, who repeated their story about Arun's tools. They accepted this without comment and turned their attention to the crime scene.

The female officer found a metal folding chair for Sonia and brought her a cup of water. "Tell me about your situation," she said sympathetically. "I understand there was a death in the family?"

While Sonia explained about the funeral, Miranda followed the other officer outside.

"Did you move anything before we got here?" he asked as they reached the broken window.

"No, sir."

Officer Rowan frowned intently at the jagged glass, then scanned the room beyond. "Do you know what's missing?"

"The cash box in the corner is empty."

He looked up. "How much do you usually keep on hand?"

"I don't know," she said. "I wasn't involved in running the business."

"So, the petty cash is gone." He jotted a note on his paper. "Was the door unlocked when you got here?"

She paused a moment to be sure of her answer. "No. My mother unlocked it."

"I see."

She followed him back inside, where his partner had finished interviewing Sonia. They spent a moment comparing notes in low voices, then Officer Rowan turned to Miranda. "We've got a small problem here. You and your mother agree that the only thing missing is petty cash, which your mother says might have been two-hundred dollars."

Miranda looked at Sonia, who shrugged. "That is the amount we kept when I did the bookkeeping."

Officer Rowan continued. "A two-hundred-dollar loss makes this petty theft."

"But what about the mess they made in here?" Sonia pointed at the overturned drafting table. "It seems to me they were searching for something."

He gave her a level stare. "Ma'am, this is a strangely isolated incident. None of the other businesses in the area reported any kind of break-in this week." He pointed at the window. "There's no evidence anyone tried to climb through that window. If they had, they would have knocked out the rest of the glass so they didn't cut themselves."

It was true. The glass around the edges looked dangerous.

Rowan went on. "There's glass inside the drawers and on top of that mess over there—" He indicated the empty cash box. "Which means the office was vandalized before the window was broken."

"What are you getting at?"

"The whole scene feels like a set-up," he said. "An inside job."

Miranda's eyes widened. "Are you saying one of our employees did this?"

"Most likely, ma'am. Someone who has a key to the office." He nodded at his partner. "Officer Martin will leave you her card. If anything else is missing after you get this mess cleaned up, give her a call."

♪

"This has to be the longest day in history," Miranda told Jason much later that night. She sat on the coat closet floor in her pajamas with the phone pressed to her ear. Mom had gone to bed, and Miranda didn't want to disturb her.

Jase was still trying to get the details straight. "So, the police think someone who had a key stole the petty cash and then staged the break-in?"

She warmed to the concern in his voice. "And then he basically said our loss wasn't big enough for the police to investigate."

"Your mom must be pretty upset."

"She seems more shocked than anything else. Disbelieving." Miranda closed her eyes. "Anyone with a key to Dad's office was also a good friend of the family."

"What did you do after the police left?"

"We swept up the glass and put a board over the window. We couldn't stay long because Arun needed to leave, and he was our ride home." She sighed. "Mom was exhausted, too."

"So, you still don't know what's missing from the office?" His voice was thoughtful.

"I told you. They took the cash."

He was quiet a moment. "Why do you think the person went to all that trouble to call attention to the theft? Why didn't he just unlock the door, take the box, and leave?"

She sighed. "I've been wondering the same thing."

"Who else has a key to the office?"

"Balan does, but he's out of the country." She thought a moment. "Dad's foremen have keys. Zac does too, I think."

"Can you rule Zac out?" Jase asked.

She hesitated. "I don't know for sure. I can imagine him stealing from the petty cash, but I don't think he'd bother to stage a break-in."

"Okay." He moved on. "What about Balan?"

"He couldn't have done it. His mother is dying, so he left for India on Friday. We think the break-in happened Friday night or Saturday." A key rattled in the door lock, and she scrambled up off the closet floor. "Zac's home. I've got to go."

She hung up as Zac came through the hall, headphones on as usual, and started for his room. "Where were you tonight?"

He stopped but didn't turn around. "What do you care? I'm going to bed."

"Not until we talk."

His shoulders slumped as he turned to face her. "Can't it wait?"

"Someone broke into Dad's office over the weekend."

His face went slack. For a moment he looked so miserable she almost felt sorry for him, but a second later the expression was gone. "I don't understand. Who would do something like that?"

She gave him a searching look. "Are you sure you don't know?"

"Why would I?" Confusion flashed across his face. "Wait. You think I did it? That makes no sense."

She shrugged. "You're supposed to be learning the business, but you obviously don't care about it. You should be taking care of Mom, but every day you run away for hours on end. And now, when I'm asking for some answers, you're trying to avoid me. So, what should I think, little brother?"

"I have a job. Okay? So sue me."

"But you work for Dad."

"Only when he makes me—" he winced "made me. And he can't do that anymore." He trudged down the hall, shoulders slumped.

"But the company is yours now," she called after him. "You can't just abandon it."

He glanced at her over his shoulder, his face unreadable. "Oh yeah? Watch me."

Eight

L ottie knocked on Cal Jefferson's office door first thing Tuesday morning. He was on the phone, but he smiled and waved her to a seat.

"Yes, Joe," he said into the mouthpiece. "She just walked into my office. Want to talk to her?" He winked at Lottie. "No? All right. Thanks again for your help. You too." He hung up and turned to Lottie. "That was a publisher who's interested in our book."

She stared at him in wonder. "You found a publisher already?"

"Yep. Your cooperation sealed the deal. They're pretty excited about it." He leaned forward, eyes alight. "Here's the best part. The editor I just talked to already knew about the Neverland."

"Really? How so?"

He checked his notes. "He hails from Shreveport, Louisiana. He said he remembers when they played there during World War II."

She gazed at him, stunned. "I wouldn't have said we were all that memorable."

Cal pushed the group photo across the desk, pointing at a man in the back row. "Can you remember this guy's name? He looks familiar."

She stared at the photo, and a snatch of memory returned. "Oh, yes. Al something-or-other. The guys called him Grease behind his back because he used so much hair tonic."

Cal scribbled a note on his paper. "I think I've seen him in the movies or on TV or something like that. Too much hair tonic, huh?"

She gave him a disapproving frown. "You can't publish every little thing I say about these guys, Cal. You'll have me on the hook for libel in no time."

He laughed. "I won't do that to you. I'm just trying to get a feel for what it was really like to travel with that band." Cal glanced at his watch. "I hate to cut this short, but I'm late for my percussion workshop."

Lottie went on her way without telling Cal why she'd stopped to see him. She'd have to find him at lunch time to warn him about Sam's illness. She didn't want Cal to bother him while he recovered.

She hadn't been back to see him since the work week began. He was better off not having visitors while he tried to regain his strength. She didn't want to hinder his progress, especially with the wedding so near.

That was what she told herself. And if the truth of the matter was a little less selfless, if she felt the need to rebuild her defenses before she saw him again, who could really blame her?

For now, she was getting her updates from Jason. Yesterday he'd reported that Sam was improving, but he wouldn't be back at work the rest of the week. That was a long time to be down for a man as strong as Sam.

She found herself praying for him at odd times, little fragmented requests as she went about her day. Martha Williams said that kind of prayer counted just as much as the beautifully worded ones Reverend Summers gave on Sunday mornings. More, Martha said, because they were heartfelt.

Rhonda Kennedy waved from her desk as Lottie crossed the third-floor atrium. The other piano professor was easier to work with these days. In fact, Lottie sometimes found her a bit too friendly. Today looked like it might be one of Rhonda's talkative days, so she buried her nose in her daily planner and kept moving.

A phone message from Ernest Fleischmann awaited her when she reached her office.

Lottie stared at the pink slip of paper. "The great man himself?" she murmured. Fleischmann did not strike her as a man who placed his own phone calls.

Tuesday mornings were busy. She didn't return the call until after lunch.

The secretary—a new one, she noted—put her through immediately. "I was delighted to learn that you're ready to visit Los Angeles," Ernest Fleischmann said in his clipped, South African-accented English. "The very idea fills me with joy. In fact, when my assistant told me you called and she didn't put you through to me, I fired her on the spot."

Lottie's eyes widened. Ernest Fleischmann had a well-earned reputation for volatility. "It's my loss. Mr. Horowitz is a worthy recipient."

"Nonsense." He sounded outraged. "Compared to you, Vladimir Horowitz has all the talent of a player piano." She started to protest, but he cut her off. "Miss Braun, if you truly want to come to Los Angeles after all these years, we would consider it an honor to be your host. I have a proposal for you."

She sat up straight, her heart pounding inside her chest. "Go on."

"As with most orchestras, we finish our regular season in May. In June we go much lower-key, with an exclusive little evening for our top-tier subscribers only. Black tie, complimentary champagne served at intermission. It's our little way of repaying their investment in the arts. Each year I bring in a surprise guest of some kind to delight the ears of the true music lovers." His voice became confidential. "It does wonders for our revenues, as you might imagine. This year I want you to be our surprise guest. We'll keep it very hush-hush." He laughed. "Because in Hollywood, keeping something under wraps is guaranteed to create a buzz."

She willed herself to speak calmly. "You say this is in June? May I have some time to think it over? I'll have to check my calendar as well, to be sure I don't have any conflicts."

"Yes, of course." He sounded ironic. "They must keep you very busy at that college of yours. You can leave your answer with my new secretary—I can't recall her name—when you call back. Oh, and Miss Braun?"

"Yes?"

"Don't keep us waiting too long."

Lottie hung up and stared at the phone, her mind in a daze. "I'm going to L.A.," she whispered. "I'm really going!"

She glanced at her watch and groaned. She was late for her next class. Grabbing her books, she hurried to her first-floor classroom and nearly mowed down Katherine in the process.

Katherine clutched Lottie's arm to regain her balance. "What's going on? You look like you just won the lottery."

"I just spoke with Ernest Fleischmann himself. He invited me to come to Los Angeles in June."

Katherine's eyes widened. "Wow. Are you going?"

She laughed. "I believe I am."

"Well, in that case, congratulations. I'm thrilled for you!"

A classroom door opened and Nathan wheeled into the hall. "Would you ladies please take your hen party someplace private? Classes are in session."

He rolled back into his classroom, letting the door snap shut behind him. Lottie shared a smile with Katherine. "Leave it to Nathan to cut me down to size."

Tuesday morning Sam felt fine. His mind was clear, his stomach was growling, and he could breathe through his nose. Four days of lazing around the house had done the trick. He couldn't wait to go to work.

Then he got out of bed.

The first cough rumbled out of his chest as he slid his feet into his slippers. By the time he reached the bathroom, he had to hold onto the door jamb to catch his breath. He made it through his shower before he lost the will to go on. Breakfast would wait. He needed a nap.

The phone woke him a few hours later. In his sleep-fogged state he thought it might be Lottie calling to check on him. He felt a nudge of disappointment when a man's voice said, "Sam? Norman Isley here. Have you given any more thought to being on the building committee?"

Sam scratched the back of his head and tried to think. He'd intended to get Lottie's take on the subject, but he'd never had the chance. "I'd be happy to help out," he heard himself say. "When do we start?"

"The first meeting is scheduled for a week from tomorrow. I have a packet of reading material for you to look over beforehand. I'll drop that off to you sometime soon."

Sam hung up in a daze. Had he really just agreed to help out the college for free? His defenses were down because he was sick. That was the only explanation.

His stomach growled. Breakfast time. No, it was closer to lunch time. Bacon and eggs would do the trick.

The phone rang again as he was flipping his omelet. This would be Lottie, he thought. She usually ate lunch around this time.

But it was Mitchell, calling from Iowa City. "I just got the results, Dad. I passed the bar exam."

A thrill of pride went through Sam's chest. "That's fantastic, son! Tell me all about it."

When Mitchell exhausted the subject of the exam and his plans for the wedding weekend, Sam hung up and slid his omelet onto a plate. In spite of Mitchell's good news, he felt a little down in the dumps.

He bit into a crispy piece of bacon and shook the thought away. Blame it on the fact that he hadn't been out of the house for almost a week. Of course, he was a little stir-crazy.

He finished his eggs and mopped the plate with a piece of toast. There was no blessed reason to want Lottie to call. He couldn't go anywhere until he got over this cough, and they weren't the kind of friends who chatted on the phone.

After lunch he retrieved the newspaper from his front stoop and took it to the living room. He had just flipped the lever on his leather recliner when the phone rang again. Jumping out of the big chair, he hurried to the kitchen.

Cal Jefferson's deep voice greeted him. "I'm calling to ask for your help. Has Lottie told you about the book my wife and I are writing about the Big Band era and little dance bands like the Neverland Orchestra?"

Disappointment sharpened Sam's voice. "She's mentioned it, but I don't think it's a good idea."

"Can we talk about why you feel that way?"

Cal's patient tone set Sam off. "Listen, professor. I know Lottie wears rose-colored glasses about that band, but it really wasn't a good life for a child. Her sister protected her from most of the bad stuff, so she didn't see all the drinking and fighting. I don't doubt your good intentions, but I'm not going to glorify a bunch of overgrown kids and their pie-in-the-sky dreams." He coughed. "I won't be part of that."

Cal hesitated. "It sounds like I've caught you on a bad day. Why don't I call back when you're feeling better?"

"You'll be wasting your time."

"I guess it's my time to waste." Was that sympathy in Cal's voice? "Get well, my friend."

"Humph." Sam hung up and stomped back to the recliner, snagging an old blanket off the sofa on his way past. He was about to sit down when an idea occurred to him.

Back to the kitchen he went and took the phone off the hook. Nobody else would bother him today.

"Wonderful!" Ernest Fleischmann said when Lottie called him after class. "This is a real coup for us. Have your secretary call mine to make all the arrangements." He rang off before she could respond.

She picked up the framed picture that sat on her desk and studied it. Mr. Schultz gazed out of it with reproachful eyes. "You're cooperating with that Tinseltown orchestra?" he seemed to say. "Is nothing beneath your dignity these days?"

She turned the photo to the wall and walked away.

Normally, Miranda would arrange a trip like this one, but in her absence, Lottie called the music department secretary for help.

"I'm not authorized for travel arrangements," the secretary told her. "I'm sorry. I'd help you if I could."

Fair enough, Lottie thought. She'd learned to open her own mail and deal with the dry cleaning. She could handle this, too. As she dialed the number for Fleischmann's assistant, she wondered once again how soon she could get Miranda to come home.

Fleischmann's assistant, whose name turned out to be Christina Dent, sounded efficient enough. "I'll take care of everything on this end, Miss Braun. I do ask that you make your own plane reservations. We'll reimburse the ticket, of course." She sounded apologetic. "It's just that you live so far from a major airport. I wouldn't begin to know how to work around that."

Lottie assured the girl that she understood and hung up. "Plane reservations can't be too difficult," she muttered. Miranda could probably advise her.

No one answered at Miranda's house. Lottie let the phone ring a good long time, just to make sure. Frustrated, she hung up and dialed Sam. He would know the travel agents in town.

Sam's line was busy, a fact that Lottie verified by hanging up and calling again. Both times the annoying signal buzzed in her ear. She received this fact with mixed feelings. On the one hand, she was glad he felt good enough to talk on the phone. On the other, she wished he was talking with her.

With a sigh, she hung up and called Patti, who laughed. "You mean you've been all over the world and never made your own reservations?"

Her defenses went up. "I used to do it when I was young, but a lot has changed since then."

"Like what?"

"I don't think I've ever dealt with plane tickets before. Back then I traveled mostly by train or bus." She thought of something else. "There's a nice young pilot in Collison who flew me to Chicago when I had to go to New York in December. I don't really know how to reach him, either."

"Last time I was home I saw a Rolodex full of useful phone numbers on Miranda's desk. I'll bet you'll find your travel agent's information there. The pilot is probably listed, too." Patti's voice was reassuring. "Miranda is the most organized person I know. You'll be okay."

Lottie ran her fingers through her hair. "You must think I'm useless."

"Not at all." Patti hesitated. "Out of practice, maybe. But definitely not useless."

Lottie thanked her niece and hung up, then frowned at the phone. That busy signal of Sam's worried her. She tried him again with the same result and decided to take action.

Picking up the receiver, she placed one more call. "Hello, Jason?"

Sam spent the afternoon in the recliner, alternately napping and staring out the window at all the work he would have to do come spring. He was dozing a few hours later when Jason barged in the front door, slamming it behind him and stomping the snow off his work boots. "Dad? Hey, Dad." He sounded worried.

"I'm back here," Sam called. "In the den."

Jase hurried down the hall. "Are you okay?"

Sam released the recliner and stood up. "What are you talking about? I'm fine."

"Lottie called and said she couldn't reach you, and I got a busy signal when I tried, too. The phone must be out of order."

Sam bit back a smile. So, she'd finally tried to call. "I took it off the hook. Couldn't stand all the nuisance calls."

Jase stood in the doorway, a look of disbelief on his face. "You mean I dropped everything because you didn't want to deal with some poor phone salesman?"

"I didn't ask you to check up on me. If Lottie was worried, why didn't you send her?"

This surprised a laugh out of Jason. "The day I tell Lottie Braun what to do…"

Sam could see his point. She didn't take direction well. "So, call her up and tell her I'm fine."

Jase frowned. "Why don't you call her?"

The suggestion gave him an uncomfortable jolt. Yes, why didn't he? "I'm sick," he said finally. "I'm going back to bed."

"Why didn't Lottie go check on your dad?" Miranda asked when Jase told her the story later that night. She was back in the coat closet, speaking in low tones.

"For the same reason Dad didn't want to call her." His voice was dry. "They're acting like a couple of love-sick teenagers."

Miranda smiled. "You know what they say. 'The path of true love never did run smooth.'"

"In other words, they'll work it out sooner or later," Jase said. "I wish they'd get it over with."

She chuckled. "They'll be happier when they do."

"But enough about my dad. What did you do all day?"

"I got up early and grabbed the car keys off my brother's dresser, for one thing." She felt a surge of satisfaction at the memory. "I figured it was my turn."

"That's something I don't understand," he said. "Why does your family only have one car?"

"Mom doesn't do much driving. We live within walking distance of the grocery and the drug store, and she would rather walk. She's terrified of highway driving, so that limits her, too. And Dad drove a big white truck with his company logo painted on the sides. It's parked at the office."

"Couldn't one of you drive that?"

She groaned. "Only Dad could tame that beast. It's hard to turn around corners, and impossible to park. Besides," she closed her eyes, "we may have to sell it to pay some bills."

"Oh yeah?"

"Remember when I told you my mom's rent check bounced?" It seemed like years ago now. "Well, today I went to the bank that holds Dad's business accounts, and they let me look at his statements. He's been losing money for months now. It looks like he was borrowing from his personal account to keep the business solvent."

"Uh-oh."

She sat up straight. "Here's the really strange part. I went to see a friend of his who owns a rival company. Dan Hollis is his name. He told me construction is booming right now. From his point of view Dad seemed to have more business than he could handle."

"Did he know of any reason why your dad would be losing money?"

"I didn't ask him that. I don't know what his intentions are, so I didn't want to give away our position."

"Spoken like a true businesswoman. Did you finish cleaning the office?"

"I did. As far as I know, nothing else is missing. It's been five years since I lived at home, so I could be wrong, but as I recall Dad's office was pretty bare to begin with. He put all his money in tools, which he kept in his workshop next door. The workshop was neat as a pin, with every tool in its place, like the robber didn't even go in there."

"So whoever broke in wasn't looking for something to fence," he said.

"But what else would they steal?"

He was quiet for a moment. "Miranda, why did you have to go to the bank to look at your dad's statements?"

"What do you mean?"

"Businesses normally keep their financial records on hand."

She frowned. "I tried to find them in the office, but the filing system makes no sense."

"That seems odd, doesn't it? Why would your dad store his files in such a complicated way?"

"Balan probably set up the system. He got his accounting degree in India. Maybe they do things differently there."

"Or maybe he didn't want anyone else to be able to find things."

"You mean he might be a bit of a control freak? That seems likely." She returned to the subject of the break-in. "Anyway, we've collected all the office keys for the time being. Dad's foremen were understanding about it."

To her surprise, Jase returned to the subject of the absent accountant. "Have you heard from him yet?"

"I don't expect him to call," she said, surprised. "He's far away, and probably busy."

Jase was quiet a moment. "I guess you're right."

Something in his voice caught her attention. "You're not jealous of Balan, are you? Just because I think he's nice?"

"No, of course not."

She warmed to his vehement denial. "Good. You're my one and only, Jase."

From there the conversation took a much different turn. They hung up a few minutes later, and she got ready for bed with a smile on her face, her family worries muted for once.

At four a.m. she woke up, feeling like an idiot. Jase wasn't jealous. He was suspicious.

Nine

ost in thought, Lottie watched the sink fill up. She tuned her ears to the babble of water hitting water, drowning out her thoughts. Steam rose to bathe her face, a welcome relief from the dry February air.

She felt embarrassed about yesterday. She'd overreacted to a simple busy signal and put Jason to a lot of trouble. He'd sounded a bit exasperated when he reported back that everything was fine.

What a silly thing to do.

She washed her dishes and let the water drain, her gaze on the scene outside her window. Across the alley a solitary figure left his house and trudged down the walk, his shadow long and dark in the early morning light. When he reached the gravel, a large orange cat slipped out of the bushes to stalk along beside him, the two shadows merging on the snow. Thomas's shoulders relaxed a fraction, and he glanced at his companion with a tolerant half-smile.

The pair disappeared from view, and Lottie turned her attention to the toy train on the windowsill. Maybe she'd return it to its original owner when she went to Los Angeles. Her heart lifted at the thought.

She closed her eyes and let herself imagine meeting Johnny again. He would be older but still handsome, and he'd meet them in his snug apartment in the city. His face would light up as they said hello, and she'd turn to Sam and say, "See? He's the same old Johnny."

Sam's face floated into view, serious and slightly disapproving. He

97

made no move to shake Johnny's hand.

Lottie opened her eyes and the scene melted away, replaced by her cheerful little kitchen. She set the green engine back on the windowsill, irritated with herself. Sam would never act that way. She left for work.

The noisy halls of the PAB made a welcome change from her silent house. Students greeted her on their way to class, and she stopped to talk with Katherine at the mailboxes. She felt sure she and Katherine were destined to be old friends someday, but for now the newness of their acquaintance made their conversations short and superficial.

That was the problem, though she didn't want to admit it. In an alarmingly short time, she'd gotten used to deeper friendships. She'd come to rely on Miranda's quiet understanding and Sam's wry realism. Now they were both fighting their own battles with no time left over for Lottie.

She missed them, and she knew in her heart things would never go back to the way they were before. Every time she talked to Miranda, she sensed the girl's distraction. With every week that passed, Lottie grew more convinced she'd be placing an ad for a new assistant come spring.

Sam was a different story. It was hardly his fault their friendship had changed.

Nathan's wheelchair blocked her way as she reached the stairwell. "Why the long face, Miss Braun?"

She stopped short, startled out of her thoughts. "What an awkward thing to say. Next you'll be telling me I look tired."

He gave her a superior smile. "I got your attention, didn't I? I hear congratulations are in order."

"What do you mean?"

"I'm referring to the Los Angeles Philharmonic. Katherine said that was what the racket outside my classroom was all about yesterday."

Oddly enough, the reminder didn't cheer her up. "Well, I am rather pleased about it."

"I gathered as much," he said. "The question is, why? Fleischmann runs a three-ring circus out there. Why do you want to be one of his acts?"

She bristled. "I have my reasons."

He gave a short nod. "They'd better be good. You can bet the public will want to know."

At six, Miranda got out of bed and tiptoed to the kitchen to make a long-distance phone call. "Hi, Tanya. What's the weather like in Chicago this morning?"

"Sunny and cold." Her favorite travel agent sounded upbeat. "So where is the Great Lottie Braun going this time?"

"Actually, this isn't about Lottie. I need a personal favor, if you've got the time."

"Go for it."

"Is there a way to find out if a person got on a flight from one airport to another on a given date?"

Tanya thought this over. "It would take some work, but I guess it could be done."

"Could you do it, if I gave you the details?"

"I could try."

"I need to know about flights from San Francisco to Bangalore, India."

"For what dates?"

"Leaving last Friday."

"You have to give me time." Tanya sounded cautious. "I need to make some phone calls, and I've got a lot of other things taking priority today."

Miranda's heart sank. "Okay. Thanks anyway."

"I can tell you this," Tanya said. "I have a client who flew round trip from Chicago to San Francisco last week, and his return flight was canceled on Friday. There were tons of weather delays because of that big storm you guys had. I ended up getting him rescheduled to Saturday morning."

"Are you telling me all flights were canceled out of San Francisco last Friday?"

"Most of them, anyway."

"Thanks, Tanya. That helps a lot."

She waited until seven before she woke her brother. "You're coming with me today."

He pulled his pillow over his head. "Can't. Have to work." he mumbled.

"Where, at your mysterious job? That's convenient." She grabbed the pillow and dropped it on the floor. "Come on. We have work to do."

"Where's Mom?"

"We're not going to worry Mom right now. I need your help to find Balan Prakash."

He sat up, rubbing his eyes. "Don't be an idiot. Balan went to India."

"Maybe he did." She swept his covers to the foot of the bed. "Maybe he didn't. I need to know for sure. You know where he lives, right?"

"Yeah. Why?"

"We're going to pay him a visit."

"That's stupid. He's not home." He sounded less certain.

She kept after him until he grudgingly agreed to go with her. "Just to prove you wrong," he said. "Then you have to promise to leave me alone."

"I'll do no such thing."

Balan's quiet residential neighborhood made a nice contrast to the busy morning traffic. Miranda parked in front of his tan stucco duplex and turned to Zac. "Let me do the talking."

"Fine." He opened his car door. "I don't want to be here anyway."

She rang the doorbell and they waited on the concrete step. "Nice neighborhood," she murmured. "How can he afford it?"

Zac threw her a sidelong glance. "He has a roommate."

The door opened, and a man in a suit and tie said, "Can I help you?"

Miranda injected some Lottie-style confidence into her voice. "We're looking for Balan Prakash. Is he here?"

The man's look changed from inquiry to faint humor. "You too? Boy, that guy got around."

The insolence in his tone threw Miranda off her stride. "He works for our father."

He shrugged. "Balan moved out last Friday. Stiffed me for the light bill, too."

"Moved out? As in, he's not coming back?"

"He'd better not." The man raised his eyebrows suggestively. "Too many women are looking for him."

She and Zac exchanged an uneasy glance. "Who else besides us?"

"A girl came by yesterday. She looked young and innocent, but when she opened her mouth—wow." He shook his head. "You should have heard the things she said about him. I sort of understood why he took off."

Miranda frowned. "Balan has a girlfriend?"

"Girlfriends. He played the field, if you get my drift. Took a different woman to Vegas almost every weekend." The man turned away. "Anyway, I can't help you. He didn't exactly leave a forwarding address."

Balan's ex-roommate started to shut the door, but Miranda stuck her foot in the frame. "How did he move his stuff? Did he rent a truck?"

"He hitched a trailer to the back of his car. He didn't have that much."

"A rented trailer?"

"Yeah, I guess so. Look, if you find him, let me know. He owes me money." He shut the door and they returned to the car.

"Now do you believe me?" she said as she pulled away from the curb.

He stared straight ahead, eyes narrowed. "Maybe he doesn't want to pay rent while he's in India."

"And the woman who's looking for him? Does that square with what you know of him?"

"That guy could have been lying. He obviously doesn't like Balan."

Miranda frowned. "Or maybe Balan was doing the lying."

"Why would he do that? We're family."

Questions crowded her mind, but the obstinate set of Zac's jaw made her rethink them. They rode in silence for a few blocks. Finally, she sighed. "Okay. Let's say he did go to India."

"He did."

"We could really use his help to solve the office break-in. Can't we call him long-distance?"

Zac gave her an incredulous stare. "You want to call Balan while his mother is dying?"

"No." She found herself over-enunciating to make her message clear. "I want to call and see if his mother really is dying."

"So, then Zac and I made a bet about where Balan went," Miranda told Jase Wednesday night. "If we find out he's not in India, Zac will help me talk to the police."

"And if he is in India?"

"Then I have to leave Zac alone."

Jase let out a disgusted breath. "If he was my brother, I'd smack him."

She chuckled. "That's the nicest thing anyone's said to me all day."

"Yeah?" His voice grew warm. "I'll say much nicer things when I see you on Friday."

Friday. She couldn't think about Friday yet.

He returned to the subject at hand. "Well? Did you find out if he's in India?"

She chuckled. "You make that sound so easy."

"It isn't?"

"Not in this case. First, we had to deal with the time difference. We got home at noon, which is midnight for India, so we had to wait until after dinner to try. Then we didn't have a direct phone number for Balan's mother because she lives in a village some distance away from the city and doesn't have a phone in her house. We called my father's sister to get the number for another family member who does have a phone."

"And then you called the village?"

She closed her eyes. "I spent a long time on the phone with my aunt, talking about my dad. She told me all kinds of things about his childhood, and how much she loved her little brother, and she wanted to know all about the funeral, and how my mom is. Then she passed the phone to my uncle and then two of my cousins. You know, just an average family phone call."

"Wow," he said. "But after that, did you call the village?"

"Yep."

"And was he there?"

"I don't know. Nobody answered the phone."

He groaned. "So, you still don't know where Balan Prakash is?"

"Nope. We'll have to try again tomorrow."

"Before or after you pack?"

"Pack?" The question slipped out before she could stop it.

"You are still coming, aren't you? To the wedding, remember?"

She drew her knees up tight and rested her head on them. "I don't know, Jase. I want to, but how can I leave here right now?"

His silence spoke volumes.

"But the ticket is non-refundable," she added quickly. "I don't want to waste it."

"You'll have to do what's best. But…"

She waited. "But?"

When he spoke, his voice was tinged with desperation. "I want you here with me again. I miss you."

"I miss you, too. So much." She cradled the phone closer to her ear. "Listen, I'll be there if it's at all possible. You can count on that. And if I can't make it, I'll call you."

Reassured, they said their long good-byes. Jase hung up, and Miranda sat for another few seconds, wrapped in the memory of his voice.

She found her mother at the kitchen table when she hung up the phone. "And how is the man from Idaho?" Sonia asked.

"He's fine." Miranda refused to be baited by her mother's loose grasp of geography. "Mom, it's late. What are you doing up?"

Sonia's small hands were wrapped around the teacup in front of her. "Are you going to marry him?" she said.

The question stole Miranda's breath for a moment. "That's the plan," she said in a low voice.

Her mother looked up, sadness in her eyes. "And he is white?"

Miranda's eyes widened. "That has nothing to do with how I feel about him."

"It will make things harder, though, my dear." Sonia gazed into her teacup with a sad smile. "Marriage is difficult enough under the best conditions. Look at your father and me. Our parents gave the matter careful consideration before they arranged for us to marry, and still we had some very hard times."

Miranda sank into the seat next to her mother. "But you and Dad were happy together, weren't you?"

"I thought we were, anyway."

Chills ran down Miranda's spine. "What do you mean?"

Sonia gave a long sigh. "All winter he wasn't himself. He was distracted, never listening when I talked to him. He lost his temper easily." She closed her eyes. "To tell you the truth, I was beginning to think I'd lost him."

"Oh, Mom." Miranda put an arm around her mother's shoulders. "That's just grief talking."

"How would you know? You weren't here."

"You and Dad had a good marriage. He knew you loved him and he loved you, all the way to the end."

Sonia raised her head. "Do you really think so?"

The lost look in her mother's eyes made Miranda's heart twist painfully. "I'm sure of it."

You can bet the public will want to know.

Nathan's parting words played in Lottie's brain like a broken record, keeping her from sleep. For hours she'd tossed and turned in the darkness, helpless to escape his brusque critique. You'd better have a good reason for going out there. People will talk.

At two a.m. she'd given up trying to sleep. Now she sat at the Steinway, pouring her heart into Mendelssohn's *Songs Without Words*, while she worked out the answer to Nathan's infernal question.

Why was she going to Los Angeles?

Certainly not for Ernest Fleischmann. At this point in her career she didn't need the L.A. Phil. They were a convenient excuse.

This wasn't about Cal's book, either. He and Teresa were competent researchers. They would make a success of their project with or without her help. She didn't need to follow up leads for them.

Which left one option. Johnny.

She tripped over a key change and frowned. Training her gaze on the opposite wall, she flexed her hands and started again.

Lottie could not shake the idea that she was meant to see Johnny again. She wanted to know how his life had turned out and tell him what happened in Santa Monica. If she could, she wanted to share God's grace with him, as Helen had shared it with her.

Finding him was a long shot. She knew that. Yet the dream persisted.

The music turned somber. Lottie had one other permanent tie to L.A, one she tried never to think about. Somewhere in a vast cemetery a small headstone marked Billy's resting place. For the first time in her life, she was ready to see it.

She broke off mid-measure and dropped her hands to her sides. She had unfinished business in the City of Angels, some of it long delayed. That was the true reason she was taking this trip.

Now, what was she going to tell the public? Because the truth would never do.

Ten

 mean it, Dad. Give yourself one more day at home."

Sam glared at his oldest son. "You can't send me home. This is my business."

"Which you taught me to run." Jason's calm manner made Sam want to box his ears. "Look, we can't have a repeat of last winter. Not with Mitch's wedding in two days. Go home and rest. We can get along without you for a little longer."

Sam put a rein on his urge to cough. "I'm going crazy just sitting around. What are you doing today?"

"I'm making a sales call on someone Diana Deering referred to us. Diana sold them a fixer-upper with a view of the river. They're looking for someone to do the fixing. Want to go?"

"Huh." This took a little of the wind out of Sam's sails. Diana Deering, real estate agent, gave him the heebie-jeebies. She talked fast, wore a lot of goop on her eyes, and was always pushing some scheme or other. Look at the way she'd tried to get Lottie to sell her house last fall. It hadn't gone well. Worst of all, Diana was divorced and on the hunt. "What else have you got? I can check in on the Donaldson job."

"I did that before I got here." Jase put a hand on his shoulder. "If you won't go home for your own sake, do it for Mitch. He needs you to be healthy this weekend."

"I am healthy," he said, then coughed.

Jase gave his shoulder a sympathetic pat. "One more day. I want you here tomorrow morning while I pick up Miranda in Cedar Rapids."

Sam stomped across the parking lot with steam coming out of his ears. The boy was getting too big for his britches. Where did he get off, telling his old man what to do?

He got in the car, breathing heavily from his exertion. This time the cough that burst out of him went on for a while. When it was over, he rested his head on the headrest to get his bearings.

On the other hand, maybe a little nap would feel good.

Once at home, he dozed off in his recliner and woke up an hour later, feeling restless. Jason's constant talk about the wedding had reminded him of a job he needed to finish.

In the garage, Sam plugged in his shop light and ran a hand over the newly painted pieces of the wooden rocking horse. He'd painted it chestnut, with a black mane and tail and four white socks. Time for a protective coat of varnish.

Before he began, he set a stack of records on the living room stereo. As the first strains of *Lottie Braun Plays Chopin* drifted through the house, he smiled. For years her albums had been his music of choice when he puttered around the workbench. He'd collected them as they were released. The fact that he now knew the artist in person only enhanced his appreciation. Now that he'd watched her play her Steinway at home, he could picture her fluid movements and supreme concentration as he listened to her records.

Nancy had puzzled over this side of him. She'd teased him about his love of classical music, but she'd also protected his right to enjoy it. She was an active woman, a hard worker without patience for a passive thing like listening to music. He should take up an instrument, she'd said. Then he could make his own music, instead of merely listening to other people play.

When she'd finally met his brother and learned that Sam could play the drums she'd been really confused. He'd never told her about Walt's band. It wasn't a thing he liked to talk about. Walt's stories had made the Neverland sound glamorous, but Sam knew better. At best it was drudgery. At worst…well, he didn't like to go there.

He dipped a brush in the varnish and set to work, methodically covering the surface of the horse.

This was the strange thing. His life with Nancy had been full and satisfying. For a while after she died, he'd thought he might as well die, too. But here he was nearly four years later, uncovering sides to himself he never needed while she was with him. He'd found out he was a pretty good cook, and he could get by in the cleaning department, too. The garden was a lost cause, but that was okay with him. Not all of Nancy's interests had interested him, either.

The cooking and cleaning were small examples. The real changes had happened in his heart and mind. Because of his grief, he'd learned to stay a lot closer to the Lord. The sense of His presence was a comfort he didn't ever want to give up, even now that the pain had gone down to a background sadness. Bob Summers had been a good friend to him through that whole process and taught him a lot about leaning on Jesus.

The real surprise, and the thing he couldn't have predicted, was the music. Not only did he listen to his records more when he was home, he caught himself humming or whistling or outright singing at odd moments. He didn't like to admit it, but sometimes he even thought it would feel good to play the drums again.

He finished the coat of varnish and set to cleaning his paintbrush with mineral spirits. The music on the stereo turned loud and joyful, and he found himself scrubbing in time to the beat.

When the brush was clean, he slid open the long drawer under the workbench and picked up the ancient pair of drumsticks that lay on top of a pile of old pictures. No one would know if he gave in to his impulse today. What's more, no one would care.

As he slid the drawer shut, a black-and-white photo slipped off the pile and lodged halfway out the drawer. He pulled it out and looked at it, the same picture as Lottie's, the one of the Neverland in its prime. Sam had found it among Walt's belongings after he died and didn't have the heart to get rid of it.

One small detail separated this photo and Lottie's: This one bore the full names and addresses of every member of the orchestra, along with updates written in his brother's barely legible hand. Walt had exchanged Christmas cards with several of the guys for years. He'd even kept up with Johnny for a while, though his last address was crossed out and the word "Moved" written next to it.

Sam shoved the photo back into the drawer. He couldn't share it with Lottie or Cal. If they wanted to resurrect the band, they'd do it without his help.

The drumsticks felt warm and familiar in his grip as he tested them on the edge of the workbench. His boys would laugh if they could see him now. They seemed to think the changes in him had something to do with Lottie. He preferred to give the credit to time and God, not some schoolboy crush on his beautiful, unattainable, new-old friend.

At ten o'clock Thursday morning, Miranda finally reached Balan Prakash's home village. The man who answered the phone said no, they did not think Mrs. Prakash was ill, but they would run down to her house and check. While he was gone, she stretched the telephone cord to its full length and knocked on her brother's bedroom door. "Zac. Get up. I need you."

He emerged from the room in shorts and a T-shirt, his eyes heavy with sleep. She pulled him close so they could share the receiver.

Half a world away, the man returned to the phone with Balan's mother, who let loose a torrent of Hindi on Miranda and Zac. When she finished, the man got back on the phone. "Did you get all that?"

"I'm afraid I'm not fluent," Miranda told him. "Can you translate for me?"

"She said she is not sick, but if she were, she would not call her son Balan, who she has not heard from in two years or more. He took her life savings to go to America, and he has never attempted to pay it back. Goodbye now."

Miranda hung up and turned to her brother. "Well, Zac?"

He pushed a hand through his thick hair. "What now?"

"We search the office for the things he really stole, and then we go to the police. Are you in?"

He gave a reluctant nod. "I'm in."

When they reached the office, they dug into the files. "What are we looking for?" Zac asked.

She looked up from the ledger she'd spread out on the desk. "To be honest, I don't really know. I never took an accounting course."

"So, we're flying blind here?"

"Well…sort of."

He frowned. "What was your job with that Lottie woman?"

"Personal assistant. I dealt with her correspondence, made copies for her classes, and booked her travel."

"Did you write checks for her?"

"Sometimes."

"If you were going to steal from her, how would you do it?"

She gave him a blank look. "I would never do that."

His eyes narrowed. "Look, I don't want to be here all day, so play along. How would you steal from your boss?"

"I would…." She closed her eyes, thinking hard. "Okay. Say I got the travel agent to help me. She could overcharge for plane tickets. I could pay her inflated bill, and we'd split the overpayment."

"Would you trust the travel agent not to spill the beans?"

"Not really." She opened her eyes. "I guess the easiest thing would be to write checks to myself and cash them. But Lottie reconciles her own bank statement every month. She'd catch me in a heartbeat, and I'd lose my job. It wouldn't be worth it."

Zac snapped his fingers. "That's how he did it. Dad had stopped reconciling the bank account statements. He trusted Balan that much." He reached for a file drawer. "We should look for those statements."

"Don't bother," she said. "I already searched. They're not there."

"That's not good."

"Don't worry." She reached into her bag. "I got the bank to give me copies of the last two years' records. You're right. They're a mess."

"Can I see?"

She opened the first envelope and removed the canceled checks. Fan-ning them out on the desk, she pointed out four made out to Balan Prakash, and not in Dad's handwriting. Altogether, they equaled four-thousand dollars. Zac stared at the evidence with growing rage. "I'll kill him."

Miranda gave him a puzzled look. "Why did we all trust this man?"

"Because he's family." Zac shrugged. "And because he was really nice to us. He loved Mom's cooking, and he worked hard at the office—or so we thought." He glanced away. "He talked to me a lot about finding my true calling. He knew I didn't want to take over the business, so he helped me find another direction. Now I know why."

Torn between anger and sympathy, she stared at her brother in silence. She wanted to yell and scream and take out her feelings on him, but she knew if she said the wrong thing now, she could alienate him for good.

The ring of the telephone cut through the silence. Miranda reached for it. "Hello?"

The voice on the other end sounded young and female, with a slight Indian accent. "May I speak with Balan, please?"

Miranda swallowed hard. "Balan is not in right now," she said as confidently as she could. "May I leave him a message?"

"Who are you?" the girl said. When Miranda didn't answer right away, she continued. "Never mind. I already know. You're the daughter of the family."

Miranda waited, intrigued.

The girl raised her voice. "Look, you probably think you're the only woman in Balan's life, but you're wrong. He may have led you to think he's interested, but he's not. We're getting married in Vegas tonight."

She spared Miranda from finding an answer by slamming the phone down in her ear. Miranda hung up with a grin. "Zac, I think we've got enough to go to the police."

Lottie blew the steam off her cup of Earl Grey and set it on the desk. She wasn't usually a tea drinker, but on her dash across campus, the cold wind had chilled her to the bone, and she needed the warmth.

Thursday afternoon was dragging by, not just because of the frigid weather, but also because it was her last day of work before the wedding weekend. Even now Patti and Sarah were driving across the flat gray interstates of central Illinois, due to arrive by supper time. Not that Lottie would see much of them tonight. No, tonight Patti and Mitchell planned to spend time alone with Sarah. They felt strongly that their little family needed to reconnect before the party started, and Lottie supported their wishes.

She should probably follow their example and spend a solitary evening centering herself, or some such modern thing, before the house filled with company, but she had too much to do. Beds made, floors swept, and bathrooms cleaned before Patti's maid of honor, a good friend from college, arrived with her husband and three-year-old twin ring bearers.

She sighed. She'd much rather spend the evening at Annie's Cafe, eating pie and arguing with Sam over whatever fool thing he wanted to fight about. But last she'd heard Sam was still sick, and she was still not Nancy.

"Are you ready for me, Miss Braun?"

Jane Lawrence, a timid sophomore, hesitated in the doorway. Lottie beckoned her inside. "Certainly, Jane. Have a seat and start warming up. I'll be right with you."

She disciplined her mind to follow the plodding pattern of the student's finger exercises. Thursdays with Sam would return soon enough. By the time they did, she planned to have enough defenses in place to safely enjoy them. Right now, she needed to teach a decent piano lesson, finish up some odds and ends, and get ready for a weekend of joyful celebration.

The hour passed quickly enough, once Jane moved on to a Scarlatti sonata. She had worked hard to attain the light touch necessary for a Baroque piece. This week she'd put the finishing touches on it, and together they celebrated a job well done. "Your performance will be a good addition to the student recital," Lottie said. "Now, let's move on to something new."

A look of dismay crossed the student's pale face. "Something new? Already?"

Lottie raised her eyebrows. "What would life be without another hill to climb?"

She assigned a short piece by a lesser-known composer and sent the girl on her way. As the door closed, she sighed. Successful artists had one trait in common: They welcomed new challenges with open arms. Performers who wanted to rest on their laurels would never rise to greatness.

Not that it mattered for Jane. Music was meant to be enjoyed by everyone, and she had acquired the skills to appreciate it more than most. She would contribute just as much to the world as a school music teacher, or church choir director, or children's piano teacher, as Lottie had as a concert pianist. More power to her.

On that positive note, Lottie marked the lesson off in her grade book, returned a phone call about the benefit concert, and tidied her office for the weekend. She was putting on her coat when Jason called, sounding hesitant. "Could you do me a favor? I'm supposed to bring Dad dinner, but I'm driving up to Cedar Rapids now so I can meet Miranda's plane in the morning."

She frowned. "Why are you going tonight? I thought Miranda's plane didn't come in until tomorrow afternoon."

"I have some shopping to do."

Something in his tone piqued Lottie's interest. "Shopping? For work?"

"It's personal." The words came out in a rush.

She resisted the urge to ask more questions. "I'm happy to help. Tell your dad I'll drop by around seven."

I hope his shopping trip has something to do with my assistant, Lottie thought as she hung up the phone.

She glanced at her watch and started to button her coat. She'd have to get a move on if she was going to have her chores done by seven.

When Patti breezed into the house an hour later, Lottie was giving the first-floor bathroom a good cleaning. She hurried to the kitchen, stripping off her yellow rubber gloves as she went, and threw her arms around her niece. "There you are! Can you believe it's finally the wedding weekend?"

Patti laughed. "We're ready for it. Aren't we, Sarah?" She lifted the little girl into her arms. "Who will you be in the wedding, sweetheart?"

Sarah burrowed her golden head into her mother's shoulder and peeped shyly at Lottie. "Fower Girl."

"The flower girl?" Lottie said, impressed. "Can I see your dress?"

"We're picking it up from the tailor tomorrow, along with mine," Patti said. "You're coming with us, right?"

"I wouldn't miss it."

Mitchell arrived to pick up his girls, and Lottie returned to her chores with a joyful heart.

Her good mood was undiminished as she pulled into Sam's driveway. The bathrooms were spotless, and the kitchen floor thoroughly mopped. Annie had been kind enough to pack her wonderful food in boxes for delivery. "Tell Sam he'd better feel good enough to dance with me at the reception," she said as she rang up the sale.

It felt good to help a neighbor in need.

Arms full of take-out boxes, she pressed the doorbell with her elbow and waited, shivering a bit in the cold night air. She had to hit the bell a second time before the porch light came on and the door opened. Sam's expression went from puzzled to surprised—though not pleased, Lottie noted—as he opened the storm door to talk to her. "What are you doing here?"

She winced at the blunt question. "Didn't Jason tell you? He drove up to Cedar Rapids tonight, so he asked me to bring you dinner."

His eyebrows drew together. "I already ate."

"You did? But Jase said you needed food."

"Well, if he'd called me, I would have told him I was all set."

Embarrassment heated Lottie's face. Not knowing what else to do, she held the boxes out. "Here. Take these. You can eat it later."

His frown deepened. "You're the one with company coming. You need it more than me."

"No. I brought it for you." She fought the urge to stomp her foot in frustration. "I'm leaving it here. Do with it what you wish." Setting the boxes on the porch, she left.

She didn't look back as she drove away. She didn't want to know what Sam would do next. In his present mood, he seemed fully capable of leaving Annie's good food on the porch all night.

Her temper cooled as she drove home, and she tried the age-old exercise of seeing things from the other guy's point of view. She could understand how Sam had been so surprised by the offer of free food that he completely lost his manners…Nope. She couldn't understand that.

She pushed the garage door button as she rolled down the alley. One positive thing had come from this evening. For the first time all week, she did not envy Nancy.

Sam stared at the boxes on his porch for a long minute. Then, with a sigh, he picked them up and brought them into the house. "That boy of mine has all the brains of a field mouse," he muttered. "First, he asks Lottie, busy as she is, to bring me a dinner I don't need. Then he doesn't bother to tell me she's coming."

That last part was what really made him mad. He'd spent the day in his recliner, and he looked like it, too. His hair stuck up in back, he smelled like Vicks VapoRub, and he had a wad of used Kleenex stuffed up his sleeve.

Worst of all the music of Lottie Braun was pouring out of his stereo speakers. He'd been playing her records all afternoon, stacking first the A sides, then the B sides to be sure he got every note.

He couldn't explain it to himself, let alone to her.

She'd taken off running as soon as she saw how bad he looked. She didn't want to be around a bad-tempered, foul-smelling old coot, and he couldn't blame her.

She'd have been really disgusted if he'd let her in. He sure hadn't spent any time cleaning this week. Pushing aside a stack of dirty dishes, he set the food on the kitchen counter. The label on the top box caught his eye. "Annie's Cafe, huh?"

A whiff of warm fried chicken reached his nose when he lifted the lid. One leg, a thigh, mashed potatoes, and green beans, his usual Thursday night meal. Annie knew her stuff. The box below it held two pieces of banana cream pie. He frowned. Two pieces? That seemed excessive. Curious, he reached for the last box. White meat, potato salad, and corn. Wasn't that Lottie's standing order?

He rubbed a hand across his stubbly chin. This put things in a whole different light. She'd been planning to keep him company and he'd sent her home hungry. What an idiot.

He reached for the phone to apologize, then put it back on the hook. What could he possibly say?

Turning off the kitchen light he trudged back to the living room and lifted the needle off the turntable. The room, comfortable enough before the doorbell rang, now seemed downright shabby. His brown recliner had a split in the leather where his feet rested, and his warm wool blanket was losing its binding.

He grabbed a stack of *Workbench* magazines off the floor and took his empty dishes to the kitchen. Feeling slightly better, he carried his medications upstairs to his room and returned with the vacuum sweeper.

Time to clean up his act. Maybe in the process he'd figure out how to apologize.

Miranda dialed Jason's number and waited for him to pick up. He was going to be so relieved that she'd gotten the police involved.

It had taken an entire afternoon of waiting, but she and Zac had finally been ushered into the presence of a San Francisco police detective named Carter. He'd listened to their story, examined last year's general ledger, which she'd unearthed from the back of a file drawer, and said, "How long has the bookkeeper been gone?"

The phone rang a fourth time.

"You probably have a case here," Detective Carter had told them, "but your perpetrator is probably long gone by now." Still, he agreed to notify the Las Vegas police, and to send a bank fraud specialist to the office to examine the rest of the books.

The phone rang an eighth time. "Come on, Jase. Pick up."

Mom still didn't know about Balan. Protecting her was one of the few things she and Zac agreed on. Since Monday, she'd only been awake for an hour or two each day, and they were not about to deepen her depression with news of the embezzlement. Give her a few more days to sleep, they thought. Then she might be able to bear this new grief.

She let the phone ring a twelfth time before she gave up. It was midnight Collison time. Jase was probably hanging out with his brother tonight, before the wedding weekend began in earnest. She'd call again in half an hour.

But he didn't answer half an hour later, or thirty minutes after that.

Miranda's alarm went off so early Friday morning she shouldn't have bothered to sleep at all. She'd stayed up far too late, trying to reach Jason without success. When she finally gave up and went to bed, sleep had been elusive. She'd split her worried thoughts between Jase, who should have been home in his own bed by now, and Balan Prakash, who might never be found at all.

A shower and a strong cup of coffee helped her feel more like herself again. Zac got up while the coffee was brewing and hugged her good-bye. He seemed to have grown up overnight, from the panicky boy who had begged her to come home to this sober young man who insisted he could handle Mom and the police investigation for a few days. "Just promise you'll come back," he said. "We need to stick together until this thing is over."

She gave him a decisive nod. "I'm coming back. You can count on that."

On that note he went back to bed, and quiet fell on the apartment as she finished packing her suitcase and re-checked her ticket. When she was ready to go, she tiptoed into her mother's room to kiss her good-bye. Sonia woke up just enough to pat her cheek in answer.

The phone began to ring as she shut the bedroom door. Glancing at her wristwatch, she hurried to answer so it wouldn't wake her mother. If it was Jase, he had terrible timing. She was already running a few minutes late. "Hello?"

"Miss Charles, this is Detective Carter. We met yesterday."

"Yes?"

"We have Balan Prakash in custody. He's confessed to killing your father. We need you to come down to the station immediately."

Eleven

This was better, Sam thought as he poured coffee into a foam cup and shook powdered creamer into it. Finally, back to work, and Jason wasn't even there to boss him around. He'd already been out to check on the flooring installation for a bathroom remodel, and now he was primed to dig into the proposals Jason had asked him to double-check.

Miranda called a few minutes later, sounding panicked. "I've been trying to reach Jase. Is he there?"

Sam glanced at his watch. "He's supposed to pick you up at the airport. Didn't he show up?"

"I don't know. I missed my flight. Sam, the police caught my father's killer yesterday. I have to stay in San Francisco until things calm down."

"Your father's killer?" he repeated, stunned.

"Yes. His accident wasn't an accident." Her words tumbled over each other. "My dad had begun to suspect my cousin Balan was embezzling from the company. When Balan realized it, he hit my dad with a wooden beam and then made it look like an accident. He's been charged with murder."

"And Jase doesn't know any of this."

"I tried to reach him last night and again this morning, but he hasn't been home at all. I'm afraid something might be wrong."

Sam rubbed his clean-shaven chin. "I think he's okay. He drove up to Cedar Rapids last night instead of waiting till this morning."

121

"He did?" She sounded surprised. "Why did he do that?"

He'd been asking himself the same thing. "There's a big mall in Cedar Rapids. Maybe Mitch and Patti asked him to pick something up for the wedding."

"Can you catch him as soon as he gets back? I need him to call me as soon as possible."

Sam gave the work on his desk a regretful glance. This was more important than looking at floor plans. "Sure."

No sooner had he finished with Miranda than the phone rang again. A leaky pipe at the bathroom remodel had halted the flooring crew. He grabbed his coat and ran out the door.

Jason was sitting at his desk when Sam returned a few hours later. The boy's head was bowed, eyes closed. "She wasn't there," he said before Sam could speak. "Miranda didn't show."

"I know," Sam said. "She missed her plane."

Jason raised his head, a blank look in his eyes. "How do you know?"

"She called here this morning looking for you. Said she tried you all night last night but you weren't home. She sounded worried."

"What happened? Is she all right?"

"They caught her father's killer."

Jase looked as stunned as Sam had felt. "His killer?"

Sam relayed the news about Miranda's cousin, and watched with relief as Jase recovered his good spirits. "How did the police find Balan Prakash?"

"They tracked him down in Las Vegas. Apparently, he's got quite a gambling problem, which is why he was stealing from the company."

"Wow! Well, I hate that she can't be here, but I understand why she had to stay behind. I just wish I could have talked to her myself."

That point was bothering Sam. "Why did you go to Cedar Rapids last night?"

Jason's eyes lit up. "Can you keep a secret?" He stuck his hand in his jeans pocket and pulled out a small velvet box. "This is why." He opened the box, and a round diamond solitaire winked in the light.

Sam gave a low whistle. "Should I be congratulating you?"

Jase shook his head. "I was going to ask her tonight."

Lottie and Sarah sat on the pink cushioned bench in Ackerman's tailor shop and watched as Patti scrutinized her wedding gown in the three-way mirror. "Does it need to be taken in another half-inch?"

"Taken in?" Lottie glanced at the tailor, who gave a silent shake of the head. "No, dear. It fits you like a glove."

"Do you really think so?" Anxiety laced her niece's voice.

Mrs. Ackerman bent to spread out the embroidered train. "I took extra care with your dress, for your mom's sake. She was a good lady." She smiled up at Patti. "She'd be real proud of you."

Patti's face relaxed into a gratified smile. "Thank you, Mrs. Ackerman." She turned to her daughter. "What do you think, Sarah? Is Mommy pretty enough to be a bride?"

Sarah pointed at the dress, her blue eyes round. "Mommy pretty."

"Thank you, dear heart." Patti performed a curtsy for her daughter and stepped into the dressing room. "I'll just be a minute, you two."

Lottie turned to the tailor. "That was the perfect thing to say," she murmured. "I only wish I'd thought of it."

Mrs. Ackerman smiled. "Everybody loved Mrs. Parker. It's a shame she's not here to see her daughter get married."

Patti emerged from the dressing room and handed her gown to the tailor. "I'll take Sarah's dress without having her try it on." She glanced at her daughter. "I'm afraid if we put her in it now, we won't get her back out of it without a fight. She's become very stubborn lately."

The tailor nodded. "Little girls love their fancy clothes. My Kathleen's youngest is about that age."

"Is that right?" Patti said. "So, Kathleen has kids?"

"Yep. She and her husband Donny have three, and one on the way." Mrs. Ackerman pulled a protective bag over the dress as she talked. "I'm closing up shop next month to help out with them."

While they chatted about Mrs. Ackerman's family, Lottie walked to the window with Sarah and lifted her up to see outside. She wanted Patti to take all the time she needed to catch up with old friends, without her fifth-wheel aunt making everything awkward.

A few minutes later Patti hung the dress in the back seat of the Mercedes and buckled Sarah in next to it. "One errand to go," she said to Lottie. "I need to stop at Annie's and break it to her gently that we added seven more people for the reception."

"I imagine she'll have a few choice things to say about that."

"What can I do? People don't understand the *RSVP* anymore."

They found Annie in the kitchen, teaching a new cook how to bread a pork tenderloin. When she saw the three of them, she washed her hands and pulled her order book out of her desk. "So, you're tying the knot tomorrow, huh?"

Patti gave her an apologetic smile. "Seven more people have told me they're coming, too."

Annie raised her eyebrows. "Seven more, huh? Wow." She looked like she wanted to say more, but she didn't.

Patti noticed, too. "I'm really sorry. I'd uninvite them if I could."

Annie's good humor came to the rescue. "We'll make it work. Think of it as my wedding gift to you and Mitch." She closed her book and turned to Lottie. "How is Sam feeling? Will he be well enough for the wedding?"

Aware of Patti's curious stare, Lottie shrugged. "I think so."

They barely made it to the car before Patti burst out, "Why did she ask you about Sam? Are you two seeing each other? Tell me everything."

Lottie dismissed her with a scornful wave. "Don't be silly. Sam and I are friends. You know that."

"I know nothing of the sort," Patti said gleefully. "Oh, this is so exciting! I knew you two were hiding something."

Lottie shook her head. "You've got a big enough romance for the both of us, Patti. Keep your mind on that."

"Sam, how are you tonight?" Bob Summers asked with concern. "I heard you were a bit under the weather this week."

Sam returned his friend's warm handshake. "I feel pretty good, Bob.

In fact, I worked until noon today. Then we closed for family business."

Bob broke into a grin. "Weddings are the best family business there is." His gaze swept over the group that milled about the sanctuary, waiting for the rehearsal to start. "Tonight is going to be very special. Now, you'll have to excuse me. It's time I got the ball rolling."

Sam looked around with deep satisfaction as the minister hurried away. All the people he loved most were in this room right now. Jason stood by the windows in his charcoal-gray suit, talking and laughing with the other groomsmen and their wives. He'd taken Miranda's news pretty well, though he looked pretty crestfallen at first. Even now he looked a little lost without her by his side.

Patti and Mitch were at the front, happily self-conscious. Mitchell's eyes glowed when they rested on his bride-to-be. Sam could see why. Patti was a dark-haired beauty like her mother, and she looked especially lovely in that bright green dress.

Sarah sat on the front row between the ring bearers, gazing from one to the other with wonder in her eyes. The twins' mother, a sweet girl named Beth, had given each child a coloring book and crayons and was doing her best to keep them interested. She had the knowing attitude of a seasoned mother, a sort of keen readiness to meet the chaos that might break out at any moment.

Sam was glad the kids had chosen the church at Westmont for their wedding. The dignified old sanctuary, with its narrow stained-glass windows and red velvet-covered pews, had an old-world charm just right for such a special occasion. It also boasted an organ, the same one Lottie had learned to play as a child, and she sat there now, fully hidden by the console, waiting for Reverend Summers' instructions. She'd been playing when Sam first arrived this evening, the melodies and countermelodies flooding the sanctuary with ancient wordless praise. He didn't have to see her to know she'd be stunning, those long, tapered fingers flying over the keyboard, with all her intensity of purpose bent on the sounds she was bringing from those pipes.

Later, he promised himself, he would find a moment alone with her to apologize for his stupidity.

Mitch and Patti had chosen Westmont for one other reason that warmed his heart. Eva Hoffman Reed, Sam's adopted mother, lived in the nursing home a few blocks away with her sister-in-law, Cora Hoffman. Both ladies were here tonight, side-by-side in their wheelchairs at the back of the room. They could not travel as far as Collison anymore, so the kids had brought the joyful occasion to them. Sam would take them home before the rehearsal dinner, to give their frail bodies time to rest up before tomorrow.

Reverend Summers called for attention, and the rehearsal began.

Lottie had been delighted when Patti and Mitchell asked her to play for their wedding. She'd been even happier when they chose the church at Westmont. Its pipe organ, an excellent instrument for such a small community, held so many good memories from Lottie's girlhood. But tonight, peeking out at the rehearsal from behind the tall console, she had to admit she felt isolated, and a little bit grumpy. She'd rather be standing in the middle of the crowd, proudly representing the bride's side of the family, not hiding where she could hardly see.

The last time she attended a wedding at Westmont Church, she'd been a ten-year-old bridesmaid in her first pair of high heels. Helen had been the bride, of course, in a hurry to marry her handsome naval officer and rush off to a new life in California. Patti looked just like her tonight, with those smooth wings of ebony hair resting on the shoulders of her jade green dress. She even smiled into the eyes of her groom the same way Helen had smiled at Bill Turner.

God willing, this union would be a happier one.

Lottie pushed away the unwelcome thought. Patti and Mitch had won their right to happiness fair and square. Their story, though different from Helen's, still contained chapters of difficulty and separation. The two of them had completely lost their way while Mitchell grieved his mother's death and Patti jumped into a mistaken marriage with Sarah's father. They stood at the altar now with more sober commitment—and greater joy—than most young bridal couples.

With decades of experience at his back, Reverend Summers ran the rehearsal like a well-oiled machine. His competent good humor kept everyone smiling as they went through the motions of tomorrow's ceremony. Even Patti, who'd suffered a case of nerves this afternoon, was beginning to relax and enjoy herself. Sarah was having the time of her life, tagging along after Jack and James, her busy new friends.

At a word from the minister Lottie began the processional. Henry Purcell's "Trumpet Voluntary"—Mr. Schultz would roll in his grave to hear it played by the wrong instrument!—was the cue for Jason and Mitchell to wheel their Grandma Eva and Great-Aunt Cora up the aisle. They took their places at the altar while the bridesmaids strolled after them one by one.

The process hit a snag with the ring bearers, who needed some persuading that the long center aisle was not a racecourse. Naturally, they wanted to see who the faster twin was, but a clever bit of bribery from their mother saved the day.

Sarah toddled happily down the aisle, her attention fixed on her new friends and the cookies they were now devouring. She reached the front, collected her reward from the mama-in-charge, and the ceremony proceeded.

Patti stepped into place, and Lottie transitioned to Wagner's "Bridal Chorus." In a twist on tradition, Patti had asked Sam to escort her down the aisle, a role he'd accepted with pleasure. Lottie could only imagine all the emotions he must be dealing with as they practiced their measured steps to the altar. He looked proud and misty-eyed, and Lottie felt the tears rise in her own eyes out of sympathy.

He must miss Nancy terribly.

Sam escorted his elderly relatives back to the nursing home, then drove to downtown Collison and parked Bessie a block off the square. After a week spent inside, the clear night air felt good on his face and hardly aggravated his cough at all.

He was the last to arrive in the banquet room at Tavern on the Square. Even the parents of small children, who had dropped them off with Martha Williams to be put to bed, had made it to the rehearsal dinner ahead of him. Maybe Bessie really was as slow as everyone said.

The tiny room was bright and overheated, and he wished with all his heart he could loosen his tie. He edged past the seated guests to reach the bride. "Where do you want me to sit?"

Patti greeted him with a kiss on the cheek. "Sit next to Lottie," she said. "Hurry. They're beginning to serve the salad."

He took his seat and smiled at Lottie. "Thanks for saving me a place."

"I didn't." She pointed to a place card with his name on it.

Before he could think of an answer, she turned to speak to Bob Summers, who sat to her left.

He looked around. The groomsman on his right, a friend of Mitchell's from law school, was busy debating the relative merits of Hawkeye vs. Cyclone basketball with an usher. The table's elaborate centerpiece hid everyone else from his view, so Sam took the safe route and concentrated on eating his salad.

He'd munched nearly all the lettuce he could stand when Lottie turned her attention to him. "Sarah really likes her new rocking horse. It's all she can talk about."

He swallowed quickly, grateful for the opening. "I'm glad she likes it. Say, you sounded wonderful at the organ tonight."

"Thanks." She sounded distant.

"Lottie, I—" he began, but she turned away again, this time to answer a question from Patti. His apologies would have to wait until later.

Conversation remained stilted through the entree and dessert courses. No matter what Sam did to break the ice, she seemed determined to keep her distance. She didn't seem hurt or mad, just polite.

He didn't like it one bit.

When the waiters took the dessert dishes away, Patti gave him a meaningful nod.

Right. Speech-making wasn't his favorite job, but he'd thought through what he wanted to say. He just hoped he wouldn't make too big a hash of saying it. Pushing his chair back, he rose to his feet, but before he could call for everyone's attention Lottie tugged his sleeve. He frowned but leaned down to see what she wanted.

"You've got lettuce in your teeth," she whispered.

Chagrined, he brought his napkin to his mouth to camouflage his tooth-scraping operation. "Did I get it?" he asked, baring his teeth in her direction.

She nodded and gave him her first real smile of the night.

The knot in his belly loosened. This speech-making thing suddenly didn't seem so difficult.

"As most of you know, Patti has been part of our family almost since the beginning. Nancy and I were blessed to have many years of friendship with David and Helen, Patti's parents, and as a result the kids grew up together." He cleared his throat. "I don't know when friendship turned to love for these two, but Nancy and I were glad it did. Even in the difficult times, and there were some, I kept the faith that someday, somehow, God would make Patti a permanent member of the Harms family. Little did I know she'd bring a sweet little girl named Sarah with her, making me an instant grandpa, but I couldn't be happier." He raised his glass. "To Mitchell and Patti. May God bless their happy home."

He sat down, relieved to have it over with, and Jason stood up to take a turn. His speech was funnier; he'd been storing up material on Mitch and Patti for years. As his stories drew waves of laughter, Lottie leaned toward Sam. "You did a good job."

"Thanks." He smiled. "You're next."

She looked horrified. "Aunts don't make speeches at these things."

Her expression surprised a laugh out of him. Had he stumbled across something Lottie Braun couldn't do? For a moment he considered putting that possibility to the test. He leaned over to catch Patti's eye, but she was fully engrossed in the story Jason was telling. When his speech ended, another groomsman jumped up to add his two cents' worth, and the moment passed.

The party broke up, and Sam helped Lottie with her red wool coat.

She thanked him and stepped back, but he kept hold of her scarf. "Can I walk you to your car?"

"Sure." She injected a world of reluctance into the single syllable.

"I need to apologize for last night," he said when they were safely out of earshot of the other guests. "I wasn't expecting you, and I didn't know you'd brought dinner for both of us. That's not a good excuse for how rude I was, but I'm sorry."

"Don't worry about it," she said when his apology limped to a stop. "This must be a crazy time for you. Mitchell's get married, and your wife isn't here to see it. I completely understand that you didn't want company last night. I'm just sorry the mix-up happened in the first place." She gave him her brightest smile. "Here's my car."

Sure enough, the Mercedes was parked right in front of the restaurant. As Sam watched her get in and drive away, he squashed a wild urge to follow her, to refute her oh-so-reasonable explanation for his lunatic behavior and make her be his friend again.

Defeated, he stomped down the sidewalk to his car, his shoulders hunched against the bitter cold. Bessie couldn't catch that Mercedes anyway. It was way out of her league.

"So, your dad walked Lottie to her car?" Miranda said on the phone that night. "That sounds hopeful."

"I guess so." Jase sounded uncertain. "She usually looks happy when she's around Dad, but tonight the look on her face was hard to read."

"Uh-oh. Was it pleasant-but-polite?"

He laughed. "Exactly. How did you know?"

"That's the way she always looked before she moved to Collison."

"So, you're saying my plan to throw them together last night didn't work?"

She couldn't help smiling. "Is that why you drove to Cedar Rapids early? So Lottie would have to bring him dinner?" They'd already talked about the missed plane *ad infinitum*, but she couldn't help teasing him a little.

"Yeah." His voice was strained. "That's why. I stayed the night with a college buddy, so it was no problem."

"Seems like an awful lot of trouble just to set up Lottie and your dad. It was sweet of you, but they'll work out their issues sooner or later."

"I guess you're right." He paused. "Man, I wish you were here right now."

"Me too. I mean that." She did, with all her heart. "Today was awful."

"I bet it was. How'd your mom take the news that your dad was murdered?"

"She's devastated. We all are." Miranda sighed. "It's horrible knowing that somebody meant to hurt my dad that way."

"And worse that it was Balan."

She laughed softly. "Actually, I can't believe how quickly my mom adjusted to that part. She went from 'Balan is wonderful' to 'Balan should get the death penalty' in the time it took the detective to explain the situation."

"Wow. That must be so hard for her."

"Not as hard as you'd think. I guess it makes a difference that he was from Dad's side of the family, not hers." Miranda smiled at the memory. "She told me she didn't trust him when he first came, but he was so respectful and kind that he inveigled her into liking him."

Jase gave a snort of laughter. "'Inveigled'? Was that the word she used?"

"My mother has a surprisingly large vocabulary," she said dryly. "I can't even repeat all the names she's called him since then. And I thought Dad was the one with the temper."

"There's something I don't get," he said. "Why did Balan wait around for all those weeks instead of leaving right away?"

"To buy time." She sat up a little straighter. "Here's the thing that's really messed up. He said he didn't mean to do any of the stuff he did. He 'borrowed' the money from the company to go to Vegas, but he planned to put it back after he started winning again. The problem was that his luck never turned around."

"That's crazy."

"I know. He also said he was relieved my dad survived the accident. Balan never wanted to kill Dad. He just wanted to keep him from thinking about the money."

131

"But when your dad died, he already had a plan in place."

"Lucky for us, it wasn't a very good plan." She yawned. "I can't believe how tired I am. I could sleep for days."

"It's been a long day," he said. "I guess we both need some sleep."

She stood up and stretched. "Hey, take care of Lottie for me. I know she doesn't show it, but she's got a very tender heart under that dignified outer shell."

Twelve

ord, show me how to do this, Lottie prayed as she washed her face Saturday morning. Show me how to help Patti today. I'm not a good replacement for her mother, but I'm all she's got. I love her so, Lord. Is that good enough?

"Lottie? Are you almost finished in there?" Patti knocked on the bathroom door. "The hairdresser is here."

"Coming." She dried her face and met her own eyes in the mirror. "You can do this," she said.

The face in the mirror didn't seem so sure.

Tying her bathrobe sash more firmly around her waist, she opened the door. "How can I help?"

Patti held Sarah out to her with a relieved smile. "Can you take her for a few minutes? She's a little overwhelmed by the crowd downstairs."

Gratitude washed over Lottie as she took the child in her arms. Just like that, she had her first job of the day. "We'll read a book together while you get your hair done. Won't we, Sarah?"

The little girl leaned into Lottie's shoulder. "Read a book," she said around the thumb in her mouth.

Lottie rested her cheek on the child's yellow curls and closed her eyes. This was what it felt like to belong.

When they went downstairs a while later, Lottie understood Sarah's shyness. The kitchen had been turned into a makeshift beauty salon, complete with the whir of a blow-dryer and the sharp scent of hairspray. The bridesmaids were taking turns having their hair done by a girl Patti had hired for the occasion.

Patti looked breathtaking, her dark hair swept up in an intricate knot, with wisps escaping to frame her face. Her lush black lashes framed luminous brown eyes that glowed with excitement. "You're next," she said when she saw Lottie. "Sit in the chair while I pour you some coffee."

Lottie sat down obediently. All this fuss over hair and makeup seemed excessive, but it made the bride happy. The hairdresser, an apple-cheeked local girl named Crystal, ran a comb through her short white locks. "You have beautiful skin, Ms. Braun," she said. "I'll bet if you let me color your hair, I could take years off your age."

A chorus of disapproval went up from all sides of the room. "Lottie's hair is her trademark," Patti said severely. "No one would recognize her if she colored it. Besides, I think the white hair is striking on someone so obviously young."

Crystal's face flushed bright pink. "I'm sorry. It was just a suggestion."

Lottie smiled at the girl. "You were only doing your job. You can't help it if people won't take your advice."

The hairdresser took her time styling Lottie's hair, and even persuaded her to wear a bit more makeup than normal. When she finished, she stepped back and handed Lottie a mirror. She took one long, critical look, and nodded. "Better than usual."

She lowered the mirror and Patti gave a whistle. "You look sensational! Doesn't she, girls?"

It was nice of everyone to nod in agreement, though Lottie didn't really believe them. Still, she did look appropriately dressy. Young Crystal had a future in her chosen field.

When Martha Williams arrived with lunch for the bridesmaids, her eyes lit up. "Wow."

Lottie gave her a grateful smile.

Martha called for attention. "I'm the schedule-keeper today. Everyone needs to leave here by one o'clock to get to the church on time."

Pandemonium followed, while they gathered their belongings. Lottie ran upstairs to put on her dress and take one more critical look in the mirror. "You can do this," she said, and this time the woman in the mirror smiled confidently back.

When she came downstairs everyone was gone but Patti, who was zipping Sarah's coat. Lottie's heart skipped a beat at the sight of the dark-haired mama bent so lovingly over her tow-headed child. "You two are just amazing," she blurted. "I'm so lucky to have you."

Patti jumped up and hugged her tight. "We feel exactly the same way."

The wedding went off without a hitch. Sam watched the church fill with guests, walked his new daughter-in-law down the aisle, and took his seat. The question, "Who gives this woman to be wed to this man?" made him choke up a little, but his answer came quickly. "I do, on behalf of her parents, and my wife." All of them, he felt sure, were together in heaven, smiling upon this day.

The music was extraordinary. He'd expected to hear Lottie's power unleashed in full on the congregation, but what she did was even more amazing. In deference to the occasion, she restrained her gift so that every note, every phrase directed attention to the bride and groom. Her self-discipline touched him as no virtuoso performance ever could. Every eye in the room was turned toward the bridal couple at the front, repeating their time-honored vows. Only Sam seemed to realize that the true miracle was sitting in the corner, behind the keyboard of an antique pipe organ.

The service ended with the traditional kiss, and the beaming bride and groom walked up the aisle hand-in-hand. Sam stood beside Mitch and Patti in the receiving line, and together they greeted each person and guided them to the church basement for the reception. Lottie slipped into place beside Patti after she finished the recessional, and though she was as quiet as could be, he knew right away that she was near. He tried not to glance her way too often, but her sapphire blue dress kept catching his eye. She'd done something new with her hair, too, though he was at a loss to know what was different.

He caught up with her at the reception, as they worked their way through the buffet. "You did a beautiful job up there."

She smiled as she spread mustard on her little ham sandwich. "So did you."

Her answer threw him off-balance. "No, I mean it."

"So do I." She looked up, sincere approval in her eyes. "It's not easy being father of the groom, or father of the bride. You had to be both today. Nancy would have been so proud of you."

His face grew warm with pleasure. Nobody said things like that to him anymore. As he followed her back to their table, it dawned on him that she didn't sound distant anymore. "Does this mean you've forgiven me?" he asked after they sat down.

"I told you last night, there's nothing to forgive. But if you insist on phrasing it that way, then yes, I've forgiven you."

She said this with such an open smile that he knew they were back on their old terms. Relieved, he gave her a cheeky grin. "I ate both pieces of pie, you know. I can't give yours back." He hadn't done so until last night when she'd refused to let him apologize, but he didn't intend to tell her that.

"That's okay," she said loftily. "I spat on one of them before I brought them over."

This was such an un-Lottie-like thing to say that he burst out laughing. She watched him with a straight face, only the glimmer in her eye betraying her amusement. By the time he recovered, they'd become a source of interest to the rest of the table. "What's so funny?" Ed Williams asked.

Sam sobered abruptly. "I think you had to be there."

Ed was on the verge of asking more questions, so Sam changed the subject. "Ed, are you still looking for a junior partner?"

"I sure am." His bushy eyebrows lowered into a frown. "Can't you talk some sense into that boy of yours? Look at him." He waved an arm at the groom. "He's having a great time in his old hometown. Why can't he see he belongs here?"

"You're on your own, I'm afraid. The boy won't listen to me anymore."

Someone rang a spoon against their water glass, and the rest of the room joined in. Patti and Mitchell laughingly complied with the traditional signal to kiss, and Ed turned to Lottie. "What's this I hear about a special concert in March?"

"We're raising money for the new PAB," Lottie told him. "You and Martha should come."

"We have to, Ed." Martha laid a hand on her husband's arm. "This will be Lottie's first concert in her hometown."

Sam looked up in surprise. Aside from today, he wanted to say. Aren't you forgetting how she played today?

Lottie's smile took in the entire table. "The whole department is exceptional. It's going to be a special show."

He loved how she made it sound like she wasn't the star attraction.

The church basement was not large, but somehow Patti had preserved enough space for a dance floor. After they cut the cake Mitchell and Patti opened the floor, swaying in time to some newfangled ballad Sam had never heard before. The next song was more familiar, a catchy tune that set his toes tapping. He watched the rotating mirror ball while he worked up his courage to ask Lottie to dance. The fact that he felt nervous irritated him, and his voice, instead of being smooth and persuasive, came out gruff. "Want to dance?"

Lottie didn't answer right away. When he turned to see if he'd upset her somehow, his jaw dropped. "Is that your second piece of cake?"

She gave a weak smile. "It might be my third. But who's counting?"

"Well, you have been kind of light on desserts this week," he said with a grin.

She punched him in the arm for that, and suddenly he wasn't nervous at all. "Dance?" he said.

"Sure."

They took the floor to Elvis singing "Hound Dog." Sam was a little rusty, but Lottie didn't seem to notice. She moved as easily as she played piano, and he had no choice but to keep up. Once or twice he stepped on her toes, but she didn't complain. Elvis ended, and Sam gamely did the chicken dance with Sarah while Lottie pulled the little ring bearers into the action. When the music changed again, he turned and drew her into his arms. Nothing else would have felt right, with "I'll Be Seeing You" flowing from the speakers. He and Lottie had learned that song together, during the endless summer in New York just before he quit the band.

She felt natural in his arms, her head coming up past his shoulder, though he was on the tall side. They kept a proper distance from each other, but it didn't matter. He was overcome by her nearness.

He'd spent months reminding himself that this beautiful, famous woman was out of his league, but tonight was different. She was just Lottie, his dearest friend, swaying in his arms, and he was waking up to all the possibilities.

He tried to catch her eye, to ask without words if she felt the same way, but her face was turned away, her gaze trained on the floor.

She raised her eyes when the song ended, and for a split second the feelings he saw there made his heart speed up. The next second she stepped out of his arms, her expression guarded. "Will you excuse me? I need some air."

Before he could say a word, she had hurried away.

Dancing with Sam was a mistake. The minute she stepped into his arms, with the beloved old standard playing in the background, all her good intentions dissolved. She couldn't stand so close to him and maintain their old friendly banter. She stared at his shoulder in dumb astonishment, at the rightness of his arms around her, and the impossibility of it all.

When the song ended, she fled up the basement steps and across the lobby to the heavy front doors. Pushing them open, she inhaled deeply, the crisp air filling her lungs. The clear night sky was full of stars, a full moon lighting the snow-covered field across the street.

"If you're going outside, you'll need a coat." Sam stood behind her.

"I guess I'll stay in, then." She let the doors swing shut and turned to face him. "It's a beautiful night."

"Beautiful." He stood too close for peace of mind, looking at her with a slight frown. "Lottie, I—" He broke off and tried again. "I don't know—"

Whatever he was going to say was lost as voices floated up the stairwell. Patti and Mitchell stepped into the lobby with a sleepy Sarah in Mitchell's arms.

"There you are." Patti hurried forward, arms outstretched. "We're ready to leave."

"Of course." Lottie slipped back into her supporting role. "I'll go get your things."

With an apologetic glance at Sam she hurried off to collect Patti's belongings. When she returned the newlyweds stood chatting with him, nodding politely as he gave them a few extra words of advice. "Remember, it's been snowing up near Chicago. The bridges might be slippery."

"We'll be all right," Mitchell said. "I'll call you when we get home." He helped his bride into her coat and took the bag from Lottie. "Thanks for everything." He kissed her cheek and turned to hug his dad. "See you in a month or so."

With a wave and a smile, they ran down the church steps to the waiting car, tucked Sarah into her booster seat, and drove away, tin cans flying out behind the bumper.

For the next few minutes they stood by the door and shook hands with the guests as they too departed. Some took longer than others to discuss the occasion, commenting on the beauty of the day and the brilliance of the couple who had found each other at last. "If only Helen had lived to see this day," said more than one doting friend.

Lottie agreed with all her heart.

Cal and Teresa were among the last to leave. "You must be so proud of your kids," Teresa said. Her gaze swept from Lottie to Sam, bringing them both into the conversation. "I'm sure Patti and Mitch will be very happy together."

Sam caught Lottie's eye and smiled. "We think so, too."

We. The inclusive little word filled Lottie with warmth. She smiled back at him, for once not minding if her feelings showed.

Cal reached out to shake Sam's hand. "I'm glad to see you're feeling better, Sam. Maybe now would be a good time to talk about that book project."

"Oh, no, honey." Teresa tugged at her husband's coat sleeve.

But Cal was not deterred. "I know you told me no the other night, but I think it would be dynamite to have your perspective in this book," he said to Sam. "It doesn't matter that you hated the band. In fact, it's an advantage. I see it this way: Lottie will present the positive side of life on the road, while you provide the negative counterpoint. It will give the whole thing depth. What do you say?"

Cal's words were met with dead silence. Beside him, Teresa's eyes grew big with horror.

Lottie glanced at Sam in confusion. "You hated the Neverland?"

He frowned and looked away. "I never said that."

Teresa took her husband's hand. "We really must be going."

"Hold on." Cal resisted her, oblivious to the tension in the room. "Lottie, I wanted to ask if you've made firm plans to fly to L.A. I have a lead on a couple of the guys we talked about. I'd like you to look them up while you're out there."

"Plans?" She dragged her attention away from Sam for a moment. "Can I get back to you on that?"

"Keep me posted," he said over his shoulder as his wife pulled him out the door. Teresa looked back and mouthed, "I'm sorry."

The doors closed. Lottie and Sam were alone. "You're not going to help with the book?" she said.

He glanced away. "They've got you. They don't need me."

"Cal says they do." She raised her eyebrows. "He says you'll provide a 'negative counterpoint' to my memories."

Sam took a deep breath. "The man does have a point. You have to admit you're a little Pollyanna about the whole thing."

"Pollyanna!" This description momentarily robbed her of breath.

He took advantage of her silence. "When did you decide to go to L.A.?"

She shrugged. "It happened while you were sick. Ernest Fleischmann asked me to make an appearance with the L.A. Phil in June."

"June? That's quick."

She glanced away. "It's really no big deal."

He raised his eyebrows. "It is a very big deal. Lottie Braun can't just sneak into Los Angeles and play a concert. Your fans won't know what to think."

His elder-brother tone set her teeth on edge. "It's my life, Sam. I'll do as I please."

"You're making a mistake," he quipped. "It'll be a media circus."

She clenched her fists at her sides. "This isn't about the media. Nor is it about my fans. I have a few loose ends to tie up in L.A. I'm free to do that now, you know."

He stared at her. "Is Johnny one of those loose ends?"

She looked away. "What if he is?"

"Why would you want to see that jerk after all these years?"

"I owe him something." She enunciated her words. "So do you, for that matter."

This brought his head up. "I do not."

"Oh yeah?" Her voice rose. "What would you have done after your brother ran away with that floozy if Johnny hadn't kept the band together?"

"Kept the—" He scrubbed a hand across his face. "Let me tell you something, sister. Johnny didn't keep that band together. He had no idea what to do after Walt left. The old man was the one who kept us on the road. With your money, I might add. You were always saving our bacon, one way or another."

She brushed away this version of events. "But Johnny was the glue. He was the reason everyone stayed."

"Hardly." He was yelling now. "He wasn't the saint you seem to think he was. Parson had to keep him from drinking himself half-blind after every dance. Parson was the one they all respected."

"Maybe Johnny wasn't perfect like Parson, but he wasn't all bad." She was dimly aware she'd raised her voice to match his. "He was nice to me, and that counts for something."

"Nice to you?" His face was flushed, his eyes burning with anger. "You bet he was. You were his meal ticket, and he knew it. Without their little child prodigy, that band was going nowhere. Besides, being nice to you made Helen happy. Why can't you see that?"

The blood rushed into Lottie's cheeks, then drained away, leaving her cold. Blindly she turned and started for the basement steps. "I've got to go," she mumbled.

"Lottie, wait." Sam caught her sleeve.

She paused.

In a quieter voice he said, "I'm sorry if I hurt you, but I don't understand your obsession with those days. You can't live in the past. You've got to move on with your life."

She moved out of his reach. "Never mind."

Downstairs, most of the clean-up was done. Jason and Katherine looked up as she entered, guilt written large on their faces. So, they'd heard. "You should go," Jason said. "We've got this under control."

Lottie gave a jerky nod. "I think I'll do that."

Sam's heart sank as she walked away. The pain in her eyes told him he'd said too much. It didn't matter that every word was true. He'd take it all back if he could.

Pulling his keys from his pocket, he let himself out the front door. He needed some time to cool off.

She was leaving the church when Sam pulled the car around. He rolled down his window and she paused beside it. "Should I stop by for you tomorrow morning?" He thought he knew the answer, but he still had to ask.

"No." She started to move on, then turned back to face him. "Sam, if I were you, I'd be careful who I accused of living in the past."

He raised his eyebrows. "Oh, you would?"

"You're a bit like the pot that called the kettle black." She reached out and flicked a chip of paint off Bessie's door. "You're not driving this old rust bucket because you like the way she handles."

She walked away, head high.

Bessie kicked up gravel as Sam sped away.

Lottie was shaking by the time she got home. Teeth chattering, she hurried up the walk on trembling legs. Pain and anger coursed through her, blotting out rational thought.

She turned on the kitchen light, shed her coat, and kicked off her shoes. She had to do something to stop the cold that seeped from her core to her very bones. Turning on the faucet she waited for the water to warm up and thrust her hands into the stinging heat.

You were his meal ticket.

Being nice to you made Helen happy.

She flinched away from the bare-knuckles truth of Sam's words. He was wrong. He had to be.

As her fingers thawed in the warm water, her doubts grew. Maybe Sam had a point. Maybe Johnny did think of her as a means to an end.

She dried her hands and started for the stairs. There was one way to find out.

She found the packet of letters in the back corner of her nightstand. The paper was more brittle than she remembered, and the ink more faded. Still, Johnny's boyish scrawl reassured her.

Back in the kitchen, she put the teakettle on to boil and freed the letters from their rubber band. Each one was brief and to-the-point. Johnny wasn't a gifted wordsmith. By the time the kettle whistled she had her answer. She sat back and sighed.

Someone knocked at the kitchen door as Lottie poured water into her mug. For a wild half-second she thought Sam might have followed her, but it was only Katherine. Lottie let her in with a rueful smile. "Have you come to hold my hand after that nasty scene? You didn't have to, you know."

"Hold your hand?" Katherine's tone was dry. "I wouldn't dare." She nodded at the kettle. "I do know how to listen, though. Especially if I can do so while sipping hot tea."

Lottie hesitated. "Are you sure you want to waste your time? I won't shatter, you know."

Katherine raised one eyebrow, a trick Lottie envied. "I know you won't. Not in public, anyway. You and I are strong women, Lottie. We only break down behind closed doors." She opened a cupboard door and took out a mug. "You didn't look so good when you left the church."

"You saw that, huh?" Lottie sat down and rested her chin on her hand. "I assume you heard the fight, too."

"Not on purpose." Katherine pulled a teabag from the jar on the counter. "Would it help to tell me what happened?"

"No. Yes." Lottie raised her head. "Maybe?" She sighed. "Oh, Katherine. I'm afraid it will sound a bit silly."

"Try me."

"Sam doesn't think I should go to Los Angeles," she said slowly. "He thinks I'll create a media storm if I play there after all these years."

Katherine poured the water and set her mug on the kitchen table. "But playing L.A. is a huge deal for you. It could start a whole new chapter in your career."

Lottie shrugged. "The actual concert isn't that exciting. I've dealt with better orchestras. I have personal reasons for wanting to go."

"And Sam doesn't approve of those, either?"

She wrinkled her nose. "You did hear us."

"You two were kind of yelling there at the end."

"I know." Lottie took a sip of her tea. "For a man who says he doesn't live in the past, he sure has strong feelings about it."

"He must have said something terrible to make you turn so pale."

"No." Lottie glanced at the letters that fanned out beside her on the table. "All he did was tell me the truth."

"About someone named Johnny?"

She nodded.

"Do you want to talk about it?"

Lottie closed her eyes. Could she talk about it? Could she articulate what it was like to be a growing girl with a half-dozen young swing musicians for friends? Johnny and Parson and all the others had made her feel like someone special when the physical evidence of her gawky thirteen-year-old frame said otherwise. She'd seen what she wanted to see, she supposed. Sam had seen the truth.

Lottie had never been the star attraction for those men. They'd been happy to profit from her talent, of course. But when it came to friendship, they'd all looked past her and focused on Helen. The evidence was right there in Johnny's letters. Not once had he mentioned Lottie or even Billy, for that matter. Helen was his only concern.

That's what she'd found tonight when she rushed home from Westmont and started tearing open the envelopes: Sappy, sordid love letters from a man with no honor, urging her married sister to run away with him.

She'd hoped for something different, something to prop up her faltering memories of a good-natured young trumpeter she'd thought of as her friend. Instead she was left to wonder if any of her memories were true.

Katherine reached out and took a letter off the pile. "Helen Turner? Was that your sister?"

"Yes," she said quietly. "They're from an old flame of hers."

"Johnny Columbus." Katherine murmured as she scanned the page. "That's a theatrical name."

This drew a half-smile from Lottie. "A stage name, yes. His real name was Higginbottom."

"I see." Katherine looked up. "This guy really had the hots for your sister."

Lottie nodded. "My married sister."

"And you loved him?" Katherine said.

"Not the way you mean." She was shocked by the idea. "I was just a kid back then. Too young to love anyone."

Katherine's eyes widened. "You don't really believe that, do you?"

"What do you mean?"

"I taught middle school music for ten years. There is no love more intense than an adolescent crush."

"A crush?" Lottie turned the word around in her mind. "I don't think…well, maybe that's what it was."

Katherine was quiet a moment. "How old were you when you went to that conservatory in Ohio?"

"Thirteen. Why?"

"I think I read some interview where you said your time at the conservatory marked the beginning of your career."

"So?"

"When people start their jobs, they stop being kids."

Lottie felt lost. "That's how it usually works."

Katherine leaned forward, her eyes kind. "My friend, most people outgrow their adolescent feelings and move on to other loves. By growing up so fast, you simply weren't given that chance."

Lottie winced. "Well, I'm over it now. I don't ever need to see Johnny—or any of those men—again."

"Don't throw the baby out with the bathwater. Maybe those guys weren't fairytale princes, but they were part of a special time in your life. Aren't you a little curious to see how they turned out?"

"Not if they all turn out to be creeps," Lottie muttered.

"Creeps or princes. Are those their only choices?" Katherine's tone was sharp. "Real-life people are more interesting than that."

Lottie plucked the letter from Katherine's fingers and stuffed it back in its envelope. "If this is what you call interesting, I can live without it."

Thirteen

ou'd have loved it, Nance." Sam settled himself more firmly on his camp stool, hands loosely clasped. "Mitch was dressed to the nines in a penguin suit, and Patti had on a lacy dress. Lace and floaty stuff. I know you always want details, but that's the best I can tell you. She's a real beauty now." He swallowed around the lump in his throat. "They couldn't stop smiling, those two. It was a real happy day."

Not everything about yesterday had been good, of course. An image of Lottie, white-faced and shaken entered his mind, but he pushed it away. Nancy didn't need to know about that.

"The music was impressive." Give credit where credit was due. "Helen would have been proud of her sister. Pass that along to her, will you?"

Sam took off his hat in the late-winter sunshine. The morning air was warm enough to melt snow off the trees, and it fell with soft plops all around him. Soon the ground would thaw and the construction business would pick up again.

"Miranda couldn't get back from California for the wedding. Jase was like a ghost of himself without her around." He frowned. "I think there's a chance she won't be coming back to Collison at all. I hate to think how much that'll hurt him."

He sat by Nancy's grave a while longer, lost in thought. Church had been pretty empty this morning, at least in his row. Jase had stayed out late with the rest of the wedding party, and Sam didn't expect Lottie to show up. Not after last night.

Reverend Summers' sermon had been unusually dry. Twice Sam's head had bobbed nearly to his chest before he startled awake again. Not too surprising. He hadn't slept real well.

After the service he'd noticed Lottie leaving by the side door. She'd been there all along, just not with him. Somehow this hurt worse than if she'd stayed home altogether.

Well, he didn't blame her. He'd said some terrible things.

Services let out at the church next to the cemetery. As people streamed out the doors, Sam folded up his camp stool. He didn't relish the thought of being stared at by strangers while he talked to his wife.

He squinted down at the gravestone. "Bessie doesn't work the way she used to, Nance. I guess I drive her different than you did. Anyway, she won't last forever."

He started for the car, oblivious to the row of kids that had formed along the cemetery fence. "Hey, mister," a little girl called.

He looked up, startled, and caught a snowball full in the face.

Kids. They never changed. Turning up his collar for protection, he strode back to the car and drove away.

Sunday morning Miranda woke to the sound of the shower running in her parents' bathroom. For the first time in nearly a week her mother was up before noon.

Miranda showered and dressed and found her mother in the kitchen, fixing breakfast. "There you are, sleepyhead," Sonia said. "Set the table and call your brother. We've got work to do."

Miranda blinked. "Aren't you going to church?"

"Not today." Sonia glanced out the window. "We're going down to your father's office. It's time to make plans."

An hour later they were in the car with Zac at the wheel. He seemed as dazed as Miranda by their mother's about-face. "What are we doing again, Mom?"

"We are honoring your father's memory."

"By going to the office on a Sunday?"

"By saving Charles Construction. Can't you go any faster?"

When they reached the office, they found Karthav, Max and Jose waiting for them. "I asked them to come," Sonia said in answer to Miranda's questioning look. "We need their help if we are to succeed."

They gathered in the office, the women seated in chairs, the men lounging against the walls. All of them were watching Sonia, who gathered her thoughts and began.

"As you know by now, on Friday Balan Prakash was arrested and charged with killing my husband and embezzling funds from Charles Construction." She looked around sadly. "Unfortunately, he will not be able to return our money, because he has spent it already on expensive living. So today we must look our problems square in the face and come to terms with the future.

"Gentlemen," She tapped the desk for emphasis. "The future of this company is bleak at best. Before we go any further, we need you to understand how things stand. Miranda?"

She sat up straight. "Yes?"

"How much money do we have in our bank accounts?"

"Four-hundred seventy-two dollars and twenty-eight cents."

Sonia turned to her son. "Zac, is it true you have neither the training nor the desire to run this business?"

Zac's eyes were wary. "That's right."

She turned back to the group of foremen. "Not only do we have no operating cash, if you continue with us, you will officially be working for a woman. If you cannot stomach these facts, I will accept your resignation without question."

Max and Jose exchanged uneasy glances. "I'm sorry, Mrs. Charles," Jose said. "I've been offered a job with another company, and I think I'm going to take it. No offense."

"Very well." Sonia gave him a regal nod and turned to Max. "Mr. Morehouse? Have you come to a decision?"

"I'll stay on a while longer," Max said, though he sounded slightly doubtful. "Your husband gave me a job even though I've got a record. I owe him for that."

"Thank you," Sonia said, though her smile was strained.

Karthav Singh threw a disgusted look at his fellow workers. "I'm staying, Mrs. Charles. What do you need me to do?"

Sonia's shoulders relaxed a bit. "My daughter has assessed the current state of affairs. She will explain what happens next."

Miranda had been watching her mother with dawning respect. Now she sat up straight, thinking fast. "We need your help to make sense of the work schedule. Which jobs are ongoing, and which have been completed? How do we read a standard contract to understand our obligations?"

Karthav frowned. "I don't know anything about contracts, but I can help you reconstruct the master schedule."

Jose levered himself upright from his place against the wall. "This is my cue to leave," he said. "See you around, guys."

"Wait." Miranda put out a hand to stop him. "Before you go, we need an accounting of the construction side of things. Can you stay an hour or two and talk about that?"

He paused. "If I stay, I'm on the clock."

Miranda narrowed her eyes. "I'll pay you twenty-five dollars flat."

Across the desk, her mother drew in a sharp breath.

"Forty," he said.

She shook her head. "Twenty-five. Take it or leave it."

After a moment, he shrugged. "Fine. But you'd better get on with it. I don't have all day."

Later, when a new master schedule was roughed in and the three men had left the family alone, Miranda asked the question that was burning on her tongue. "Mom, why did you put me in charge of that meeting? How did you know I'd been thinking about our next step?"

Sonia gave her a weary smile. "You are the obvious choice to lead this company, my dear. That became clear when you spent last week chasing down Balan Prakash."

"But you told Karthav and Max that you would be their boss."

"Not true." Her mother raised her eyebrows. "I said their boss would be a woman. And so she will be."

"But I—" She turned to Zac. "Is this okay with you?"

He flashed her a relieved grin. "More than that, it's a load off my mind."

Miranda looked at her mother and brother with growing excitement. The trust in their eyes filled her with indescribable warmth. She couldn't wait to tell Jase how this day had gone.

As soon as the thought was formed, her heart sank. Yes, what would she tell him? And what would she do about Lottie?

Pushing aside those questions, she smiled at her family. "I can't wait to get started."

For the next few days Miranda spent every waking hour at the office, studying contracts, calling customers, and putting out fires. The electrical and plumbing departments continued to fulfill their obligations, though with fewer day laborers due to the shortage of cash. But the carpentry was a problem that stole Miranda's sleep when she did go home at night.

That and what to do about her life in Iowa. Out of fairness to Lottie, she needed to resign, but she couldn't stomach the permanence of that action. What if, despite her best efforts, Charles Construction was a failure? What would she do without Lottie to fall back on?

Her torn feelings about Lottie paled in comparison to her agony over Jase. Without question he was the most important person in her life, but she couldn't turn her back on her family's needs. When the time came to make a choice, she did not know which way the needle would point.

Tuesday morning at breakfast, her mother gave her a level stare. "That man from Iowa called last night. I told him you were still at the office."

A chill ran down her spine. "Thanks," she mumbled into her coffee.

"Miranda," her mother said. "I wish you would tell me what is bothering you."

Miranda looked up. "I've got a million things on my mind, Mother. Which one do you mean?"

"The one that makes you look so sad when you think no one is around."

She blinked. "I don't know what you mean."

Sonia reached across the table and patted her hand. "It takes more energy to worry about your problems than it does to face them."

Miranda gave her a reluctant smile. "I'll keep that in mind."

That evening she made it a point to be home for supper. After the dishes were dry, she called Lottie.

"I already know, my dear," Lottie said when she gave her resignation. "I figured you'd be quitting when you didn't come back for the wedding."

"I'm so sorry—"

"Not at all." Lottie's voice was kind. "I'll miss you, of course. You're the best assistant I've ever had. But your family needs you right now. That is much more important than keeping my sheet music straight."

Miranda smiled. "If there's anything you need while you're training someone new, don't hesitate to call."

"What will you do about your townhouse?"

"I haven't really thought about it." She bit her lip. "I guess I need to hire someone to box up my stuff and put it in storage until I can afford to have it shipped." Where she'd get the money to do that, she didn't know.

"I'll take care of it," Lottie said quickly. When Miranda protested, she added, "What are friends for?"

She hung up, encouraged by Lottie's generosity.

The conversation with Jase didn't go as smoothly.

"You mean you're not coming home at all? Ever?" He sounded shocked.

"Jase, I am home." She was trying to be as gentle as possible.

"So, this is it for us?"

She wasn't sure how to answer. "I don't want it to be."

"But you're not coming back."

"No." The word came out small and pebble hard.

A long, suffocating silence later, Jase's voice came out in a croak. "Then I guess there's nothing else to say."

The following week the weather turned surprisingly. Early spring sunshine melted most of the snow, leaving deep puddles in the potholes around Collison. Lottie's spirits sagged in spite of the weather. After all the wedding excitement, life seemed sadly flat. She hadn't heard from Patti, of course. Newlyweds seldom remembered to call their maiden aunts. Miranda also had her hands full at home. Besides which she no longer worked for Lottie and had no reason to call.

Wednesday morning a patch of purple crocuses brightened the quad. She noticed them on her way into the PAB and felt amazed that she knew their name. Aunt Cora must have taught her that for it to stick so well.

Cora and Eva seemed to have a very nice time at the wedding. Cora wasn't sure who the bride and groom were, of course. But she'd been wide awake for once, and mildly entertained by the proceedings.

Eva knew. Her bright gaze had followed every movement of the wedding party, the orchid corsage on her lapel rising and falling with her breath. After the ceremony, they had been picked up in the nursing home van, two exhausted old ladies with stories to tell the nurses.

The new department secretary was the only person in the office. She sat behind her desk, still wrapped in her coat and scarf. "It's colder in here than it is outside," she said when Lottie commented on her outfit. "The heat's out again. I've called for a repairman, but you know how that goes."

"All the more reason to build a new PAB," Lottie said cheerfully.

The girl's eyes lit up. "I heard about that. Nice work, Miss Braun."

Lottie gave her a puzzled smile. She often felt like she'd missed something after a conversation with the new secretary.

Cal passed her on the stairs and stopped to talk. "I need to apologize for the things I said at the wedding. I shouldn't have brought up the book when I did. My wife says my timing was way off."

"Don't give it another thought," she said. "You didn't do any harm. I've been meaning to talk to you about the Neverland project, though."

"Oh? What's on your mind?" He looked startled.

She took a deep breath. "I'm afraid I can't participate in your research right now. It's stirring up a lot of old feelings, and they're becoming too much for me."

Cal took a moment to digest this news. "This is a disappointment,

Lottie. I don't think I can keep my publishing deal without your support."

She took a deep breath. "I feel terrible about that, Cal, but I'm sure some other project will come along for you."

"Just out of curiosity, did Sam talk you into changing your mind?"

"No. This is my own decision." She hesitated. "Speaking of Sam, can you remember exactly what he said when you asked for his help?"

Cal shrugged. "He said something about not glorifying the pie-in-the-sky dreams of a bunch of lost boys."

She bit her lip. "I see."

"I wanted to use that quote as the title: The Lost Boys of the Neverland." He glanced away. "But I guess that doesn't matter now."

Cal's words followed her through the day. Lost boys indeed. Well, maybe they had been lost, all but Parson.

The sun was low in the sky when she left work, and long shadows swallowed up the crocus patch. The air had a cold late-winter edge, and Lottie was grateful for the comfort of the Mercedes.

She passed Thomas on College Boulevard, trudging along with his hands in his pockets. Pulling over, she called, "Going home?"

He looked up. "Yeah."

"Get in." She didn't need to ask him twice. "I see you walking everywhere," she said when he was settled.

He shrugged. "My mom needs her car to go to work. It's not a big deal."

"You're always by yourself these days. What happened with Faye?"

"I dunno." He looked out the window. "She said she wanted someone more fun."

"More fun than the front man in a rock band? I can't imagine that."

His fleeting smile was her reward. "I think what she meant was, she wanted someone with a car."

She wrinkled her nose. "Then I say good riddance. Girls should like you for who you are, not for what you have."

He shot her a glance of disbelief. "I guess it's been a while since you went to high school."

Fourteen

ust like always, the first warm spell of the year brought a slew of calls for remodeling estimates. Ordinarily Sam liked to go out and size up a new project. He and Jase made a good team, and the prospect of new business always put them in a good mood.

This week, good moods were hard to come by. Jase hadn't smiled since the wedding. What's more, he'd nearly taken Sam's head off for asking if he'd talked to his girlfriend lately. Something had gone wrong, that much was clear, but he wasn't dumb enough to ask for details.

Sam wasn't feeling too whippy either. His cough, which had stayed away during the weekend, was back in full force, and it made him tired. He wasn't about to bring it up with Jase, though, for fear the boy would try to send him home again. Instead, he slogged through the days as best he could and went on home to bed.

He made an exception for the first PAB committee meeting Wednesday night. He figured since he'd been roped into doing it, he'd better be there at the start. Dr. Isley had kept things mercifully short, limiting himself to introductions and passing out materials to read for next time. All in all, not a bad bunch of people, if he didn't count Nathan Bartholomew. The sarcastic professor had made a point of wheeling himself over to Sam afterward. "So, you're the plant," he said. "I figured there would be one."

And then he left.

Thursday afternoon Sam and Jase called on a homeowner out in the county. The couple wanted a kitchen remodel, complete with custom cabinetry and new french doors to their fancy deck. French doors were a bad choice within the limits of the space, but the woman of the house had her heart set on them.

Sam had taught his son not to argue with the customers, but today Jason was ignoring that policy. "Sliding glass doors will take up less room," Jase told the homeowner. "French doors swing inward, so your table will have to be smaller."

"Those doors are the focal point of my design scheme."

Jase frowned. "They might look all right, but you'll have to move the furniture whenever you want to open and shut them."

"I understand that," she said with a hint of steel in her voice. "Are you saying you won't put them in?"

"No ma'am," Sam said before Jase could keep up the fight. "Put that in your notes, Jason. French doors in the kitchen."

"Yes, sir." Jase took out his notebook with that it's-your-funeral look that made women so mad. "French doors in the kitchen."

Later, on the way back to town, Sam confronted him. "What were you thinking? You could have lost us that job."

The boy hunched his shoulders and glared across the steering wheel. "I was trying to do the right thing."

"More like trying to pick a fight. Over french doors. What is wrong with you?"

He didn't answer, but the truck leaped up the highway like the police were chasing after it.

"Slow down," Sam said when they reached the outskirts of town. "You're gonna get a ticket."

Jase shot him a hostile look, but eased up on the pedal. "Looks like they're having a sale at the Ford dealership."

Sam followed his gaze. "I like the look of that F150."

"Which one?"

"The red one on the end of the row. I always liked red for a truck."

"Not shopping for a new truck, are you, Dad?" Jase said, surprised.

He didn't like Jase's sarcastic tone. "It don't cost anything to look."

A hint of a smile crossed the boy's face. "True."

The phone was ringing when they reached the office. Jase reached it first. One of their suppliers was on the line, explaining that an order was going to be late.

Sam poured a cup of stale coffee and listened while his son raked the poor guy over the coals. Until now, they'd had a good relationship with this company, but Jase seemed determined to cut all ties. He finally slammed down the receiver, breathing hard.

Sam stirred powdered creamer into his coffee. "Feel better?"

"Nope." Jase bit off the word and stalked out.

Lottie heard the drip-drip-drip Friday morning, as she passed the music room on her way to make breakfast. She found the source easily enough: A rivulet of water had found its way around the top of a brand new window, and now dripped steadily onto the shadow box that held the little purple dress.

"Oh, mercy." She rushed to get the dress out of harm's way, but she was too late. Water had already seeped inside the frame. The dress was ruined.

Since Harms and Sons had installed the window, she had to call them to repair it. She sent up a little prayer as she dialed. "Please don't let Sam answer."

No luck. His deep voice came on the line right away.

"Hi, Sam. This is Lottie." She hurried to reassure him this was a business call. "I've got water coming in the music room windows. Can you send someone over to take a look?"

"Sure thing." His tone was clipped. "Jase can get there around noon."

Relieved, she hung up and went to find some towels.

"The gutter was installed wrong," Jase told her after he looked at it. "The thaw caused it to fill with melted snow, but instead of running the water to the downspout, it buckled right above that window. That's where your water is coming from. I bent it back in place and ran some new caulk around the window frame. It should hold for a while. I'll get in touch with my installer, and he should have it fixed by tomorrow afternoon."

She thanked him and he turned to go. "One more thing," she said quickly. "Are you busy tomorrow?"

He looked back, his face guarded. "Why do you ask?"

"I need a help with a chore." She did her best to look helpless. "I'm packing Miranda's furniture to ship to California."

Anger flashed across his face. "You've got the wrong man for that job. Why don't you ask my dad? He seems to have a lot of free time this week."

For a second or two they eyed each other carefully. Then Lottie cracked a reluctant smile. "Touché." She held the door a little wider. "Now that we've got that out of the way, would you please step in here a minute and tell me what's going on?"

He hesitated. "What do you mean?"

"Miranda Charles is miles deep in love with you. Yet you are here, and she is three thousand miles away. Why?"

"Guess you're wrong about that first part."

"I am not. Listen, I know stubbornness is like a religion in your family, but in this case, it's not doing you any good. Miranda's up to her neck in problems—problems you could help her with if you wanted to—and you don't even see it."

"What am I not seeing?" he asked, his face uncertain.

The tension in her shoulders eased. She finally had his attention. She pushed the door open wider. "Come inside."

He followed her into the kitchen and leaned against the counter, arms crossed defensively. "All right. I'm listening."

"She's heading her family's construction firm."

"I know. She told me."

"Did she tell you they've got very little operating capital and they're short-handed?"

"Yeah." He looked away.

"Miranda is smart and motivated, but she doesn't have the experience she needs to make things run smoothly." Lottie shook a finger at her guest. "You've been running a similar company for what? Six years? You have the answers to all of her questions. You could make all the difference."

His expression remained unyielding. "She doesn't want me. She chose her family business over me."

"Why can't she have you and the business?"

His head came up. "What do you mean?"

She gave him a long, assessing look. "Jase, I think you have to ask yourself a question. Do you love Miranda? Or do you just love the way Miranda looks when she's hanging on your arm?"

"That's unfair. You know I love her."

"Well, what are you going to do about it?"

He left a minute later in a state of confusion. As she listened to his tires crunch on the gravel, she wondered two things.

Did he have the courage to stand by her sweet friend?

And would he remember to call his gutter installer?

Doris greeted Lottie by name at the dry cleaners. "Are we picking up or dropping off today?" she asked cheerfully.

"Both." Lottie set the damaged shadowbox on the counter. "This little dress is a family heirloom. Can you save it?"

Doris removed the dress and examined the water stains. "There's not much here to save." She lifted a corner of the skirt between two fingers. "The fabric is too fragile. It'll fall apart if I try to wash it."

Lottie's heart sank. "Isn't there anything you can do?"

Doris looked thoughtful. "I could send it out to the company that preserves wedding dresses for us. They'll treat the fabric and send it back in an airtight box. You won't be able to hang it on the wall again, though. It needs to be stored somewhere dark."

Lottie sighed. "I guess it's time to let it go."

"Sometimes, that's how it goes. Now, what are you picking up today?"

"You've got my black beaded dress." Lottie handed her the ticket. "I need it for the big benefit concert next week. Are you going?"

Doris nodded. "I've got a nephew in the choir."

♪

Saturday morning, Sam ran a few errands around town, spent good money at the grocery, and slowed down on his way past the Ford dealership to see if the red pickup was still there.

It crossed his mind to stop in at Lottie's and make sure the gutters were fixed—out of professional pride—but he thought the better of it.

He was fixing a peanut butter sandwich for lunch when Mitch called.

"How's married life treating you?" Sam asked, happy to hear his younger son's voice.

"It's great," Mitch said. "Patti and Sarah are the best."

"And the new job? Do you like it?"

Mitchell hesitated. "They've got me working some pretty long hours. I've got a lot to learn, I guess."

"That's how it is when you're starting out," Sam said. "It should ease up at some point, right?"

"Yeah, I guess I'm just low man on the totem pole." He changed the subject. "Any idea where Jase is? I've been trying to call him."

"Nope. I try not to be too nosy about his life."

"Right." There was a hint of laughter in Mitch's voice. "Well, if you see him, tell him to call me."

"Will do."

They hung up, and Sam bit into his sandwich. He was glad his sons were friends. It wasn't a given with brothers. Walt hadn't wanted anything to do with Sam when they were young. He'd been more interested in night clubs and women than looking after his little brother. He wouldn't have needed to, either, if Sam had been a little older when he was orphaned. Thirteen was a hard age for a boy to lose his mom.

Those had been different times. People didn't talk about grief back then. He'd been expected to stuff those feelings down and forget about them, and for the most part he'd succeeded. But once in a while things had gotten pretty lonely.

The Neverland had been his training ground for keeping that stuff to himself. Those guys didn't miss a chance to poke at his weak spots. If he'd ever let on how much he missed his mother, he never would have heard the end of it. God bless Eva Reed for rescuing him from that life. Without her, he didn't know how bad things might have gotten.

Sam came back to the present with a start. He never thought about those days. At least, he never did before Lottie came back into his life. With all her cockeyed notions about the Neverland, maybe it was a good thing they weren't seeing so much of each other anymore.

After lunch he gathered all the quarters he could find and drove Bessie to the self-serve car wash. He wasn't the only person with that idea, so he had to wait his turn. Bessie looked much better when all the salt and dirt were washed off.

As he drove home along Main Street he waved at Thomas Allen, walking as usual. Lottie was right. Thomas was always out walking, sometimes pretty far from home.

Sam was so intent on watching Thomas that he didn't see the giant pothole that swallowed up Bessie's right front tire. One minute they were bowling along at 30 miles per hour. The next, they were airborne. When they came down, the engine coughed and died. Sam sighed as traffic backed up behind him on the busy street. He hated car trouble.

Thomas ran up beside the car and tapped on the window. "Can I help you, Mr. Harms?"

Sam frowned. "I'd like to move out of traffic, if I can. Do you think we can push the car around the corner?"

Thomas squared his shoulders. "We can try, sir."

"All right."

Sam put the car in neutral, and Thomas planted his feet behind the vehicle. Seeing their efforts, the driver behind them got out of his car to help. Pretty soon, they had enough manpower to turn poor Bessie onto the quiet side street. Sam thanked his helpers, and they went back to their cars.

Thomas stuck around. "Will you be all right from here?"

"Sure. I'll walk up to the Sinclair station and call a tow truck."

"I'm going that direction. I can make the call, if you want."

"No thanks, but I'll walk with you that far, if you don't mind."

As they started down the sidewalk, Thomas glanced back at Bessie. "She's a sweet old car. Do you think they can fix her?"

"They usually do."

Thomas nodded. "I guess owning a car isn't as simple as it looks."

"A car is a good thing to have, if you take care of it right."

"I will." Thomas shrugged. "Someday, I mean."

They parted ways at the gas station, and Sam went in to use the phone. He reached the garage right away, and they promised to collect Bessie.

He had a harder time finding himself a ride home. Jase wasn't answering his phone, and he couldn't call Lottie, of course. He should follow Thomas's example and walk home, but it was a bit of a hike.

Ed Williams picked him up a while later. "What's the matter? Is your son too busy to help out his old man?"

"He's got a girl on his mind. You know how that is."

Ed chuckled. "Boy, I wouldn't be single again for a million bucks."

Sam couldn't quite muster a smile.

"Looks like we've found your missing son," Ed said when they reached Sam's house.

Sure enough, Jason's red Mazda sat in front of the garage. Sam waved good-bye to Ed and let himself into the house. "Jason?"

"Out here, Dad."

He found Jase on the back deck, gazing at the river. "I forgot how much I love this view."

"Where have you been?" Sam joined him at the rail. "I've been trying to call you."

"Lottie needed my help this afternoon." Jase turned to look at him. "Dad, I've got something to tell you."

Miranda woke up Sunday morning to the sun shining in her eyes.

She'd been so tired the night before she forgot to lower the shade. Pulling the pillow over her eyes, she rolled over to go back to sleep, but it was too late. Sleep would not return.

A week ago today, she'd become the director of Charles Construction. She couldn't believe how much things had changed since then. Dad's foremen had given her a crash course in the electrical, plumbing, and carpentry aspects of commercial spaces, including how to order materials, the hiring of day laborers, and which developers they had the most respect for.

Their help was priceless, but it only went so far. They had never negotiated contracts for new work or handled the financial side of the business. Mom had unearthed several boxes of records from before Dad hired Balan Prakash, but they weren't an adequate guide for establishing new bookkeeping practices.

A thousand times a day she wanted to reach for the phone and call Jase. He knew the answers to most of her questions. She could picture him explaining each matter in his usual deliberate way, making sure she understood every detail before he moved on to something new. But she'd burned that bridge.

She'd even thought about calling Sam, but that didn't feel right, either. She couldn't stay in touch with the family of the man who had broken up with her. No, she was better off figuring things out on her own.

Today she would take a breather from work, but only because her mother insisted on it. "We worked straight through last Sunday," she'd said. "We need to rest if we are to keep up this pace." For Sonia, that meant attending church in the morning and napping in the afternoon. Miranda agreed to the first part of the plan but not the second. Sunday afternoons were meant for planning.

Zac was reading the paper in the living room when she got back from her morning run. She snared the color comics on her way to the kitchen, and he grunted in protest. "Hey, I was going to read that next."

"You snooze, you lose, little brother." She poured a glass of water and returned to the living room. "You're up early. Do you have to work today?"

"Never on Sundays. I'm going in to pick up my paycheck, though.

Want to come?"

She looked up, startled, and caught his wary gaze. He looked skittish, like a wild animal who might bolt if she made a sudden move. "Sure. Yes." She smiled. "When are you going?"

He tried to frown at the newspaper, but his lips twitched in a pleased little grin. "After lunch, I guess."

The morning passed in slow motion, first the familiar church service, conducted by their scholarly minister, then the drive home and a simple lunch. Finally, when the dishes were put away and Sonia had gone to her room to rest, Zac picked up the car keys. "Ready?"

Miranda kept her voice level. "Let me get my purse."

They drove around the city to a road that led into the foothills. Finally, Zac parked in front of a square cinder block building and turned to Miranda with a stern look. "This is where I work. Don't ask questions until we're back in the car."

The sign in front of the building said, "KTLM Radio, 89.1." She gave him a stunned nod. "Anything you say."

Zac led the way around back to a door that took them into a dark business office. Though the place seemed deserted, some kind of jazz was playing on the speaker overhead. Miranda followed him down the hall to the control room, where a man in a Hawaiian shirt removed his headphones and greeted them. "Well, if it isn't Mr. Zac Vindaloo Charles," he said. "What are you doing here? And who's the lucky lady?" He gave Miranda an admiring leer.

"Ian Riley, this is my sister, Miranda." He turned to her with a rueful smile. "Miranda, this is Ian Riley. He does an oldies show on Sundays."

"Oldies?" Ian looked surprised. "I only play the classics, my man." He gave Miranda a confidential grin. "This guy. He thinks everyone wants to listen to that Indi Pop stuff. He doesn't get that some people like instruments that don't have to be plugged in."

Mystified, she glanced at her brother. "Right," she said slowly. "Indi Pop. He's always talking about it."

Ian slid his earphones back in place. "Well, guys, I've got a show to run." As the song ended, he turned a button on the panel and spoke into the mic. "This is Ian coming at you this Sunday afternoon and we're living the life of Riley, with all the hits from the nineteen-thirties, forties, and early fifties, before rock and roll was the name of the game."

They left on tiptoe, back to the office where Zac found his paycheck, and then out to the car. As he turned to go back the way they'd come, Miranda let out her breath. "You're Vindaloo Z."

He shot her a sideways glance. "Wait. You've heard of me?"

"A couple of times."

"Weird, huh?"

She felt like she'd wandered into the deep end of a swimming pool. "I mean, radio? That's pretty good. Isn't it?"

"It's a great job," he said earnestly. "I'm good at it, too. The numbers for my show are the best at the station."

"How did this happen, Zac? You just wandered in the door one day and they put you on the air?"

"I took a communications class in college. The professor was some kind of frustrated actor or something, so he had us do a lot of acting and speaking, not so much writing." He shrugged. "I'm good at talking fast and putting on voices. I've got a voice I do on the air to sound older, like I know what I'm doing."

"But how did you get from classroom assignments to a job with a radio station?"

He smiled. "You just met the prof."

"Ian Riley?"

"Yeah. He teaches community college during the week. That's why he does the Sunday afternoon show." He was talking fast, trying to convince her of his future. "It's a little independent station, and they don't pay me much. But I'm learning a lot, and I'm going to apply at the big stations around here soon. Ian says they'll hire me."

"Mom knows, doesn't she?" At his nod, she added, "Did Dad?"

He hesitated. "I was working up the nerve to tell him when the accident happened. I saw the way he treated you when you defied his wishes. I didn't want the same thing to happen to me." He glanced at her. "I'm not as brave as you."

"Or as stupid," she murmured.

"Balan was the reason I applied for the job at the station, you know." He grimaced. "The pressure on me eased up a lot when he came. I guess that's why I was so accepting of everything he did."

She frowned. "I can't say I'm happy about that."

"I'm not asking you to."

"But I understand why you did it." She turned to face him. "Look, I guess I'm a lot like Dad in the way I see Charles Construction. I can't imagine why you'd want to do anything else. But I won't stand in your way. In fact," she narrowed her eyes, thinking. "Do they sell advertising at that station of yours?"

He laughed. "Nope. But you can sponsor a show if you want."

"Can you get me a deal?"

"It's a donation. You can write it off your taxes."

"That could work."

"You're really something, Miranda. I'm glad you're home."

Tears sprang to her eyes. "Thanks, little brother."

Lottie stuffed her hands deeper into her coat pockets, grateful for the warmth against the pre-dawn chill. Jason was taking his time, double-checking the connection between his truck and the Toyota Corolla he planned to haul cross-country. The little car, secured to a flat-deck trailer, would add significant weight to his journey.

"How far will you get today?"

"I think to Denver. Dad and I planned my route last night."

"Denver?" She raised her eyebrows. "Don't you think that's a stretch?"

"Not on the first day." He tucked a corner of tarp more tightly around the load in the back of his truck. "I figure it'll be slower going once I reach the mountains, so I'd like to put some miles behind me on the front end."

"Drive safely," she said through teeth that were beginning to chatter. "You won't do her any good if you don't get there in one piece."

"I will. I promise." With a grin, he reached out and enveloped her in a bear hug. "Thanks for making me breakfast."

She leaned into his shoulder. "You needed something better than a McMuffin for the road. Take care of our girl."

"I will if she'll let me." He climbed into the truck and started down the alley, tires crunching on cold gravel.

She waved until the trailer lights pulled out of sight, then headed for the house. "Well-begun is half-done," she murmured. "You're halfway there, Jason Harms."

As she reached the porch steps, she saw a curtain twitch next door. Nathan was up early today. She gave him a jaunty wave, and the curtain fell back into place.

She wished she could tell Sam how impressed she was with his oldest son. Jason's hard work and determination had made all the difference at Miranda's place on Saturday. He'd brought a couple of friends to move furniture, a job they'd done many times before. The real surprise was his chosen destination: not the storage unit Lottie had rented, but his own truck. "I'll deliver it to her myself," he'd said, and her estimation of his character had gone up several notches.

It sounded like Sam approved of this move, which surprised her even more. He was so intent on bringing Mitchell back to Collison, she couldn't quite believe he was willing to let Jason go. Maybe she'd misjudged him, too.

Not that it mattered now.

She checked her watch as she headed upstairs. For once she was running early for work. If she hurried, she could get in an hour of piano practice before her first class.

Fifteen

Tuesday morning Sam woke before dawn, pulled on an old flannel shirt and some work pants and ate breakfast on the run. He needed to pick up some supplies at the office and be at the newest job site by eight o'clock. The homeowners were skittish about the demolition phase of work in their historic South Hill mansion. Sam wanted to be on-hand to direct the crew and do whatever hand-holding was necessary.

Yesterday had been one for the history books. Without Jase to share the load Sam had run from job site to office and back again, working through his normal supper time. He'd forgotten what it was like to be the sole proprietor, the last word on every decision that must be made. And there were dozens. Jase had spent Sunday afternoon bringing him up to speed on his projects, the men he supervised, and the potential problems he anticipated in the near future.

He'd be gone two weeks, maybe longer. Long enough to haul Miranda's Corolla to California, meet her family, and bring her back to Iowa. At least that's the way it played out in Sam's mind. Jase had said something ridiculous about evaluating her family's company for growth opportunities, but that was just his lovesick heart talking. Sam figured he'd be thinking more clearly after three or four days on the road, towing a car over the mountains.

Sam had Lottie to thank for that harebrained scheme. Apparently, she'd talked the boy into following his heart to San Francisco. Which reminded him: He needed to call the gutter installers.

He drove Bessie to the office and parked her in the lot, where she'd sit all day while he drove around in the company truck. Jason had offered him the keys to his little red sports car while he was gone, but Sam wasn't interested. Hot cars with old men at the wheel always used to make Nancy laugh.

The morning flew past, a combination of supervision and pitching in to get the work done. Lunch was a salami sandwich at his desk, while he checked the numbers on an estimate. He was taking his last bite when Martha Williams called to ask him to dinner on Friday. He refused the invitation, pleading work, though the fear that she'd invite her next-door neighbor without telling him did flash through his mind. Martha was a matchmaker at heart. It must be killing her to see them avoid each other at church and not know why.

It wasn't his fault they still weren't on speaking terms. He'd tried to bury the hatchet last Sunday after the service, but she'd turned and walked away before he could reach her. He wasn't going to make a fool of himself to get her attention. She had a right to choose her own friends. It was a relief, really. This Thursday he could take his banana cream pie to go and eat it in the peace and quiet of his own kitchen. Unless he was working, which seemed likely.

Man, he loved this life.

Wednesday was identical to Tuesday, with the addition of that infernal building committee meeting. By the time he reached the paneled conference room he was bone-tired and not in the mood to waste time. He'd studied the two reports: The wish list of every department that would occupy the new building, and the information on several architects they might solicit for bids. The wish lists contradicted each other in spots, and most of the architects didn't impress him. Not that he planned to say so. Tonight was just for listening and forming opinions.

Nathan Bartholomew sat across from him at the big walnut table. True to form, he saw fit to comment on every agenda item. As they moved from introductions to setting procedures to dividing up the current phase of work, Nathan dropped little gems of wisdom every step of the way. Sam held his tongue, contented instead to glare ever more fiercely at the pages in front of him, and press a little too hard with his ballpoint pen as he took notes.

Near the end of the meeting, Dr. Isley turned his attention to the list of recommended architects. "I'd like to have a couple of you divide up this list and contact each firm, then report back as to their interest in bidding, their time frame, and your overall impressions." He turned to Sam. "With your expertise, I want you to take the lead on this. Would you mind?"

Sam nodded. "I can save you a little bit of time." He pointed to the first name on the list, an architecture and engineering firm out of Iowa City. "I've seen this company's work over the years, and cleaned up after it, too. They seem to sprout lawsuits wherever they go. Rumor has it they're bankrupt. I'd steer clear, if I were you."

Dr. Isley broke into a pleased smile. "I knew you'd be a good addition, Sam. Strike them off the list, then."

Nathan cleared his throat. "I object." All eyes turned to him as he continued. "I thought we needed five bids to comply with college guidelines. Won't it narrow the list too much if you strike them off?"

Dr. Isley frowned. "We can add another firm if we need to—"

"Besides," Nathan continued, "they may or may not be all the things Mr. Harms says they are. You've only got his word about that. I move we investigate them anyway."

Sam stared at the man across the table. "That would be a complete waste of time."

"Maybe. Maybe not." Nathan turned to the college president. "What do you say, Norm? I'll take it on if you want."

"All right, Nathan." Dr. Isley looked relieved. "I don't object if you'd like to talk to them."

The meeting limped to a close. Sam listened with half an ear as assignments were made and the group adjourned. He caught up with Nathan on his way to the front door. "What was that all about?" he demanded. "Why were you questioning my motives for ruling out that firm?"

"Oh, come on. Everyone knows you're not your own man. I don't see why we should pretend."

"What do you mean?"

"Are you trying to pretend you don't know?"

Sam wanted to shake the man. "Know what? What are you talking about?"

Nathan's smile was superior. "You've never been asked to volunteer for the college before. Why now?" He slapped the arm of his chair. "Obviously because Lottie Braun wants it that way. You're Lottie's puppet on this committee, and I don't trust you."

Annie's Cafe was a busy place on Thursday nights. Even though she'd called ahead, Lottie had to wait a few minutes for her piece of pie to be boxed up. She shared a bench near the door with an elderly couple who were waiting for a table.

A family paid and left, and the couple's name was called. The young cashier apologized for keeping her waiting. Her pie would be ready in a minute.

She watched the girl fold a box and pull the pie from the glass case. She was settling one perfect piece in its cardboard nest when the door opened with a jingle, and Sam walked in.

Lottie shrank deeper inside her coat, but she needn't have bothered. He walked straight up to the counter without looking around. "How are you tonight, Mary?" he said to the cashier. "I see you've got my pie ready."

She smiled up at him. "Sorry, Mr. Harms. This one is for Ms. Braun."

Lottie gave him a weak wave. "Hi, Sam."

If she hoped for an answering smile, she was doomed to disappointment. Sam gave her a stiff nod and stepped away from the counter. "Sorry."

She tipped her head toward the box. "You can have that one, if you're in a hurry. I've got time."

"I'll wait my turn."

She hesitated. "Have you heard from Jason? Did he make it to San Francisco?"

"He got stopped by a snowstorm in Utah," he said politely. "He expects to finish his trip tomorrow."

"Well, I wish him the best." Lottie paid for her pie and left, brushing Sam's coat sleeve on her way to the door. "See you around, Sam."

He didn't answer.

The work week flew past. Miranda hadn't accomplished half the things on her to-do list by Friday. She'd spent much of her time visiting the job site and badgering her two remaining foremen with questions in order to understand their duties, and what they expected of their laborers. They said they didn't mind, but she knew the sooner she was up to speed and out of their way, the better. Max and Karthav were working overtime, trying to fill in the space left by Jose's departure, a fact they reminded her of regularly. "The most important thing you can do for us," they told her, "is get a new carpentry foreman."

Miranda had advertised for a new carpenter, but with the construction boom in the area, applicants were few and far between. The ones who had bothered to show up for an interview either had unexplainable gaps in their work history or were unsuitable in other ways.

Her mother had spent the week in the office, setting up a new bookkeeping system. Dan Hollis had loaned them his office manager for a few days, and together she and Sonia had put together an efficient office. "As soon as we have the money for it, I want a computer," Sonia told Miranda after a day or two. "It will make everything so much easier."

Miranda was happy to see her mother's force of personality put to such good purpose. She was less thrilled with Sonia's role as self-appointed chaperone. "I do not feel comfortable leaving you alone in the office, Miranda," she said the first day. "You are a beautiful young woman. There is no telling what might happen in this neighborhood."

Miranda had laughed. "Mom, if someone wanted to hurt me—and I don't believe anyone does—what exactly could you do to protect me?"

"There is safety in numbers, Miranda."

Sonia would not be moved, so if Miranda went to work early, Sonia went with her. If Miranda stayed late, Sonia did, too. By the end of the week, Miranda was feeling claustrophobic, but she was trying to pick her battles carefully, and this was not a hill she wanted to die on.

Every night they went to bed tired, and every morning they stumbled around half-awake until their first cup of caffeine. Miranda continued the coffee habit she'd acquired in college, but her mother stuck with her traditional cup of milky chai. Then, as the sun rose higher in the sky, they drove to work in the big white truck with Charles Construction painted on the side. Miranda was getting pretty good at taking corners in the behemoth, and Sonia insisted it was free advertising.

Now that Zac's life was an open book, he settled down to do his part for the family. He talked to his station manager about becoming a program sponsor and contributed his meager paycheck to the household budget. And on Friday, his one day off, he offered to work on the drywall crew.

The business was now on firmer footing. The Charles family was united in purpose and strength. Miranda knew she should be happy, but when she let herself stop for breath, sadness washed in like the tide. So, she made it her policy never to stop for breath.

"You're going to work yourself to death," Sonia said on Friday afternoon as the work crew returned from the job site. "Why don't you close an hour early, go home, and put your feet up? I'll make dinner."

Miranda smiled at her mother. "I can't leave yet. I've got someone coming for an interview at four-thirty. Why don't you go home with Zac? He's outside with the rest of the crew."

"You know very well I can't go home until you do."

"You mean you won't go home."

They were still arguing the point when a stranger walked into the office. "I'm here for my interview?" He looked around with a puzzled air. "Is this the right place?"

"It certainly is." Miranda walked around the desk with her hand extended. "I'm Miranda Charles, and this is my office manager, Sonia."

"Nice to meet you." He shook her hand but looked past her with an expectant smile. "Am I early? I can sit over here to wait."

Miranda's smile froze. "I am the owner, Mr.—" she looked at the application on her desk "—Johnston. Your interview is with me."

The man blinked. "I see."

Miranda's heart sank. She knew by this point that continuing the interview was an exercise in futility. This man, like several of the others, was simply not interested in working for a woman. Still, she made herself go through the motions. She couldn't change her sex, but she could still maintain a level of professionalism.

"I'll call you in a few days," she told Mr. Johnston fifteen minutes later, and watched with despair as he made his escape. "Mom, what are we going to do? We have to fill this position soon, or we'll have a mutiny on our hands."

"Maybe Zac could do the interviews," Sonia said.

"Mom!"

"No?" Sonia gave a tiny sigh. "Do you have any other candidates?"

"No." Miranda slumped behind her desk. "Maybe I should run the ad again."

"Maybe." She didn't sound hopeful.

Zac walked in and pointed at Miranda. "There's a guy out here who wants to talk to you."

She attempted a smile. "Is he a carpenter? If so, we're hiring."

Zac looked confused. "I don't know. I'll ask."

"No, wait. I was joking." She jumped to her feet as her brother turned to go. "Send the guy in. Let's see what he wants."

Sonia frowned. "It's late in the day for a sales call, isn't it?"

"I agree—" The words died on her tongue.

Jase stood in the doorway, ball cap in hand, gazing straight into her eyes. "I have a delivery for Miranda Charles?"

She swallowed hard, her throat suddenly dry.

"One Toyota Corolla, a set of bedroom furniture, table and chairs, and eight boxes of personal effects." His lips turned up in a faint smile. "Minus one bottle of perfume that broke when my truck ran off the road in Utah."

175

Somewhere in the back of her mind, she heard her mother gasp.

A note of uncertainty crept into his voice. "Where do you want me to leave everything?"

Still she couldn't speak, couldn't quite believe her eyes. She opened her mouth and shut it again. The silence stretched on.

Finally, the light went out of his eyes, and he turned to go. "I guess I'll start unloading."

He left, and she stared after him, unable to tear her gaze from the door. Behind her, Sonia spoke. "Is that your man from Iowa?"

Miranda nodded, relieved. So, her mother had seen him, too.

"Isn't he a carpenter?"

"Yes," she whispered.

She felt a firm hand in the small of her back. "Well, you'd better run after him before he drives away."

Sixteen

f he'd heard it once, he'd heard it a thousand times. "Sam, when is that boy of yours coming back?"

All kinds of customers and contractors wanted to talk to Jase. When Sam offered to answer their questions in his absence, some of them looked a little skeptical. "Did he bring you up to speed?" they asked.

It was enough to make a man question his own competence.

Truth was, Sam didn't know when Jase was coming back. He was pretty darned happy in California, by the sound of things. Miranda had welcomed him with open arms, and she'd put him straight to work, too. Jase had called home over the weekend, and Sam couldn't remember when he'd sounded so excited. "Business is booming out here, Dad. Miranda's doing great, but she's really got her hands full."

"How did her mother react?" Sam asked.

Jase had laughed. "Surprisingly well, but I think that's because they needed a carpenter and I fit the bill. She's a nice lady. We're getting along just fine."

Sam was "getting along just fine," too. He was a little surprised at how much he liked being in charge again. No more twiddling his thumbs at the office while Jason directed the job site. Two years ago he'd handed over the reins so the boy wouldn't get restless and leave. Now that he was back in the driver's seat, Sam wasn't sure that had been such a good idea. Oh, it had been good for Jase, all right. Just not good for Sam.

Tuesday evening Sam was at the drug store, looking for a bottle of aspirin when Norm caught up with him. "Did you see the headlines in the paper today?" Norm said. "Looks like you were right about that builder from Iowa City." Dr. Isley gave him a thumbs-up. "They're no good, just like you said. See you tomorrow night."

Sam picked up a copy of the paper at the check-out counter. "CEO Indicted on Five Counts of Fraud." The headline brought a smile to his face. He hoped that fool Bartholomew was satisfied. Sam Harms might not be a college professor, but he did know a thing or two about his chosen field.

He savored his sense of vindication for a minute or two before the truth sank in. All week he'd been planning to pull out of that commit-tee. Now he was more stuck than ever.

But maybe it was worth it. Someone had to stand up to Bartholomew.

Thursday afternoon the Performing Arts Department came together to rehearse for the benefit concert. Classes at the PAB were canceled for the afternoon, and the auditorium was abuzz with students either performing in ensembles or working behind the scenes. Faculty members bunched together in small groups, critiquing the action amongst themselves.

Lottie sat with the music professors while she waited her turn to play. Their conversation revolved around work, a subject they all knew inside and out. She sat back and listened and enjoyed a newfound sense of belonging. This was her world, where well-trained musicians spoke the same language and valued similar things. Tomorrow night, dressed in her beaded gown, she would show the good people of Collison what a consummate professional could do.

Katherine nudged her arm. "Enjoying yourself?"

Lottie smiled at her friend. "This must be how Mickey Rooney and Judy Garland felt in those 'Let's Put On a Show' movies."

Nathan leaned over to add his two cents' worth. "You've done a bit more than just put on a show."

Lottie raised her eyebrows. "Oh?"

"There's that little matter of a large donation to the building fund."

Katherine shot him a warning look. "Nathan…"

Lottie's jaw dropped. "What are you talking about?"

Nathan shrugged. "Don't get me wrong. You've done us a favor."

She turned to Katherine, who looked apologetic. "This is Collison, Lottie. There are no secrets here."

"What I don't get," Nathan continued loudly, "is why you can't come right out and admit you've got an interest in the project, instead of putting your boyfriend on the planning committee."

"My boyfriend?" Lottie's head was beginning to spin. "I don't have a boyfriend."

Nathan looked disgusted. "There's another secret you've failed to keep. Sam Harms is always at your house. I have eyes, you know."

"Is that so?" She raised her eyebrows. "How many times have you seen him at my house in the past three weeks?"

Lottie turned her attention to the stage, her mood ruined.

"So, you've broken up?" Nathan said finally.

She kept her gaze on the performers. "We were only friends, and I had nothing to do with him being on the committee."

Nathan's eyebrows drew together in thought. "I wish I'd known that. I may have said some awkward things at the committee meetings."

She turned to glare at him. "Maybe you should apologize."

He snorted. "Apologies are not my strong suit."

"Practice makes perfect."

The last thing Sam wanted to do after a long work week was go to a concert. He was tired, his back ached, and the forecast called for rain mixed with snow. If he had his way, he'd spend the evening in his recliner with a good book.

Instead here he was in a suit and tie, sitting at the end of the row of committee members. At least he'd managed to grab a seat far away from that fool Bartholomew. The last thing he needed tonight was that guy's running commentary buzzing in his ear.

He made short work of the program in his hand. Six different ensembles—two dance, two theater, two music—meant he was in for a long night. He didn't care much for dance, and the theater department was doing selections from Shakespeare, which he'd never understood. Cal Jefferson's jazz ensemble looked all right.

His mind skimmed over the last act of the evening. He had trouble thinking about Lottie right now. If Bartholomew was right, she'd played Sam for a fool, tricking him into thinking he'd been appointed to a civic committee on his own merits. He didn't take kindly to being made a pawn in some kind of power game.

But every time he saw her his heart betrayed his will. If she so much as stood in the same room with him, he knew it. His face turned red and his hands got clammy, and he felt like a love-struck schoolboy.

He made himself sick.

The curtain rose on a dark stage, and Sam caught his breath. There she stood in the spotlight, majestic in a form-fitting black dress that did something to his senses. Drat her.

She took her time, drawing in the audience with her Mona Lisa smile. "Good evening, my dear friends." Was she looking straight at him? "Welcome to the Collison College Performing Arts Building. Seventy years ago, this auditorium was the cutting edge in entertainment venues. Tonight, we hope to honor its history with another wonderful show." She paused and looked around, her expression rueful. "And perhaps to highlight how times have changed. So sit back, get comfortable, and enjoy the show."

She walked off-stage and Sam could breathe again. The lights came up to reveal Cal Jefferson with his back to the audience, arms raised to hit the downbeat on his first number.

When Sam settled back in his seat, his knees nearly touched the row in front of him. He would have liked to stretch his legs into the aisle, but good manners got the better of him. Instead he sat up straight to make the most of the wooden folding seat. Behind him, a little girl whispered, "Mom, I can't see," and Sam slumped forward, elbows on knees to accommodate her.

By intermission he felt like a human pretzel. He was also hotter than Billy-blue heck in the under-ventilated room. When the house lights turned on, he made a bee line for the front door for a breath of fresh air.

The sight that met his eyes made his heart sink. Cold bullets of rain fell in slanted sheets, turning the lights on the quad a hazy silver. Here and there a drop of solid slush clung to the frozen steps of the PAB. If temperatures fell much farther, they'd have a mess on their hands.

If they left now everyone would have a chance to make it home before the roads got slick. The concert organizers could make an announcement from the stage and end the show early. It was the only safe thing to do.

He let the door fall shut behind him and went in search of Lottie. She'd know who to talk to.

She was standing in the hall outside the stage door, talking to Bartholomew. More like scolding him, complete with her index finger waving in his face. The fool looked like a teenager caught out after curfew. Sam hesitated to get in the middle of that.

He waffled a moment too long, and found his way cut off by Norman Isley. "Great concert," Dr. Isley said. "It's going exactly as I hoped."

"What? Oh, yes." Sam turned his attention to the man in front of him. "Norm, there's a storm brewing."

Dr. Isley chuckled. "You could put it that way, Sam. A perfect storm. Stuffy room, bad microphones, terrible lighting. No one could miss the point we're trying to make. A storm indeed."

"No, I mean—"

The lights blinked, and Dr. Isley gave Sam two thumbs-up. "That's the sign for the second act. Gotta go."

The man hurried away to his waiting wife, and Sam looked around. The hallway was empty.

Against his better judgement he returned to his seat. There was nothing he could do right now, he told himself. He might as well stick around to help sand the parking lot after the show.

By the start of the second act Lottie could sense the audience's goodwill. The students responded with rising excitement, determined to give their best to an appreciative public. Even when the stage lights flickered and the speakers sputtered the show went on with gusto.

Sam Harms was the sole exception. She watched him from the wings, hunched forward in his seat, his eyebrows lowered in a perpetual frown. He seemed to grow gloomier as the show went on, as though an evening of light entertainment had offended him in some way.

The technical problems grew worse in the second act. For a full thirty seconds during Hamlet's first soliloquy the lights failed completely, leaving the actor—a senior with a bright future on Broadway—to carry on in the dark.

Lottie stood backstage with Katherine while she waited to go on. "Is this par for the course?" she asked her friend.

Katherine shook her head. "I've never known it to be this bad."

The lights flickered and came on. A sigh went through the audience. The student director gave them a thumbs-up as he scooted past. "Everything's under control," he whispered. "You're up next, Miss Braun."

Lottie squared her shoulders and drew a deep breath. Time to make the case for a new PAB.

She walked to center stage and raised the mic to her height. "Now that you know our good ol' PAB the way we know it—warts and all—we want to ask for your help. As you leave tonight the ushers will hand you a pledge card for our building fund. Won't you help us build a better performance space for Collison College and the city we call home?"

With that she settled at the piano and placed her hands on the keys, the opening chords of the Chopin scherzo taking shape in her mind. Sending up a prayer for the sound and lights, she bent her head.

The room plunged into darkness as she struck the first chord. Someone gasped, and a general murmuring rolled through the room.

Lottie froze. The piece she'd chosen covered the keyboard from top to bottom, not a feat she could pull off in total darkness. Yet if she quit playing the restless audience might panic. It would be the same as yelling "fire" in a crowded theater.

Thinking fast, she turned her first fortissimo chord into a progression that marched down the keyboard to C sharp minor and became the *Moonlight Sonata*. Beethoven's lyrical masterpiece was a composition she could play for as long as it took to fix the lighting.

Right away she felt the audience relax. They seemed to believe she was in a playful mood, the inky blackness a parlor trick designed to entertain them.

Fair enough. She played until a flashlight beam appeared in the wings. Then, as quickly as she dared, she brought her performance to a close.

The last lyrical note died away, and the audience responded with loud applause. The flashlight bobbed across the stage and stopped beside Lottie. "We're in the middle of an ice storm," the student director told her. "The electricity is out all over town. We have to get these people out of here safely."

Lottie read panic in the young man's eyes. "Courage," she said. "Follow me."

Taking the flashlight from him, she led the way to the middle of the stage and called for quiet. "Ladies and gentlemen, it seems we have a situation on our hands. I've just been told that we have no electricity in the entire building, but there is no reason to be afraid. Please stay in your seats until the ushers have opened the doors and turned on their flashlights. They will dismiss you in an orderly way so you won't step on one another's toes on the way out." She turned to the student director. "The ushers do have flashlights?" she murmured.

His guilty face spoke volumes. "I'm not sure."

For the first time a prickle of worry ran down her spine. If one person chose this moment to panic, pandemonium might break out.

As the noise level rose to a roar, the center doors opened at the back of the room. Sam stood there, his face lit up by the high-beam lantern he kept in the trunk of his car. Four ushers marched in behind him and began dismissing the rows.

Lottie turned to the young man next to her. "Well? What are you waiting for? Get down there and help."

When the lights went out on Lottie's performance, Sam knew immediately what must have happened. The college was always losing power in storms. At first, he was angry that she kept playing. She should have stopped and told everyone to go home. Then he saw the opportunity in it. While she held the audience's attention, Sam felt his way up the aisle and slipped out to the parking lot.

He returned with his emergency work lantern and the pen light he kept in the glove compartment. The warm flaps of his good hat now securely covered his ears, and his suit was protected by a plastic rain poncho.

A group of student ushers milled anxiously by the main doors. "Aren't you supposed to carry flashlights?" Sam asked.

They looked startled. "I know where they're kept," said one.

Sam handed him the pen light. "Go get them. Hurry."

The kid ran off, and Sam turned to the other ushers. "We need to get all these people out of here safely. This is what we're going to do."

Armed with flashlights and a plan, the ushers lined up behind Sam. As soon as the applause died away, he opened the doors. Time to get to work.

Within fifteen minutes the auditorium was empty. Sam stayed until the last student left, then made a sweep of the aisles just to be sure.

Only a handful of cars remained when he got to the parking lot. The red Mercedes was not one of them. He told himself he was glad. He wished Godspeed to all his neighbors on this dangerous night, including Lottie Braun.

Norm Isley pulled up next to him while he was scraping Bessie's windows. "Your quick thinking saved our bacon in there," he said. "I've never seen anything like it."

Sam stuffed his hands deeper in his coat pockets. "It was nothing."

Norm shook his head. "Sam, you're a heck of a guy. I knew you were the right man for that committee. I knew you had a cool head the first time I ever heard you talk about your job. And tonight, you proved me right." On that note he rolled up the window and drove away while Sam stared after him, mouth agape.

What a night, Sam thought later as he crept home at a snail's pace. Lottie had done a wonderful job under the worst conditions. The fact that she continued playing in pitch darkness was a mark of pure class. Someday, somehow, he'd find a way to tell her so.

Lottie heaved a sigh of relief when she finally reached her own dark house. She didn't have much experience with the dangers of driving on ice, but the short trip from campus had made a believer out of her. She hung up her black dress and brushed her teeth by flashlight, then added another quilt to the bed before retiring for the night. To hear the locals tell it, the power could be out for a couple of days, and she was already getting cold.

Sam had been a hero tonight. When he walked in with that lantern, looking like Norman Rockwell on a rainy fishing trip, she could have kissed him.

Her heart filled with pride and broke a little at the same time. Sam was the salt of the earth, equipped for every emergency. Lottie didn't belong in his world, and he didn't have much use for hers. No wonder they couldn't sustain their friendship. It simply wasn't meant to be.

And on this depressing thought she fell asleep.

Three hours later she woke in the glare of her overhead light. The electricity was back on.

Seventeen

Saturday morning the world had turned to crystal. Lottie's breath caught at the glint of sun on the ice-coated landscape outside her bedroom window. Her tree-lined street looked like something from a Nordic fairytale. She let out her breath as the sand truck passed, tossing dirt on the pristine snow.

After breakfast she put on her coat and boots and headed outside to clean up.

Ed Williams waved to her from his back porch, where a fallen branch had taken out the wrought iron railing. "Come spring we'll be building that deck I've been dreaming about," he called, his breath making white puffs of vapor in the air. "There's no way Martha can stop me now."

Lottie had to laugh. "That's looking on the bright side."

He jerked his head toward her yard. "You got off pretty light."

She shrugged. "The guys removed a couple of trees to build the music room. I was sad to see them go, but I guess it had its good side."

Martha opened the kitchen door. "Phone's for you, Ed. They've got trees down at church."

"I figured." He waved and turned away. "Duty calls."

Lottie waved good-bye and walked up the property line to the front yard. Now that she stood at street level, the wonderland looked more like a disaster area. Up and down the street, homeowners were awakening to a day of cleanup and repairs.

The oaks that shaded Lottie's front walk were largely intact, but when she reached the side she shared with Nathan, her heart sank. The big sycamore between their houses had dropped its limbs everywhere. Most of them had fallen harmlessly on the lawn, but a good-sized branch now teetered on her porch roof above the front steps, where it could easily roll off and conk the mailman in the head. Better not leave it there.

She headed for the garage to fetch a ladder. Passing Nathan's dining room, she gave an automatic wave, just in case he was watching. Sure enough, he leaned into the bow window and raised his coffee cup in response. No doubt he'd have some blistering comments for her about the mess in his front yard. She could wait till later to have that conversation.

Sam waited until he heard the sand trucks before he moved a muscle out of bed. He'd had enough of the ice last night. No need to drive on it this morning.

He didn't have much to clean up in his own yard. His trees had come through pretty well. A birch in the back yard was bowed to the ground, but it would spring back into shape once the temperature rose.

Bob Summers called shortly after eight, looking for help with the cleanup. "We've got several flowering crabs and a pear tree that lost limbs," he told Sam. "Bring your chainsaw."

Even with the sand, the road out of town was uncertain. Sam passed five accidents on his way to the church. Bessie wasn't handling too well so Sam crawled along, shoulders hunched, muttering under his breath every time someone went around him. His eyes never left the road, but when he passed the Ford dealership, he could have sworn that shiny red four-wheel-drive truck flashed its headlights at him.

A crew of elders and deacons had assembled at church by the time Sam arrived. They sent up a cheer when he pulled both of his chainsaws out of the trunk. "Thank God for power tools," Bob Summers said fervently. "Now we can get down to business."

Sam raised an eyebrow at his friend. "Did you ever use one of these things before, Bob?"

The minister grinned. "Don't let my credentials fool you. I'm an old farm boy at heart."

"Good. Let's take care of that mess by the entrance."

Bob was like a kid at Christmas with that saw. He went after the downed limbs the same way he parsed a scripture passage, first sizing up the job, then going after it piece by piece. Sam contented himself with carrying the logs to the edge of the lot and watching his friend enjoy himself.

They'd finished with one tree and were moving on to the next when Martha Williams showed up with a thermos of coffee and some donuts. "I thought you boys could use a warm-up," she said. She handed a cup to Sam and one to Bob and moved on to the others.

Bob blew the steam off his coffee with a thoughtful air. "I remember when Nancy was the refreshment gal on days like today."

"That's true."

"I'll bet you miss her."

Sam shot him a sidelong glance. "I sure do."

Bob squinted toward the horizon. "I didn't see Lottie at church last week. Any idea where she's been?"

Ah. Sam fixed his eyes on the same far spot. "You should ask her, Bob. She's your parishioner."

Bob turned to Sam, his gaze full of compassion. "It's all right to move on, my friend. You know that, don't you?"

"Yeah, I know." Sam crumpled his coffee cup and threw it on the sidewalk. If only it were that simple.

Marmalade joined Lottie as she carried the ladder out of the garage. He'd been out hunting in the snow and looked quite self-satisfied. "Hello, old fellow," she said to her orange friend. "Catch anything today?"

"Meow."

"I'll take that as a yes."

He sat down behind the rose bushes to wash while she settled the ladder against the house. She wanted it as steady as possible before she climbed, so she leaned her weight against the legs to anchor them evenly in the grass.

As she put her foot on the first step, Nathan knocked on the window behind her. She glanced back and he threw up his hands, his expression outraged. She gave him an exaggerated shrug, and he answered with a thunderous frown.

Clearly, he had no faith in her. She'd show him.

Turning her back on the man in the window, she began to climb. She settled on the fifth step and looked around to get her bearings. From her perch she could easily touch the branch. If she leaned out just a little, she'd be able to push it to the ground. The stoutest part rested in the gutter, a fact she hadn't noticed from the ground, but she thought a little force would dislodge it.

Grabbing the ladder firmly with her left hand, she leaned out and shoved the branch with her right. It shook but did not fall. Another push would do the job.

She leaned out to try again and felt the ladder tip. Suddenly off balance, she lost her grip and scrambled for something to break her fall. The ice-coated gutter held her weight for a split second before her hands slipped away. On the way down her body bounced against a post, careened into the railing, and landed with a thud in the ice-covered grass.

Eighteen

Sam stowed his tools in Bessie's trunk and raised a hand to the few remaining elders on clean-up duty.

"Thanks again," Bob called.

"No problem, Pastor."

He drove home in a good mood. The morning sun had done its job on the roads. They were now merely wet instead of slick. Already the trees were beginning to drip. By tomorrow all that would be left of the storm was the damage it had done.

When he reached the edge of town, he took a long look. Sure enough, the red pickup still anchored the corner of the car lot. "Aw, what the heck," he muttered, and made the turn into the dealership.

"You've got a good eye, sir." Young Brett Rowley, an old friend of Jason's, said when he'd stated his business. "That baby's the real deal. Would you like to take a test drive?"

Sam could hear his heartbeat pulsing in his ears. "I sure would."

"You all right, Ms. Braun?" The voice was barely audible over the pounding in her ears.

She raised one eyelid. Thomas Allen's face swam into view. "I really got the wind knocked out of me."

"Oh, thank God." He straightened and gave a thumbs-up to some-

191

one she couldn't see.

Somewhere far away, sirens wailed. She closed her eyes against the sun's glare. "You can go home, Thomas. I'll get up in a minute."

He stuck his hands in his pockets. "You better hold still. You don't know what's broke."

"I want to go inside." Those sirens were deafening now. She moved one arm to pull herself up, and pain erupted in white-hot flashes. She heard herself yell.

Somewhere out of sight, a man swore long and fluently. "Keep her down, kid. They're almost here."

Thomas crouched next to her on the grass. "Relax," he whispered. "The ambulance is here."

The sirens cut off mid-wail. Footsteps approached, and the boy's pale face disappeared from view. She heard voices overhead but couldn't follow the conversation. Pain radiated from her shoulder—no, her neck—or maybe it was her head. She couldn't figure out where she hurt.

The two EMTs had a natural air of command. They questioned her closely while they checked her limbs, then informed her that they were taking her to the hospital. She held back a scream—at least she thought she did—when they moved her to the stretcher.

The ride across her lawn was bumpy but mercifully short. Boots crunched on gravel, the stretcher was airborne, and Lottie found herself secured in the back of the ambulance.

Metal doors clicked shut, blotting out the sun. The deep, commanding voices dropped to a murmur and a clinical silence took over. Somewhere a machine beeped.

She slipped from consciousness.

Sam had a lot to think about when he left the dealership. He needed to drop by the library and look up the blue book value of the truck. It wouldn't hurt to check *Consumer Reports* while he was there. Knowledge was power when it came to negotiating.

Bessie needed a new home, of course. Trading her in was out of the question. They'd rip him off and sell her to the junkyard for parts. She was old, sure, but she'd been taken care of. She'd make a good starter car for a high school kid.

He knew just the right kid, too.

Sam turned left at the light and pulled up in front of Thomas Allen's house. As he got out of the car, a flash of red and white caught his eye. An ambulance in the alley? His heart skipped a beat.

By the time he reached the back yard the ambulance was gone. Thomas stood in his back yard, staring after it with a defeated expression. When he saw Sam, his face brightened. "So you got the message?"

"What message?"

"About Ms. Braun. Mr. Bartholomew said he called you."

Sam's chest tightened with fear. "What happened, Tom?"

"She fell off a ladder." Thomas bit his lip. "I wanted to go along in the ambulance, but they wouldn't let me."

"Come on. I'll give you a ride." He was already striding toward the street, a thousand frightening images crowding his brain. "Fill me in," he said as they rolled down the alley. "Did you see her fall?"

"No." Thomas swiped his bangs out of his eyes. "Mr. Bartholomew did, but he couldn't do anything about it, y'know." He glanced at Sam to see if he understood. "He yelled to me from his back porch, and I ran over to help. She was out cold."

Sam's breath caught in his throat.

"But finally, she opened her eyes. Mr. Bartholomew yelled at me to make her stay still—I did the best I could."

"Is she all right?"

Thomas hesitated. "I dunno. She screamed when the EMTs moved her to the stretcher."

"So she stayed conscious?"

"Yeah, but she wasn't making a lot of sense." His eyes lit up. "She mentioned you."

Sam glanced at him. "She did?"

"Yeah. She said, 'Sam was right.'"

"Huh." This stunned him for a minute. "Now, those are words a man seldom hears."

"Boy, don't I know it."

Sam raised his eyebrows. "You're a little young to be so wise."

"I had a girlfriend for a while."

They reached the hospital and hurried into the emergency room. "Lottie Braun?" Sam said to the nurse on duty.

"You can take a seat," the nurse said. "They just wheeled her into X-ray. We'll let you know when family can see her."

Sam didn't correct her assumption. Technically he and Lottie were family: first cousins by adoption. He sat down in a molded plastic chair against the wall, and Thomas sat beside him. "Hey, I just thought of something," Thomas said. "If you didn't know Ms. Braun was hurt, why did you stop by?"

"I came to see you." It seemed like hours ago now. "I wanted to know if you'd be interested in a good used car."

Thomas hesitated. "What kind of car are we talking about?"

"My car. The one we drove here in." Sam gave him a sidelong glance to gauge his reaction. If the kid showed one iota of disappointment in Bessie, Sam would withdraw the offer.

Thomas's eyes lit up, but he kept his cool. "Depends on how much you want for it. I don't have any money saved up."

"Do you consider yourself a hard worker?"

"Sure."

The knot in the pit of Sam's stomach relaxed a notch. "Maybe we can come to terms."

The nurse approached. "You two can see Miss Braun now. She's resting in Room 4 while we wait for the doctor's orders."

She led them down the hall and knocked on the door. "Miss Braun? Your family is here." She gave them a businesslike nod. "Keep your noise to a minimum. She hit her head pretty hard."

Sam pulled up short. What would Lottie think of him announcing himself as family? After the last few weeks, he barely qualified as her friend. Maybe she'd rather he didn't show his face.

Thomas had no such qualms. Brushing past Sam, he entered the dimly lit room. "Hey, Ms. Braun," Sam heard him say softly.

"Hi." Her voice sounded rough.

"Hope you don't mind me being here. I wanted to make sure you're all right."

"Thank you, Thomas. You're a good boy."

Sam wavered at the door for another minute, torn between running for his life and walking inside. He decided to stay, not for any noble reason, but because he knew the duty nurse would notice if he left. Heck, she might even stop him and ask where he was going. Anything Lottie dished out would be easier than that.

Besides, he thought as he stepped into the quiet room, she needed him. Simple as that.

She was propped up on pillows, her right arm strapped to some kind of contraption to hold it still. Her face looked paler than usual, except for a big purple bruise that bled into her hairline and tired blue smudges beneath her eyes. He stood at the foot of the bed and let the wave of relief crash over him. No permanent damage here. "Hullo, Lottie," he said as steadily as he could.

She opened her eyes a crack. "That you, Sam?"

He stepped forward. "I'm here."

"You were right."

"I know. The sycamore was dead. I should have cut it down."

"I should've listened." Her words were slurred.

"Not necessarily." He wasn't that smart. He slipped past Thomas and took her good hand in his. "You gave us quite a scare."

"Did I?" she said. "Sorry."

"Accidents happen, Lottie. It's all right now."

Her eyes drifted shut and her hand relaxed in his, but he didn't let go.

Someone had taken a hammer to the inside of Lottie's head. She squeezed her eyes shut to fight the throbbing pain. Maybe if she stayed very still, she could find her way back to the oblivion of sleep.

The next time she woke up the throbbing had receded to a dull ache. Her nose itched, but she couldn't move her arm to scratch it. Her whole body felt like one big bruise.

Reluctantly she opened her eyes. She lay cocooned in the hospital bed, its metal sides raised in the safety position. Her right arm lay on top of the covers, permanently bent at the elbow by a complicated sling. Outside her window the sky was streaked with pink as daylight lost its battle with the dark.

Someone moved beside her. "You drifted off again."

She slanted her eyes toward the deep, familiar voice. "You're still here."

"Yep."

He'd been here all day, through the endless waiting for a doctor's exam and the transfer to a private room. He'd stepped outside—but hadn't left—when the nurses came to do their rounds. She did not know what miracle had given her Sam on this worst of all days, but she was grateful.

"Are you hungry? They brought your dinner a while ago."

She tried to smile through chapped lips. "You're not going to make me eat that stuff, are you?"

"Not if you don't want it." He reached for her call light. "We'll ask the nurse to take your tray."

A young nurse answered the call. "What can I do for you?"

"I don't want my dinner tray," Lottie said. "Could you take it away?"

"Sure thing." She turned to pick up the tray, and spotted Sam for the first time. "Oh, hello, Mr. Harms." She sounded surprised. "How in the world are you?"

"Hi, Erica." Sam smiled at the young woman. "Good to see you."

"Gee, what's it been? Three years?"

"Nearly four. So they moved you off the oncology floor?"

"I needed a break." Her smile faded. "It wears on you after a while."

"I know what you mean."

They exchanged a look of quiet understanding. Then Erica seemed to recollect herself. "Well, I'd better..." She picked up the tray and looked back at Lottie. "You hit that call light if you need anything, Mrs...." She glanced at the big name sign by the door. "Miss Braun."

Erica whisked out with the tray, and Sam reached for the remote. "Should I turn on the TV?"

"Sam..."

He didn't meet her eyes. "It's after six. We could catch the news."

Lottie reached out with her good hand. "Sam, I'm sorry."

He frowned. "Stop apologizing for that stupid tree."

"That's not what I meant." She caught his gaze and held it. "I'm sorry you had to spend one minute inside this hospital on my account. I'm sorry you know the nurses on the oncology floor, and I'm sorry you lost your Nancy, especially in such a sad way."

He shook his head. "You don't have to—"

"Yes, I do." She set her cold fingers atop his warm hand. "I'm sorry we ever had that stupid fight, and I'm sorry I said mean things about Bessie." She blinked away the sudden moisture in her eyes. "It's none of my business what you choose to drive."

His throat moved when he swallowed. "I'm the one who should apologize. I wish I could take back all the things I said that night. You belonged to the Neverland. I had no right to take that away just because I didn't."

"No, you were right." She closed her eyes. "They tolerated me because I helped the bottom line. And because of Helen. Johnny and Parson—all the guys—they loved Helen best. I know that."

He smiled, and his whole face transformed. "If it's any consolation, I liked you better than Helen. You were my friend."

One tear spilled over and rolled down her cheek. "Can we be friends again, Sam?"

"Yes." His voice was rough, but she read relief in his eyes. "Yes, please."

Nineteen

Sam left for the night, and Lottie called the nurse to help her get ready for bed.

"Can you manage with your left hand?" Erica asked as she squeezed the toothpaste onto Lottie's brush.

"I'll give it a try."

The toothbrush felt like a foreign object as she raised it to her mouth. She gave the inside of her cheek a vicious poke before she finally connected with teeth and gums. She swished up and down in a clumsy imitation of the nightly ritual, and spit in the little plastic basin with a sense of relief. "There. That's over with."

"The first time is the hardest," Erica said with a smile. "You'll get better at it as you go along."

Lottie looked up, startled. "I won't have this sling long enough to get much practice. Will I?"

"That's not for me to say." Erica busied herself arranging Lottie's pillow. "The doctor will come by in the morning. Meanwhile if you need anything, press your call light." She turned out the light and left.

Lottie stared into the darkness, the nurse's words on replay in her mind. The first time is the hardest. How long would she have to live without her right arm? A week? A month?

Forever?

Sheer exhaustion carried her off to sleep, but a few hours later she woke up, her mind and body gripped with fear.

How bad was her injury?

She tried to remember what the attending physician had said all those hours ago. He'd called it a separated shoulder and told her not to move. "The orthopedist is out of town today. Sometime tomorrow he'll be in to talk to you about treatment options."

His bedside manner had been vague but reassuring, and she'd been too fuzzy headed to ask questions. She was pretty sure he'd said she would recover just fine, but then he didn't know what she did for a living. Any injury to arms, hands, or fingers could alter the course of her career. Without full strength in her right arm, the famous Lottie Braun style would be a mere memory. Eyes wide in the darkness, she stared down the possibility that she'd just sacrificed her livelihood to a stupid household accident.

As the flood of terror spread through her mind, one tiny island of rational thought remained. You're blowing things out of proportion, it said. Three a.m. is the worst time to analyze your problems. You can't solve anything until morning. Stop worrying and go back to sleep.

The voice made sense. She needed to distract herself. Clamping her eyelids shut, she set about alphabetizing all the composers of the Romantic period. Berlioz, Bizet, Brahms...

What if she never again walked onto a stage, took her place at the piano, and nodded to the conductor to begin? What if she never lost herself in the movement of phrases, outlining every nuance of thought and emotion with the action of her fingers?

...Debussy, Delius, Donizetti, Dvorak—No, she'd forgotten Chopin.

Could she still teach? Would the college want a professor who could not demonstrate the techniques she'd been hired to instill in her students?

To be fair, they probably would. She was still Lottie Braun. She could be the department spokeswoman—a high-profile side show, at the very least. Depressing.

...Chopin, Debussy Delius, Donizetti...

This wasn't working.

She opened her eyes. "Lord God? This is Lottie." He knew that, of course. "I'm scared to death. Can you help me?" She took a shaky breath, not sure what else to say. "Well, thanks. Amen."

This time, when she closed her eyes, they stayed shut of their own accord. Lethargy overtook her muscles, relaxing them one by one.

…Field, Franck, Faure, Grieg…

She slept.

Sam had to hurry to get to church on time. Last night had been a late one, and he'd overslept.

Not that he minded. He wouldn't trade the memory of yesterday for all the tea in China. He and Lottie were friends again—real, count-on-me-when-the-chips-are-down friends. The knowledge filled him like a helium balloon.

He would have headed straight back to the hospital this morning if she'd asked him to, but she had other ideas. "Go to church," she'd said. "Tell God how grateful I am that all I got was a headache and this broken wing."

"You can tell him that for yourself right here," he said.

"I will." She smiled into his eyes, and his heart skipped a beat. "But there's something sacred about Sunday morning church."

She was right, he thought when he took a seat behind Ed and Martha. These were the people he'd spent his life with, who knew his history and his faults and accepted him anyway. He counted it a privilege to worship with them every week. As they rose in unison to sing the first hymn, his heart filled with praise.

After the service he stopped to tell Ed and Martha about Lottie's accident, but the news had already spread. "Thomas told us what happened," Martha said. "How is she?"

"She'll live." The words brought a smile to his face. "Her head aches a little, and that arm will take some time to heal, though."

Frown lines appeared on Martha's forehead. "Poor thing! Is she well enough for visitors?"

He wanted to say no, to keep her to himself, but he didn't have the right to do that. "I'll bet she'd like that," he said instead.

It was funny, he thought as he pulled out of the church lot. Nobody seemed surprised that he was the one taking care of Lottie. What a contrast to the way he felt inside. He was surprised every minute that a woman like her would stoop to be friends with someone like him.

He passed the cemetery on his way into town. Someday soon he'd have to stop and see Nancy. Today he had other things to do.

The squeaky wheels of the meal cart woke Lottie up. She opened her eyes to bright daylight and a profound sense of relief. Even though every muscle in her body ached, the long night was over.

"Breakfast," said a chirpy voice. "Cereal, toast and applesauce."

Her neck screamed in protest as she turned her head. "What kind of cereal?"

The voice belonged to a tiny, white-haired woman in a food service uniform. "Bran flakes. They're good for the digestion." She whisked the covers off the dishes and scurried out.

As the meal cart squeaked on down the hall, Lottie frowned. If brushing her teeth with her left hand was hard, eating a drippy bowl of cereal would be impossible. She'd have to content herself with toast and juice.

The orthopedist showed up just as she was finishing her last bite. Dr. Ferber was portly and pink-faced, with wire-rimmed glasses and a fringe of white hair. "I'm honored to meet you, though not under these circumstances," he told her. "My wife and I are big fans."

Lottie smiled. "How nice."

"I've had a look at your X-rays," he continued. "Technically, you have a Grade III separation of the AC joint. In other words, you separated the top of your scapula from your clavicle when you landed on the ground. For a case as severe as yours I highly recommend surgery to repair the torn ligaments."

Surgery. The word set off ripples of fear in her brain. "How soon?"

"Normally I'd do it right away, but your case is complicated by that concussion." He peered at her over the rim of his glasses. "First things first, Miss Braun. Let's give your head some time to heal. We'll work on your shoulder after that."

She took a deep breath. "Will I be able to play piano again?"

"I believe so." He gave her hand a reassuring pat. "Of course, there are no guarantees, but the majority of these cases get back to 90% full movement. In six or eight months, you should be as good as new."

Six or eight months. She stared at him, speechless.

"We'll schedule your follow-up appointment before you leave the hospital. I'll go over your treatment plan at that time."

She brightened. "Does this mean you're letting me out of here?"

"You could go home as far as I'm concerned," he said. "That bump on your head is the real concern. The internist wants to keep you under observation for one more day." He scribbled a note on her chart and left.

Lottie stared after him, her thoughts in a whirl. Dr. Ferber's bedside manner was reassuring, but his words were not. She hated the thought of surgery, but it sounded like she had no other option. And six or eight months of recovery? It might as well be forever.

She wanted to talk this over with Sam. He could help her sort everything out. At the same time, she was scared of what he'd say. She already felt stupid for climbing that ladder. If he offered even one 'I told you so,' she'd be crushed.

She glanced at the clock on the wall. Half an hour until church let out.

He had a few stops to make before he went to the hospital. First up, the dealership.

It was closed. He stood outside the locked showroom door for a minute, shaking his head at his stupidity. By Iowa law, you couldn't buy a car on a Sunday. He'd have to wait until tomorrow to put his plan into action.

Disappointed, he turned away. This threw a real monkey wrench in his plan. Now he needed to rethink his next step.

Behind him a voice said, "Can I help you, Mr. Harms?"

Startled, Sam looked over his shoulder.

Brett Rowley stood in the doorway. "You look like a man on a mission. I'm catching up on paperwork this afternoon. Do you want to come in?"

"It can wait until tomorrow."

"Are you sure?" The young salesman raised his eyebrows. "You and that truck are made for each other. I'd hate to see it go to someone else."

Sam laughed and shook his head. "Me too, but I don't want it bad enough to break the law."

"Oh, I can't sell it to you today." Brett held the door a little wider. "But under the right circumstances I might be able to let you have it on an extended test drive."

Sam turned around, his attention caught. "That sounds promising."

With Bessie as collateral and a handshake deal on the sale of the truck, Sam drove it off the lot. He'd be back first thing in the morning to sign the paperwork and hand over a check.

Mary Allen answered his knock. "What's this about a car for my Thomas?" she asked as she let him inside.

"I'm selling my '72 Dodge Fury. It's old, but I've taken care of it."

She gave him a tired smile. "I appreciate you thinking of him, but we don't have the money to buy him a car right now."

"I'd like to talk to you both about that," he said. "I've got an offer I think you'll approve of."

A note of suspicion entered her voice. "We don't take charity, Sam. I thought I made that clear years ago."

"Hear me out."

Reluctantly she called her son, who appeared looking downcast. "Hi, Mr. Harms."

Sam gave him a nod. "Thomas."

"If you're here about the car, I guess I'll have to pass."

"Not so fast, Tom." Sam stuck his hands in his coat pockets. "With my son away in California, I'm taking on more help at the office. Now, I know you don't have any experience, but you can still help out with odd jobs after school." He shrugged. "I figure a smart guy like you will pick up on how we do things pretty fast."

Thomas looked interested. "I'd like that."

"Let's say I give you three months' probation. During that time, I'll hold back your wages. At the end of three months, though, if you've done a good job, you will have earned enough to buy my car."

"What happens to the job after three months?" Mary asked.

"He'll become a regular employee and draw a paycheck every two weeks, just like everyone else." Sam raised his eyebrows. "If he still wants it."

Mother and son exchanged a long look. "Your schoolwork still comes first," Mary said softly.

The boy's face split into a radiant grin. "Yeah, I know." He turned to Sam. "When can I start?"

Sam left the Allens' house by the back door and crossed into Lottie's yard to take a look at the fallen tree. To his surprise, the only thing left was the stump. The yard had been cleared, the brush stacked neatly by the curb for pick up by the city. The street was quiet, not a soul in sight, but he wasn't fooled. He knew he was being watched.

He knocked and waited, and Nathan eventually opened the door. "How is she?" he said without preamble.

"She'll recover, thanks to you."

Nathan snorted. "Any fool can call an ambulance."

"But you're the fool who did," Sam said. "So, thank you."

"Since we're being polite, it seems I owe you an apology." Nathan rolled his chair back and forth in place. "Lottie had nothing to do with putting you on that committee. Improbable as it seems, I guess you were chosen on your own merits."

Sam shrugged. "I know." But the confirmation felt good.

Nathan fixed Sam with a hard stare. "I hope you know what a rare breed that woman is. People who've lived in the public eye usually come with egos and demands. I have yet to see signs of either in Lottie Braun."

Sam couldn't quite hide his smile. "I know."

"She's out of your league, you lucky son of a gun." Nathan rolled back and prepared to close the door. "You'd better take care of her."

He was gone before Sam could reply.

♪

With the help of a nurse, Lottie managed the basics of her morning routine. Sure, her hair had a permanent flat spot from the pillow, and makeup was out of the question. But after a bit of work she felt adequately prepared for Sam's visit. She emerged from the bathroom to find a single pink carnation on her bedside table. The card said, "Sam told me what happened. I'll be there as soon as possible. —P."

The message warmed her heart. She hoped Patti wasn't too worried. The poor girl had enough to handle without adding a trip to Collison into the deal.

Soon after church let out footsteps sounded in the hall. Lottie sat up straight and tried to suppress a little thrill of excitement.

"Knock, knock! Mind if I come in?" It was Norm Isley, looking jovial. "I hear you had a little accident."

The excitement died. "Hello, Norm."

Norm held out an enormous vase of white roses. "These are from me and the board of directors."

White roses reminded her of funerals. "Sorry about the way the concert ended, Norm. We didn't get to hand out the pledge cards."

"Don't apologize." He set the vase on the windowsill. "We got our point across. The rest is out of our hands."

Lottie glanced toward the door. More footsteps, but these shoes were unmistakably crepe-soled. Rhonda Kennedy burst into the room, red-cheeked and panting, dragging a yellow-haired urchin by the hand. "I came as soon as I heard. Poor Lottie! That was such a close call. Thank goodness you weren't seriously hurt. I just don't know what we'd do without you." She spied the college president and stopped short. "Hello, Dr. Isley. My goodness, what are you doing here?"

"The same thing as you, I believe." He turned to Lottie with a smile. "Having mercy on the sick. But I'd best be going…" His sentence died away as Katherine, Cal, and Teresa walked in. "Well, if it isn't the rest of the music department. Why don't you all sit down and have the monthly faculty meeting?"

"Very funny," Katherine said, setting a vase of daisies next to the roses. "We didn't plan this. We just have good timing."

Norm said his good-byes and left while Katherine rearranged the two bouquets. "Daisies are so cheerful, don't you think?" She gave Lottie a conspiratorial smile. "Besides, they were all I could find at the grocery. Couldn't you have fallen off that ladder on a weekday?"

Lottie chuckled. "Sorry to inconvenience you."

"You did better than me," Rhonda said brightly. "I didn't think about flowers. Although I did bring my little girl to brighten Lottie's spirits. Chelsea, get down from there." She reached for her daughter, who was swinging from the bed rail.

Teresa stepped forward, her brown eyes full of sympathy. "This is a tough break, Lottie. Will you be here for long?"

"No." Lottie glanced past her to the empty doorway. "I'll be discharged tomorrow."

Rhonda patted her hand. "You mustn't come back to work right away. You've been through a trauma."

Lottie caught Katherine's eye and smiled. "I really haven't had time to figure out what I'll do. I'm sure I'll need your help with the piano lessons, Rhonda. That is, if it's not too much trouble."

Rhonda brightened. "I'd be happy to help. Chelsea, don't do that." She snatched a pill bottle out of the little girl's hands with an apologetic smile. "Maybe it's time to take her home. Bye, everyone." She swung her daughter into her arms and hurried away, crepe soles squeaking.

Cal shook his head as her footsteps died away. "That woman is the life of every party."

Teresa gave her husband a warning look. "Oh, shush. She does the best she can."

Lottie smiled. "That's true." Rhonda's willing spirit was a contrast to the angry woman who had fought Lottie tooth and nail for the corner office last fall.

"Cal, the jazz band did a wonderful job at the concert. It ended so abruptly I didn't get a chance to say so afterward," Katherine said.

Cal looked gratified. "The whole show went well, until the ice storm ruined it. Do you think we raised any money?"

Katherine shrugged. "Time will tell."

The talk turned to the storm and the damage it had done around town. Cal and Katherine competed for most sensational story, and Lottie enjoyed the friendly banter. It distracted her so well that she only glanced toward the door six or seven times during the whole conversation.

Ed and Martha showed up next. They brought fresh banana bread, which Martha sliced and handed out on star-spangled party napkins. "They're left over from the Fourth of July," she said, "but who cares?"

Nobody did.

Sam walked across the hospital lobby, whistling under his breath. He'd parked at the back of the lot, across two parking spaces to protect his new truck from possible dings. It would never do to scratch the red paint before he'd officially bought it.

He couldn't wait to tell Lottie. She was certain to say something pithy.

He stopped whistling when he reached the general medical floor, out of respect for the patients who needed peace and quiet. As he passed the nurses' station, one of them called out, "Are you going to the party?" He gave her a puzzled smile and kept going.

When he reached the end of the hall, he suddenly understood what she meant. People stood two-deep in Lottie's room, blocking his line of sight from the door to the bed. His heart sank. This was not how he had pictured this moment.

As he stood unnoticed in the doorway, he was struck by how quickly Lottie had made good friends. She'd lived in Collison less than a year, yet all these good people were willing to visit her on a Sunday afternoon.

He frowned. Maybe she had enough visitors right now. After all, she probably thought of him as just another friend. If she'd been anticipating his visit, surely, she would have noticed him hovering in the doorway by now.

Before this thought could dig in too deep, the people parted and he caught sight of the patient: Sound asleep amid the hubbub of voices. They'd worn her out.

He took a step back and tried to figure out what to do next. He wanted to be here when she was awake so he could show off his new toy, but not with all these people around. They'd hear about his revolutionary purchase soon enough, and when they did, he would never hear the end of it.

The scent of hothouse flowers drifted into the hall. He hadn't even thought about bringing her a gift unless you counted the truck, and he was pretty sure Lottie wouldn't.

It seemed to Sam that flowers had been a bit overdone. She probably wouldn't notice if he bought her a little bouquet from the gift shop downstairs.

He spied her untouched lunch tray, and inspiration struck.

Lottie woke up to peace and quiet, and the tantalizing smell of french fries. Sam sat in the chair by her bed, his coat off and sleeves rolled up, with a big white McDonald's bag on his lap. His smile, when she opened her eyes, warmed her right down to her toes. "Hungry?"

"Starved."

Without another word he divided up the food: two cheeseburgers each, with enough fries to feed a harvest crew.

She didn't give a thought to her clumsy left hand as she plowed through her dinner. When she finished, she sat back with a happy sigh. "That was perfect."

"You've got ketchup on your face," he said, and swiped a finger across her cheek.

The gesture sent a tremor through her, but he sat back with a sudden smile. "I have a surprise for you."

She felt like a kid at a birthday party. "You do? Where is it?"

He flashed a grin. "I brought it with me, but they made me leave it outside."

She looked past him toward the hall.

He gave a shout of laughter. "It's not out there. I bought a new truck."

Her jaw dropped. "You did? What about Bessie?"

"I thought it was time to find her a new home."

The look in his blue eyes stole her breath. "Good idea."

A commotion in the hall broke the mood. They turned toward the door as Patti rushed into the room. "Poor Aunt Lottie! I'm here to take care of you."

Twenty

Miranda couldn't concentrate. She turned the pages of the supply catalog spread before her on the kitchen table, and tried to fill out an order form, but Jason's one-sided phone conversation claimed all her attention.

"Yeah, Dad...She is? She must be pretty tired...Miranda will call her in the morning, then...What's that? No, I don't think so. I'm sure she'll want to, but we're pretty swamped here...I love you too. Bye."

"What happened?" she said as soon as he hung up.

"Lottie fell off a ladder yesterday. She separated her shoulder and got a concussion." He turned to her with a bemused smile. "My dad didn't sound too upset by the whole thing."

Miranda raised her eyebrows. "So, he's the one taking care of her?"

"He was, until Patti showed up and sent him home."

The news brought a smile to her lips. "Well, it's about time."

"He called for another reason. Lottie is going to need some help around the house for a few weeks, and he wondered if you'd be able to get back to Collison for a few days." Jase shook his head. "I didn't encourage that idea."

She frowned. "Jase, when are you going to tell him you're quitting?"

"Give me time." He sat down and covered her hand with his own. "I stand by my decision, but it's going to be a shock to my dad."

"It isn't fair to string him along, either," she said. "You need to give him a chance to hire more help before peak construction season."

A flash of pain crossed his face. "I'm letting him down, Miranda. Give me time to do it gently."

The front door opened and Sonia walked in, her face half-hidden behind the groceries she carried. "Hello, you two." She looked from one to the other and her expression changed. "Who died?"

"Nobody," Miranda said, as Jason hurried forward to take the bags. "Lottie Braun is in the hospital."

Sonia's eyes widened. "Will she be all right?"

"Eventually."

"Good." Sonia turned away, losing interest. "Did you two finish the work schedule for this week?"

Ignoring Lottie's protests, Patti stayed overnight at the hospital. "I left Sarah in Chicago with Mitch so I could give you all the time you need," she said. "I don't care how long this takes. You're family."

The discharge process took forever, but they finally reached home around noon on Monday. Patti helped Lottie get settled in the living room and made lunch. While they ate, she went through a list of reminders. "You need to wait three days before you take off that sling. Try not to move the arm at all. You have a doctor appointment on Thursday. And call Martha and Ed if you need help. They'll come right over."

"I'll be all right," Lottie said. "Stop fussing and go home to your family."

"I'm coming back this weekend," Patti said for the tenth time. "You just have to fend for yourself until then."

Lottie waved her away. "Go home, Patti. I'm fine."

She listened to Patti's tires crunch on the gravel as she headed down the alley. It was sweet of the girl to come all this way, but Lottie knew how busy she was at home. She couldn't justify taking up more of Patti's time. Besides, Lottie had work to do. She settled deeper into the chair, reached into her book bag…

…and woke with a start. Late afternoon sunlight made patterns on the front curtains. Her mouth tasted like the entire Dust Bowl, and pain was shooting up and down her neck. She levered herself upright and tottered unsteadily to the kitchen for a drink of water.

When her glass was empty, she set it down and clutched the edge of the counter for support. She'd been warned about dizziness.

She kept a hand on the wall for support as she trudged back to the living room. Up to this point, she'd been the most worried about her arm. Now she wondered if her brain would prove to be the greater injury.

A new fear wormed its way into her thoughts. What if her shoulder recovered completely, but she couldn't memorize music?

Ordinarily this question would have occupied her mind for hours, but not today. By the time she reached her soft recliner and pushed it back for full comfort, she was too exhausted to think. This time, when sleep claimed her, she was ready.

The ringing telephone dragged her back to consciousness.

"Did I wake you?" Sam sounded concerned. "It's only eight o'clock."

"No, I'm awake." Her thoughts were muddled. "How was your day?"

"Busy. The ice storm caused a flood at one of our job sites, and we didn't find it until this morning." He paused. "I can't stop by to check on you tonight. Are you okay?"

"Yes." She tried to organize her thoughts. "I'm pretty tired anyway. I think I'll go on to bed."

"Good." He sounded relieved. "I'll drop by tomorrow morning, then."

"You don't need to. Katherine's coming by to pick up some things."

There was a short pause. "Sounds like you've got it covered."

"I think I do, Sam."

She hung up and Marmalade jumped onto her lap, meowing pitifully. She rubbed his ears, and he bumped his head against her hand. "Has it been a while since you ate, old boy?"

He jumped off her lap and led her to the kitchen where an unfamiliar casserole dish waited, a note taped to its lid. "Your door was unlocked. Hope I didn't wake you. —Martha."

The dish was no longer hot, but the mix of beef, tomato sauce, and noodles smelled divine.

Marmalade trailed her upstairs after supper and sat washing himself while she tried to change into her pajamas. True to her word, she didn't mess with the straps that held her arm. Instead she worked one-handed to remove her sweatshirt and knit pants and put on her striped flannel pjs. By the time she succeeded, she was sweating, and saying words under her breath that would have raised the hairs on the back of Aunt Eva's neck.

She tucked herself into bed, ready for another round of healing sleep.

Ten minutes later her shoulder began to ache. She got up and took some pain reliever and went back to bed.

Twenty minutes later the Velcro strap was torturing the tender skin at the nape of her neck. She sat up, adjusted it, and lay back down.

Thirty minutes later the darkness was too dark, and the quiet house too still. Where was Thomas's garage band when she needed it?

With a sigh, she got up, put on her slippers and shuffled downstairs.

She awoke to sunshine streaming in the living room's east windows. The rich aroma of coffee wafted in from the kitchen as she set her recliner upright. She followed her nose, and found the table set for breakfast.

Katherine was humming a light soprano version of Gilbert and Sullivan's "Major-General Song" as she buttered a piece of toast. She broke off when she saw Lottie. "Hello, sleepyhead. Are you hungry?"

Lottie's eyes widened. "You didn't have to do all this."

"I wanted to." Katherine emptied the pan of scrambled eggs onto a plate and set it at the table. "Dig in. I promise I can cook."

"Want to stay and have a cup of coffee?"

Katherine shook her head. "I've got an interview with a prospective student this morning."

"Right. The midterms I told you about are next to my chair in the living room. There's also a note for you to put on my office door. To let my students know why their lessons are canceled."

Katherine chuckled. "You don't need to explain. They'll just be happy you canceled. That's how college students are. No, don't get up."

She gently pushed Lottie back into her seat. "I'll get your stuff. Is there anything else I can do?" she asked when she returned to the kitchen.

"I'm fine." Lottie did her best to sound convincing. "I plan to be back at work in a few days."

"Give yourself time, my friend. You need to rest."

She left, and Lottie sat back with a sigh. The empty day stretched out before her like a prison sentence. Most people would jump at a few days off from work. "I guess I'm not like most people," she told Marmalade.

The morning crawled past. Lottie warmed up a plate of leftover casserole for lunch and spent the afternoon dozing in front of the TV. "Is this how people live?" she asked the cat, who gazed at her through half-closed eyes.

She was watching the sun set from the music room windows when the phone rang. She rushed to answer it, knocking over a stack of music in her haste.

"I've got office mail for you." Nathan sounded put out. "I'd deliver it myself, but your house isn't exactly accessible."

Lottie stuck her arm in one coat sleeve and pulled the rest of it around herself as best she could. Cold air nipped at the edges of this get-up as she crossed the lawn in the gathering dusk.

Nathan met her at the door, a big brown envelope in his hand. "Special delivery from the L.A. Phil," he said. "Looks official."

"It's my itinerary for June." Lottie took the envelope without meeting his eyes. "I'll have to call and tell them things have changed."

"I'd like to be a fly on the wall for that conversation," he said. "Fleischmann uses some pretty creative language when he's mad."

The amusement in his voice raised her hackles. "It's not like I fell off that ladder on purpose. He'll understand these things happen."

Nathan laughed. "Of course. Ernest Fleischmann has a very understanding nature. Just out of curiosity, what kind of recovery time are you looking at for that arm?"

"The doctor gave me six to eight months."

"Eight months!" He sounded outraged. "Is he serious?"

All her fears rushed back in. "Y-yes. He wants to do surgery to repair the ligaments next week—"

"You need a second opinion."

She stared at him. "This doctor seems to know what he's talking about."

"They always do." He fiddled with the wheels of his chair. "If you were smart, you'd see a specialist in Iowa City. That's what everyone else around here does."

"And if you were smart, you'd mind your own business." She turned on her heel and marched home with the heat of her outrage to keep her warm. "That man is an interfering old busybody," she told Marmalade, "with an infuriating knack for reinforcing my own worst fears."

"Meow," said Marmalade, and rubbed his furry back against her ankles.

She crouched to scratch his furry neck. "I'm glad you agree."

The cat raised his chin and stared into her eyes. "Meow!"

"What's the matter, old boy?" She glanced up at the clock. "Aha. You weren't making polite conversation."

As she shook a box of dry food over the bowl, she glanced out the window at the house next door. Nathan did have a point. A second opinion would be prudent before she consented to surgery. But Dr. Ferber said time was of the essence, and she had no idea how to work the University of Iowa medical system.

She set the cat's bowl on the floor and turned away. She didn't have to decide tonight. She'd figure it out tomorrow.

Sam's week unfolded in a series of crises: First the flood at the kitchen remodel, then a lost order of hardwood flooring that left him scrambling to reschedule his crew. He was still working on it when a customer called to express his displeasure over the navy-blue paint job in his dining room. "It's too dark. You'll have to do it over."

He didn't point out that the homeowner had chosen the paint. He simply agreed and added a new paint job to his to-do list.

Some weeks were like that: Just run, run, run, without a break. Every day he went to work early and came home late. Every evening he called to check on Lottie and breathed a sigh of relief when she told him she was fine. "I'll be back to work in no time," she said cheerfully.

He had no choice but to believe her.

Jason called on Thursday night. "Wish me happy," he said. "Miranda and I are engaged."

"Congratulations!" Sam couldn't stop grinning. "That's just great, son. Let me know when you set a date, and I'll reserve the church."

"That's sort of what I'm calling about." Jase hesitated. "We're getting married here in San Francisco."

Sam took a deep breath. "That makes sense," he said slowly. "Miranda's family is there."

"You'll fly out for it, won't you?"

"Sure. I wouldn't miss it."

"Good." Jase sounded cautious. "I've got something else to tell you."

"Oh, yeah?"

"We're not coming back to Iowa, Dad. We're going to stay in San Francisco."

He felt like he'd taken a sock to the gut. "Say that again?"

"The market out here is crazy," Jase said. "Miranda's dad positioned this company for growth, and it's really taking off. We want to see how far we can take it." He paused. "And then there's her mom, who needs the support right now. We really feel that staying is the right decision. I hope you understand."

A few minutes later Sam hung up and stared at the receiver. "Boy, I didn't see that coming," he muttered. He'd always known Mitch would move away someday, but Jase? Jase was on track to grow old in Collison.

He turned out the light and started upstairs, surprised that he wasn't more upset. There was no sense stewing about it. He needed a good night's sleep to tackle tomorrow's problems.

Twenty-One

Engaged! Oh, Miranda. That's wonderful." In her excitement, Lottie was shouting into the phone.

Miranda held the phone away from her ear and rolled her eyes humorously at Jase.

"Have you set a date?" Lottie asked.

"We want to do it in June, to coincide with your trip to L.A."

"How thoughtful."

She sounded less enthusiastic than Miranda expected. "That's all right, isn't it? You don't mind extending your time in California? We do want you to come to the wedding."

"No, no. It's fine. I'm just…overwhelmed. I'm so happy for you."

"We owe it all to you," Miranda said. Across the table, Jase nodded his agreement. "If you hadn't made Jason see the light and come out here, I don't know what would have happened."

"You'd have found each other eventually," Lottie said. "True love conquers all, or so they say."

Miranda smiled happily at her beloved. "That's how we feel, anyway."

She hung up a minute later and turned to Jase with a frown. "Lottie doesn't sound like herself."

He shrugged. "She's probably still in pain. Give her a week or two to get back to normal again."

"Hey, you two." Zac walked into the kitchen. "Are you still making wedding phone calls?"

"Get used to it," Miranda said. "Weddings don't plan themselves. Where are you off to?"

"I'm filling in for Ian Riley tonight."

She smiled. "Will you play the "Boogie Woogie Bugle Boy" for me?"

Zac rolled his eyes. "Not in this lifetime. The old fogies who tune in are gonna get a shock tonight." He grabbed an apple and left, slamming the front door behind him.

Jase grinned at Miranda. "I like that kid."

Lottie slammed the cat food box on the counter so hard a few pieces bounced out of the top. "Don't look at me with those pitiful eyes. You know I can't work the can opener."

Marmalade yowled and shied away from her raised hand, and tears sprang to her eyes. "Sorry," she muttered, but the cat had already darted under the table.

She'd spent the day in tears for one reason or another. The walls were closing in on her, and there was no escape. She couldn't drive one-handed. She'd run out of schoolwork, she didn't like to read, and the daytime TV schedule drove her crazy. The house grew dirtier by the day, but she inevitably came to grief if she tried to do more than dust.

Five times a day she rearranged her To-Do pile: The bills needed to be paid by checks she could not sign. The jazz curriculum committee report needed penciled-in notes she couldn't write. Her black beaded dress should go back to the dry cleaners. If only she could be sure she'd ever need it again.

At the bottom of the pile, the big envelope from the L.A. Phil sent a thrill of fear through her every time she looked at it. She couldn't bear to open it, couldn't even think about calling Ernest Fleischmann.

Miranda's phone call last night had heightened her anxieties. What if they asked her to play for the wedding and she had to tell them no? She couldn't stand the thought.

She might have been able to deal with all the "what-ifs" if she weren't so lonely. Since her squabble with Nathan, her only visitor had been Rhonda Kennedy, who brought her a lasagna on Thursday afternoon.

"I've been wanting to talk with you about something," Rhonda had said as she settled on the living room couch. She pulled a book out of her purse. "I did my doctoral research on the piano repertoire for left hand alone. It has a long and fascinating history. Do you know how many great composers wrote pieces for left hand?"

Lottie murmured that she remembered hearing something about it, though in truth she didn't.

Rhonda offered Lottie the book in her hands. "This is my dissertation. I included three of my favorite left-hand-alone compositions in an index in the back. I think it could be really useful to you."

Lottie took it without enthusiasm. "I'll take a look at it."

"Good." Rhonda rose to leave. "Who knows? This could be a turning point in your career."

As Rhonda toddled down the front walk to her car, Lottie shook her head. Was this what she'd come to? A once-great pianist, reduced to playing with only one hand?

She went to the music room and shoved Rhonda's book under a stack of sheet music on the bookcase. She'd rather die.

Sam was working long hours—she understood that—but it didn't stop her from wishing he would visit. Last night, after the ecstatic phone call from Miranda announcing her engagement, she especially longed to talk to him. She could only imagine how upset he must be over Jason's new plans.

She could have called him—probably should have—but it was hard to make the first move when she felt so needy. To use a tired cliché, she didn't want to be a burden.

In a way, she felt grateful Sam was too busy to show up in person. Mirrors had become her nemesis. After three days, she'd finally been able to remove her sling and take a shower, which helped her feel human. Washing her hair proved tricky, though, and blowing it dry it was impossible. It stuck up permanently on the crown of her head because she couldn't tame her cowlick.

She couldn't blame the cat for running and hiding from the monster she'd become.

Grabbing the kitchen counter for support, she lowered herself to sit cross-legged on the linoleum. "Marmalade," she called softly.

He stuck his head out from under the tablecloth, gave her a timid glance, and withdrew.

"Come on, kitty. I didn't mean it." She reached out with her good hand. "Please?"

Marmalade's face appeared again. This time he seemed to accept her apology. In response he stretched, first his neck, then his body toward her, and butted his head up against her palm. Purring, he stepped into her lap and sat down.

"Oh, sweetie!" She stroked his orange back and let the tears fall.

This was the woebegone scene that met Patti's eyes when she burst in a few minutes later, calling, "Aunt Lottie? I'm home. I took the afternoon off—" She pulled up short. "What's wrong?"

For a split-second, Lottie considered saying she was fine, despite her red-rimmed eyes and wet cheeks. Then little Sarah peeped out from behind her mother's legs, and with wide blue eyes exclaimed, "Aunt Wottie!"

Which for some reason started the tears flowing all over again.

Patti knelt and threw her arms around her. "I came back as soon as I could," she said, her cool cheek pressed against Lottie's hot one. "Has it really been that bad?"

Lottie groaned. "Look at me."

Patti pulled back and gave her a critical stare. "Hmmm. I see what you mean." She smiled. "Well, don't you worry about a thing. Sarah and I will get you all straightened out."

"I feel terrible, putting you to all this trouble," Lottie said Saturday morning. They were working in the kitchen while Sarah played at their feet. "You should be at home with your husband, relaxing on the weekend."

Patti looked up from the checkbook with an ironic lift of the eyebrow. "Mitchell and I don't relax on weekends. We run around like hamsters on a wheel, trying to make up for lost time."

Lottie's heart sank. "That's just not right."

"But that's the way it is. There. We've paid all your bills." Patti set down her pen and picked up the last envelope. "This big one from the L.A. Philharmonic is the only thing left in your mail pile."

"Don't worry about that," Lottie said quickly. "I'll take care of it."

Patti set it aside without comment. "Is there anything else you need me to do around here?"

"I hate to ask, but can you help me clean the bathroom? It's driving me crazy."

"Sure I can. Though I don't understand why you haven't hired a cleaning lady to do it."

Lottie blinked. "The thought never crossed my mind. I've always cleaned my own place."

"But you always lived in apartments, didn't you?"

"Yes, or housing provided by whatever university I was working for at the time." She felt a little sheepish. "Now that I think about it, the university houses usually had housekeeping services."

Patti gave a decisive nod. "That settles it. You need help with this big old barn. I'll call around today and see who I can find."

"Thanks, but I really never—"

But Patti had moved on to the next problem. "I noticed your fridge is empty. When is the last time you got groceries?"

"Last Friday." She was getting irritated. "I can't drive yet. Remember?"

"And nobody offered to help with that?"

Lottie glanced away. Martha had offered, but she didn't want to be a bother.

Patti seemed to guess what she was thinking. "Look, would it help if we arranged to have your groceries delivered? I think Nash's Market will do it, if we talk to the owners. They sponsored my softball team in middle school."

"That would be fine." She didn't have the strength to argue.

"Now I understand why you have an assistant." Patti scribbled a few notes on a pad of paper. "When are you going to hire a new one?"

"I don't know." She tried to speak lightly. "Are you in the market for a new job?"

Patti's pen went still. "Not really."

Lottie looked up, startled by her wistful tone. "What's wrong?"

"Nothing." The cheerful smile was back in place. "What are we getting at the grocery?"

Swept up in Patti's positive energy, they spent the morning knocking items off the to-do list. By lunch time Lottie had full cupboards, clean bathrooms, a grocery delivery scheduled for next week, and a new cleaning lady with impeccable references.

"She'll have her work cut out for her around here." Lottie wiped a cobweb out from under the upper cupboards. "This house seems to manufacture its own dirt."

Patti spread butter on a slice of bread for Sarah. "What's next?"

Lottie yawned. "A nap."

Patti's eyebrows drew together with concern. "Your accident really wiped you out, didn't it?"

"More than I want to admit."

"Go ahead and lie down," Patti said. "Sarah and I will find something to do."

Sam parked next to Patti's car and sat for a moment, gathering his thoughts. After the busiest week he could remember, he finally had a minute to drop in and see Lottie. He'd been thinking about it for days. Heck, he'd even changed into his new blue jeans and his best checkered shirt in the middle of a Saturday. He just hadn't bargained for Patti. Maybe he could turn around and go home and come again tomorrow after she was gone.

Before he could act on that plan, Patti opened the back door and waved. He was stuck.

"Great truck," she called as he crossed the yard. "Is it yours?"

"Yep. I bought it last weekend."

His daughter-in-law looked impressed. "Why didn't you tell us? Mitch is going to love it."

"It's been a busy week," he mumbled. "Did he come with you?"

"Nope. I'm just here to take care of Lottie. That's why we didn't call."

"Oh." He tried to look past her. "Is she okay?"

Something in his voice must have given Patti the wrong idea. She crossed her arms and looked at him with that knowing expression some women had. "She's asleep right now. You look nice, Sam."

He stuck his hands in his pockets. "All my other clothes are in the laundry."

She looked like she wanted to laugh, but to his relief she controlled herself. "Why don't you come back for dinner? I'm cooking."

"Oh—okay. Sounds good."

"Dinner's at six," she said. "Bring some flowers for the table."

He turned and ambled back down the yard before he could sort out what had just happened. He would have liked to go in and wait, and maybe talk to Patti about how Mitch's job was going. But here he was back in the alley instead. There was no crossing that girl when she put herself in charge.

Thomas Allen caught up with him before he opened his door. "Hey, Mr. Harms."

"Hi, Tom."

Thomas held up a bottle of blue liquid and a rag. "I'm going to wash the windows on the car. I noticed they were pretty smudged."

"Good idea. See you Monday."

"Sure thing." Thomas went on his way, whistling.

"Aunt Lottie. Wake up." Patti tapped her gently on the arm. "We've got things to do."

Lottie blinked in the afternoon light. "What's going on?"

"You're having company tonight, and you aren't ready."

She tried to clear her fuzzy thoughts. "What? Who?"

"Sam's coming over for dinner."

Her eyes flew open wide. "He is?"

"Uh-huh."

"Oh, no." She sat up. "Patti, I look terrible."

"I know." Patti's laugh was not unkind. "Remember the girl who did our hair for the wedding?"

"Who, Crystal?"

"I gave her a call. She'll be here in half an hour."

"Oh, thank goodness!"

"Why don't you take a shower? By the time you come downstairs, she'll be set up and waiting for you."

Crystal traveled with an industrial-strength blow dryer, an assortment of curling irons, and a pink tackle box full of supplies. "I was so surprised to get Patti's call," she confided to Lottie as she tied the plastic smock around her neck. "I didn't think you'd ever want to see me again after what I said about coloring your hair."

"Don't be silly," Lottie said with some of her customary crispness. "You've got a gift, child. You make women feel beautiful."

Crystal's plump cheeks went pink with pleasure. "That's what I try to do," she said earnestly. "I really want to bring out the best in my clients."

"I like your commitment." She waved her good hand over her hair. "You have your work cut out for you today."

Crystal left a while later with Lottie's gratitude and an appointment to return late in the week. As she drove away, Lottie turned to her niece. "I'm so glad you called her."

"She'll keep you young." Patti closed the back door. "By the way." Her tone was elaborately casual. "Sarah and I have been invited out for dinner. Can you entertain Sam by yourself?"

Lottie shot her a suspicious glance. "A change of plans?'

Patti's smile was bland. "Remember Mrs. Ackerman, the tailor? Her daughter Kathleen was one of my high school friends. I ran into Kathleen at the grocery this morning. She called just now and asked us over.

I hope you don't mind."

"Looks like I don't have a choice," Lottie said, exasperated. "Have you always been such a schemer?"

This surprised a laugh out of her niece. "I have no idea what you're talking about."

At six o'clock sharp Sam rapped lightly on Lottie's back door and waited. He fiddled with the bowl of flowers in his hands and wondered again if it was too fancy. The florist had sold it to him cheap because the customer who ordered it had changed her mind. It was beautiful, with all kinds of colorful blooms he couldn't identify, but he felt a little silly standing here with it. Plain old Sam, with this hothouse bouquet. Ridiculous.

He'd like to put the whole thing back in the truck, except it would freeze there. He couldn't waste money like that.

His thoughts had reached this impasse when the door finally opened. Lottie stood there smiling at him, and he forgot all about the dumb flowers. She was elegant, even with one arm in a sling. "You look great," he said, and instantly wished he'd been more eloquent.

Her smile deepened. "And you're a sight for sore eyes. Those flowers are magnificent."

He set them on the hall table and shrugged off his coat. "I hope they're not too much."

"They're just right." A twinkle lurked in the depths of her eyes. "They'll look beautiful on the dinner table."

He followed her into the dining room, where china and crystal shone in the candlelight. "I don't think I'm dressed right," he said, suddenly off-balance.

"That's not surprising," Lottie murmured. "Nancy Reagan wouldn't know what to wear to this soiree." She set the flowers down and turned to him with a rueful smile. "This is Patti's idea of Saturday night supper."

"Hmm. Where is she, by the way?"

"She ditched us." Lottie looked faintly embarrassed. "An old friend invited her and Sarah to spend the evening. There are children involved, and Patti decided they should go."

Sam was beginning to get the picture. "So, in other words, she set us up." He nodded at the table. "Candlelight, flowers, and all."

"Oh, were the flowers her idea, too?"

"To tell you the truth, I was scared not to bring them."

She chuckled. "I know how you feel. Patti can be terrifying." She glanced at him. "She thinks she's helping us along. Your kids all seem to think we're...y'know..."

Chagrined, he said, "Yeah, I'm sorry about that. They have no right to make you uncomfortable."

She was quiet for a moment, her face unreadable. Then, "You're right, Sam. They just don't get it." Swiftly she leaned over and blew out the candles. "Turn on the light switch. It's right behind you."

He did as she asked, and suddenly the room looked normal again. "That's better."

"It sure is." She led him into the kitchen. "Let's eat in here like we always do."

Her voice sounded strained to Sam's ears, but she looked as composed as ever. "Sounds good."

"Dinner's ready, by the way," she said brightly. "Patti cooked for us before she left."

A thought occurred to him. "Hold on a minute."

He went back to the dining room and picked all the pink roses out of the bowl. In the kitchen, he stuck them in a glass of water and set it on the table. "That's better."

Her whole face lit up when she smiled like that.

They ate roast beef and potatoes off the everyday dishes and left the serving dishes on the stove to keep warm. "Patti will understand," Lottie told him. "She might be bossy, but she's not unreasonable."

"I'm glad she's been here for you. I know I wasn't much help this week."

She shrugged. "No need to apologize. You're a busy man."

"Especially now," he said with a grin. "Can you believe that boy of mine ran off and got engaged behind my back?"

"I knew he and Miranda would work things out. How do you feel about them staying in California?"

"I didn't expect it, but I don't really mind. I didn't realize how much I missed being the one in charge."

"You didn't?" She gave him a teasing look. "I think the rest of us saw that pretty clearly."

"What about you? You'll have to start looking for a new assistant."

She took a sip of water. "I think I'll hold off on that for a while. I'm doing all right without one. I recently learned how to book my own plane tickets." A fleeting smile crossed her face. "Next week I'll figure out how to cancel them."

He frowned. "What do you mean?"

"I'm not going to L.A. in June. My arm won't be healed in time."

He set down his fork and stared at her. "That's a real shame, Lottie."

She looked away. "It can't be helped."

"Are you sure? What did the doctor say about it?"

"Dr. Ferber wants to schedule surgery for a week from now. Recovery from that will take at least six months."

Sam thought this over. "What happens if you don't have the surgery? Is there an alternative?"

"Are you suggesting I get a second opinion?"

"Yes." He frowned. "Why are you laughing?"

"Because for once you and Nathan Bartholomew agree. He was quite adamant that I go up to Iowa City for a consult."

He gave her a reluctant smile. "The old fool is right about this. Collison General is a good city hospital, but the University of Iowa does cutting-edge research. They'll be able to tell you if there's another way to approach your injury. You should go talk to them."

She sighed. "I'll think about it."

"I mean it." He tapped his finger on the table for emphasis. "Don't cancel that plane ticket until you to talk to them."

Lottie raised her eyebrows. "I'm surprised at you, Sam. Somehow I thought you'd be pleased that I'm not going to L.A."

"Well, I'm not." This surprised him, too. "I don't think you should give up so easily."

A teasing note entered her voice. "What about your rights as a Lottie Braun fan? Didn't you say you were disappointed in me for going?"

He looked up and caught his breath. Her cheek curved upward when she was amused, and her eyes sparkled with fun. She made him want to reach out and touch that flawless skin, to see if it was as soft as it looked. He'd loved her for months, and the effort to hide it was killing him inside. It would be a relief to take her hand in his and tell her how he felt…

He lowered his gaze to his plate and gave himself a mental shake. They'd just gotten back to their old friendly footing. He could imagine how uncomfortable she'd be if he acted on his impulses now.

"Sam? Are you all right?" The laughter had faded from her voice.

He glanced up but couldn't quite meet her eyes. "I can't imagine anyone being disappointed to see you face your fears, Lottie. That's why I think you should go to L.A." He scooted his chair back and reached for his coat. "Thank you for a nice evening. I should really go before Patti gets back."

Lottie was watching the local news when Patti tiptoed through the living room with Sarah asleep in her arms. "How'd it go?" she whispered.

"Fine," Lottie whispered back. "Go put Sarah to bed and come back."

Patti took her daughter upstairs and returned ten minutes later in her nightgown and robe. "Now," she said, curling up on the couch. "Tell me everything."

Lottie gave her niece a tolerant smile. "Sam came over, we ate a delicious dinner, had a nice talk, and then he went home."

"That's it?"

Unfortunately. Lottie moved to the couch and took her niece's hand. "I need you to understand something," she said. "This thing between Sam and me has to unfold in its own time. You were sweet to try to give it a push, but it doesn't work that way. I need you to resist the urge to manage us and let us muddle along on our own."

"So, you admit there's something between you and Sam. That's progress, anyway." Patti's eyes sparkled with fun.

Lottie groaned. "You're impossible."

"I promise I won't interfere anymore." Patti squeezed her hand. "But I do wish you two would hurry up."

She made it sound so easy.

Twenty-Two

"Are you sure you'll be all right?" Patti asked as she buckled Sarah's car seat Sunday morning.

"I'll be fine."

"Sam's picking you up for church?"

"Yes."

"And you'll call Martha Williams if you need to run errands?"

"Of course. Now, go home and kiss that sweet husband of yours."

"Okay. Call me if you need me. I can come back in a few weeks." Patti gave her a quick hug.

"I know."

Lottie waved and smiled as they drove away. She wouldn't need to call Patti for help any time soon. She now had help for every task of daily living. She had people on call to buy her groceries, style her hair, and drive her around town. Her house had been rearranged to better serve a one-armed human. Even the cat could once more enjoy his favorite dinners, thanks to a brand new electric can opener. The girl was a whirlwind of organizational energy. What could possibly go wrong?

Sam showed up an hour later to escort her to church. "You look spiffy this morning," she told him. She liked him in his Sunday best.

"Thanks," he said briefly, and lapsed into silence.

She gave him a puzzled glance. Last night they'd been on easy terms, until that odd bit at the end. She never should have teased him about being a Lottie Braun fan. For some reason he was sensitive about that.

Today he was acting like a stranger, all buttoned up and quiet on his side of the truck.

It made for an awkward church service, enduring so many interested glances from around the sanctuary when she knew their assumptions were false. She kept her eyes on her Bible, her mind on the sermon as much as possible. When church let out, she let Sam take her home as quickly and quietly as possible.

Sam breathed a sigh of relief when he finally helped Lottie out of the truck and watched her cross the lawn. This business of being Lottie's friend was taxing, when every minute he might slip up and give away how he really felt. He wanted to put his feet up and take a nap.

The phone was ringing when he got home. He ran to pick it up, half-hopeful and half-scared it might be her, but the person on the other end was a stranger.

"Sorry to bother you, sir." The man had a strong New York accent. "My name is Emmett Carlyle. I'm looking for Mr. Sam Harms, who had a brother named Walter Harms."

Sam sat down hard on a kitchen chair. "You found him. Carlyle, is that really you?"

"Yeah, Sammy, it's me. Boy, it's been a long time."

"It's good to hear your voice." Sam felt like he was dreaming. "What can I do for you?"

"I've got a funny question for you. I'm not bothering you, am I?"

"Nope," Sam said, ignoring his hunger pangs. "I'm listening."

"Bobby Richards called me up a while back and said there's a guy who wants to write a book about the Neverland Orchestra." Carlyle chuckled. "Ain't that a kick? We couldn't even get gigs back in the day. Now they want to write a book about us. Anyhow, Bobby wanted my opinion on that. Said he wasn't too sure he should talk to the guy."

"Oh, yeah? What did you tell him?"

"I said to ignore him and maybe he'd go away, but then I got the same letter as Bobby. This professor in Iowa wants to write about the Neverland. Well, I got to thinking about how he even knew about us and I remembered the note you sent me about your brother's passing. I was sorry to hear about that, by the way."

"Thanks."

"Anyways, I remembered you live in Iowa too. My wife kept the letter—she keeps everything—so we got it back out and found out this guy lives in your town."

Sam closed his eyes. "Is his name Calvin Jefferson?"

"That's him. So, you know him?"

"I sure do."

"Is he a good guy, Sammy? Should we help him out?"

"Cal's all right. He's a jazz professor at Collison College and he wants to cover the whole subject of small-time dance bands, not just the Neverland. It's up to you if you want to get involved or not, but he's a bona fide professional."

Carlyle hesitated. "Has he interviewed you?"

"No," Sam said. "I don't want to get involved. Lottie's the one who told him about the band. Remember little Charlotte Brown, who played the piano for us?"

Carlyle laughed. "How could I forget? She had more talent than the rest of us put together. Plus, she's the only one of us who ever got famous."

He hesitated. "You know about that, huh?"

"What, that little Charlotte grew up to be Lottie Braun? Come on. I'm dumb but I'm not stupid. We all know, just like we know that for some reason she doesn't want that fact spread around."

"Wait a minute." The conversation was moving too fast for Sam. "Who is this 'we' you keep talking about?"

"Me and Bobby and the other guys from the band," Carlyle said. "There aren't too many of us left, but we keep in touch."

"And none of you ever felt like selling Lottie's story to the gossip rags? Not even in the sixties, when she was in them all the time?"

"Course not." Carlyle sounded disgusted. "She was a cool kid, same as you. We wouldn't want to hurt either one of you. That's why I'm not sure about talking to this guy Jefferson."

"I appreciate that," Sam said. "Lottie will, too, when I tell her."

"So, you two are in touch?"

"Yeah, we're friends."

"No kidding? Gee, I'd love to see her again." Carlyle sounded nostalgic. "You could tell way back then that she was going to have an interesting life. Is she nice? The papers always made her sound like a snob, but I couldn't believe that."

"She's great," Sam said, his thoughts elsewhere. "Say, Carlyle, I understand why you guys don't want to talk about Lottie. But what did you mean when you said you wouldn't want to hurt me? I didn't grow up to be famous."

Carlyle was quiet for a moment. "You remember how it was, Sammy. We all treated you like somebody's stray mutt. All the practical jokes and the name-calling seemed like good fun at the time, but I know you hated it." He cleared his throat. "I wouldn't blame you if you hated us."

"I did," Sam said quietly. "Some of the time, anyway. Do you remember that day in Indianapolis?"

"When we left you at the train station? Yeah, I remember. Johnny and Walt thought that was hysterical."

"And you didn't?"

"I probably laughed at the time." Carlyle sounded regretful. "Looking back, I knew it was a rotten thing to do."

Sam swallowed around a lump in his throat. "What changed your mind?"

"I had kids of my own who didn't always fit in. When they hit high school, they reminded me of you." The Neverland trombonist sighed. "Parson was the cool one, you know. I've often wished I'd followed his lead."

"Me too, Carlyle. Me too."

"He was furious when he found out they'd left you behind."

"I know." The memory made Sam smile. "He came back for me eight hours later. I was still sitting in the station, wondering what to do next. Parson put his arm around my shoulders, bought me a sandwich, and got us both on the next train to St. Louis."

"That sounds like him," Carlyle said. "He was a man worth knowing."

"Yes, he was."

Carlyle sighed. "For what it's worth, Sam, I'm sorry."

Lottie spent the afternoon in her recliner, recovering from the exertion of attending church.

The doorbell woke her up. Nathan sat in his chair on her front porch, accompanied by Thomas Allen.

She blinked and rubbed her eyes with the back of her hand. "How did you get up here?"

Nathan jerked a thumb over his shoulder, where a plywood board covered the steps. "I had the kid build me a ramp." He handed Thomas a folded bill. "Wait in the yard, please."

Amused, Lottie watched Nathan's new chauffeur retreat to a safe distance. "So, Thomas works for you now? How in the world did you manage that?"

"Boys with cars need gas money." Nathan dismissed the subject with an impatient frown. "Did you make an appointment in Iowa City yet?"

"We've been over this, Nathan. It's none of your—"

"None of my business. Yes, I know." He glanced away. "Do you know why I'm in this chair?"

"You already told me." He'd cornered her at the office Christmas party after one too many glasses of eggnog. "It was a ski accident."

"That's not quite true." He glanced at his useless legs. "My fall did a lot of damage, but it took a botched surgery to finish the job."

Lottie swallowed hard. "I'm sorry."

"I didn't come for your pity." He fished a scrap of paper out of his pocket and held it out to her. "I did a little research, and this guy is supposed to be the best in his field. Lucky for you, he's also a Lottie Braun fan."

"How do you know that?"

"I spoke to him on Friday."

"Oh, you did?" Torn between laughter and irritation, she stared at the paper in her hand.

Nathan gripped the wheels of his chair. "Look, I know I'm an interfering old so-and-so. But in this case, I know what I'm talking about." He turned and waved to Thomas, who started up the walk. "Call his office in the morning. They're saving an appointment for you."

Twenty-Three

Monday morning Lottie canceled her appointment with Dr. Ferber and made one with the orthopedist at the University of Iowa Hospitals and Clinics. She called Martha Williams, who said she'd be happy to take her to Iowa City on Thursday. "I've got a cousin who runs a yarn shop up there," she said. "She lost her mother to cancer a couple of months ago. I'll visit with her while you're at the doctor."

Which was the most classically Iowa thing Lottie had heard all day.

Her next phone call wasn't nearly as friendly. Ernest Fleischmann met the news of Lottie's accident with controlled rage. "You can't back out on me." His voice hissed in her ear. "Too many people know you're coming."

"I thought my appearance was supposed to be a surprise."

"Don't be naïve. I had to leak the news to boost attendance. People are falling all over themselves for an invitation to this thing." He cackled with glee. "Our endowment is about to go through the roof."

Lottie bit her lip. "That makes it all the harder to disappoint you, Ernest, but my arm won't be strong enough to perform by the end of June. Can't you postpone my appearance until next year?"

"You'll come in June or else," he roared. "You won't make a fool of me, Miss Braun."

"How do you expect me to entertain your guests?" she said, exasperated. "Card tricks?"

239

"You can whistle "Dixie" for all I care. Just show up."

With that, Ernest Fleischmann hung up in her ear.

Sam had begun to enjoy the building committee. He liked the mental challenge it presented. The new Performing Arts Building was expected to serve many different purposes, while staying within a prescribed budget and allotted space on campus. The committee had spent hours looking for the best contractor to fulfill those requirements. In the process, Sam had gained a certain respect for his fellow committee members.

He liked to think their respect for him had grown, too. For instance, Nathan had stopped picking fights with him in the middle of meetings. And Sam, for his part, had quit calling Nathan 'that fool Bartholomew,' except in his private thoughts.

Tonight, he sat next to his former adversary and opened his notebook. "I hear you talked Lottie into getting a second opinion."

"So, you do check in with your girlfriend once in a while."

Sam didn't correct the man's assumption. "I don't know what you said to her, but I'm glad you got her to change her mind."

The professor looked pleased with himself. "You're not the only one around here who knows how to get things done."

Norm Isley called the meeting to order. "I have good news tonight. We have received a steady stream of donations to the building fund since the night of the concert. As of this afternoon, we stand at seventy percent of our goal."

"Thank you for doing this," Lottie said as Martha guided her car onto the highway Thursday morning.

Martha shrugged. "I don't mind."

Lottie didn't believe her. "I'm sure it's a sacrifice, dropping everything to spend the day ferrying me around."

Martha looked at her, a smile in her eyes. "You're a lovely person to spent time with. Believe me, this is more fun than ironing pillowcases, which is what I'd be doing if I'd stayed home. Are you nervous?"

"Not really." Lottie gazed out the window at the passing fields. "I'm more excited than anything else. I'm hoping this doctor will give me a shorter timeline for recovery."

"I'll pray for that."

"But enough about me." Lottie smiled at her friend. "How are your grandchildren? Are you still taking care of them once a week?"

"I certainly am." Martha glowed when she talked about her grandchildren. "I've been teaching the older ones a few Bible verses. They have wonderful memories."

Lottie relaxed in her seat, glad for a change of subject.

The orthopedist was thin and tan, his light hair self-consciously combed over a growing bald spot. Golf trophies lined the shelf behind his desk. "The diagnosis is correct," he told her after his examination. "You have a severe separation of the acromioclavicular joint in your right shoulder." He looked up from his notes. "You hit the ground hard, Miss Braun."

She wrinkled her nose. "I'm aware of that. Will I need surgery, doctor?"

He shook his head. "That's certainly one option, but these days we favor a more conservative approach. We'll wait and use surgery only if nothing else relieves your pain. Now, let me see..." He checked his notes again. "This happened nearly two weeks ago, and you have very little swelling around the joint today. That's a good indication that you're ready for physical therapy."

"Already?" She blinked. "That sounds painful."

He smiled, and crow's feet blossomed around his eyes. "We have an excellent team of physical therapists connected with in our clinic. You'll be in safe hands. You can make your first appointment before you leave today."

"How long will I be in treatment?"

"Not more than twelve weeks, I'd say." He shrugged. "It's hard to predict how any one case will go."

Her heart sank. Twelve weeks would take her into July. "Can I play the piano before then?"

"That depends. Do you mean finger exercises or full-on Tchaikovsky concertos?"

She stared at him.

He grinned. "I've seen you in concert, Miss Braun. You bring a lot of athleticism to your performances. If you push yourself too hard too soon, you could re-injure that shoulder. Understand?"

She nodded.

"Good."

"I'll be back to normal after that, though, right?"

He tented his fingers together and looked out the window. "I'm going to level with you. Performing may never feel as free and painless as it did before your injury. But technically, after a full course of physical therapy, you should be healed."

When Lottie got in the car to go home, Martha wasted no time in asking, "How did it go?"

"Pretty well. No surgery. I start physical therapy on Monday."

Martha glanced at her. "Will you need me to drive?"

"The doctor released me to drive right away. He seemed surprised that I was still wearing a sling all day."

"That's good."

"I guess so." Lottie turned her face to the window. "He couldn't guarantee a complete recovery, though. He said I might always deal with a certain level of pain."

"What a shame." Martha sounded sympathetic. "Our bodies find all kinds of ways to let us down."

Sam watched Lottie take a sip of coffee and set down the cup, her expression woebegone. "Twelve weeks doesn't sound too bad," he said cautiously, "compared to the six months Dr. Ferber gave you."

"I don't know, Sam. I guess I was expecting a miracle. I wanted this guy to promise he could fix me up better than new by next week."

Miracles were rare things in his experience. "He said you'd get to perform again, right?"

"With a certain level of pain, probably." She looked up with a frustrated groan. "Sorry. I'm whining."

He studied her downcast face in silence. Something else was bothering her. He could feel it. "What's your worst-case scenario?"

Her eyebrows drew together. "My what?"

"It's a question I ask myself when I'm making business decisions. In your mind, what's the worst thing that might happen in relation to your arm?" He warmed to his topic. "Is it the risk of re-injury? Or chronic pain? Or—or—" He cast about in his mind for more possibilities.

"I probably won't play like I used to," she blurted. "Pain or fear will most likely keep me from attacking the notes. My worst-case scenario is that people will come to my concerts and leave disappointed. I'll be a has-been." Her gaze flickered up to his face and back down again. "That's it. Pretty shallow, huh?"

"Change is scary, especially when you didn't choose it." He caught her gaze and held it. "Right now, you're facing the end of your entire way of life. But at this point, you don't know what's going to happen. A year from now, you'll probably be just fine."

Her blue eyes filled with tears. "But what if I'm not?"

He reached across the table and took her hand. "Then God has another plan."

Twenty-Four

Sam found himself thinking about Lottie's situation at odd moments. Her fear of becoming irrelevant made him sad. She seemed to believe no one would care about her if she couldn't play the piano. If only she'd heard the way Carlyle talked about her—a cool kid—maybe she'd think differently.

Something held him back from telling her about Carlyle. He wanted to think it was concern for Lottie's feelings. She was going through a personal crisis right now. He felt selfish talking about himself.

Deep down he knew his hesitation had nothing to do with Lottie. Carlyle's phone call had eased Sam's mind like nothing else in years. He was afraid he'd diminish its power if he told someone else about it. Even if that someone was Lottie.

He was thinking about the matter on Saturday morning as he loaded his truck to go to Thomas Allen's house. Thomas had proven to be a hard worker. Sam was ready to hand the car keys over to him, but first the kid needed a lesson or two in general maintenance. Good thing he'd bought that crate of oil back in January. It would work for today's lesson.

He stowed the crate and a set of car ramps in the back of the truck and headed over to see Thomas. The kid met him in the alley in work clothes, and Sam handed him a drip rag. "You want to stay as clean as possible," he said. "No sense ruining your clothes if you don't have to."

Thomas gave him a businesslike nod. "Yes, sir. Where do we start?"

Sam lifted the ramps out of the truck and set them on the gravel.

"First we pull the car out of the garage and set her up on these."

"Cool." The boy's smile was reserved, his eyes alert.

In the end, Sam didn't know who enjoyed the morning more: Thomas, or himself. It felt good to pass his skills on to this smart young man who liked the attention even if he didn't want to show it. Sam's sons had outgrown these lessons long ago. He was proud of their self-sufficiency, but sometimes he missed the old days.

When the oil was fully drained and a new filter installed, Sam sent Thomas for the crate of oil. He brought it back with a doubtful look on his face. "The cans look pretty old. Are you sure they're okay to use?"

Sam nodded. "I bought them at an auction a while back. They're dusty because they were in somebody's barn." He pulled a metal tool out of his box. "Use this key to take the lids off."

After they finished the job, Sam let Thomas back the car off the ramps and put it away. The boy emerged from the garage, wiping his hands on his drip rag. The satisfaction in his face was good to see. "One more month and she's mine."

"I've been thinking about that," Sam said. "You've been working pretty hard, Tom. How would you like to take possession a little early?"

The boy's eyes lit up. "Sure. When did you have in mind?"

"Does today work for you?"

For once, Thomas forgot to be cool. "Wow. Really? Sure!" He shoved the bangs off his forehead with an agitated hand. "I've got to tell my mom."

Sam couldn't hide a grin as the kid ran for home. He couldn't re-member when he'd enjoyed a day more.

He stacked the ramps and lifted them into the back of the truck. Time to clean up his tools and see if Lottie might want to go get lunch.

The last thing he picked up was the empty crate. With its weathered boards and antique construction, he still hoped to keep it for some future project, provided he could get rid of the reek of motor oil. The dirty plywood board that lined the bottom seemed to be the source of the odor, so he pulled it out and walked it over to the Allens' trash can. When he returned, he raised his eyebrows. "What's this?"

An old wooden cigar box lay in the bottom of the crate, hidden until now by the plywood board. Sam pulled it out and traced with one finger the fancy Spanish words burned into the top. He hadn't seen a box like this in years. The faint scent of tobacco reached his nose when he opened the lid.

There wasn't much inside. Two black and white pictures and a program from a concert lay in the bottom. A gold crucifix, the plainest he'd ever seen, slid around on top of them. The only other item was an oval-shaped medallion hanging from a safety pin. It bore the image of a woman and the words, "Saint Monica, Pray for Us."

He picked up the photos. The first showed a young farm family from fifty years ago or more. The second was a formal portrait of a young man Sam recognized. He flipped it over, and the words on the back, inked in sloping cursive, sent an arrow through his heart: Our Johnny. Bring him home. Pray for us, Saint Monica.

All morning Lottie kept an eye on the oil change from her kitchen window. She loved the professional way Sam carried out the lesson, and Thomas's respectful attention to every word he said. Sam Harms was a living example of the Bible's command to love thy neighbor.

She planned to tell him so after the lesson was finished, but he went home before she could. It was odd. One minute he and Thomas were standing next to Bessie, surrounded by tools, and the next the alley was empty. She didn't know what to make of it.

The doorbell rang while she was mulling it over. Rhonda Kennedy stood on the front porch, looking apologetic. "I was in the neighborhood, so I thought I'd pick up my lasagna pan. If you're done with it, that is."

Lottie hesitated. She remembered just enough about small-town manners to know she should wash the pan before giving it back. "Come in," she said finally. "Why don't you have a seat on the couch while I get it?"

She hurried to the kitchen, plugged the sink, and turned on the faucet. "Hurry up," she murmured to the stream of water. "Heat up already."

"I don't expect you to wash it. Not with your arm in that sling."

Lottie turned to find Rhonda in the doorway. "I should, though."

"I know what to do." Rhonda took the dishcloth out of Lottie's hand. "I'll wash it. That way you can feel better about giving it back clean." Without further discussion, she picked up the dirty pan and put it in the water.

Lottie had no choice but to stand and watch while her colleague washed, not just the lasagna pan, but all the dirty dishes on the counter. "Thanks," she muttered.

"No problem." Rhonda glanced over her shoulder at Lottie. "Have you had time to take a look at my doctoral thesis?"

"I—No. To be honest, I haven't looked at it."

Rhonda turned back to the dishes. "I figured you wouldn't."

"You did?"

She nodded. "Your face said it all when I gave it to you."

"Oh." A flush of embarrassment crawled over Lottie's skin.

"I've come to expect that reaction." Rhonda sounded philosophical. "I know what my colleagues think of me. I'm silly and over-emotional, and I talk too much. Why would you take my research seriously?"

"I—We—" Lottie searched for the words to refute this charge, but it was true. They both knew it. "Rhonda, I'm sorry."

"It's all right." Rhonda unplugged the sink and reached for a hand towel. "I've always been a little out of step with the world. I don't let it get to me."

"That's something we have in common," Lottie said quickly. "I've always been out of step with the world, too."

Rhonda gave her a tolerant smile. "Yes, but you're beautiful and out of step. I'm—not. It makes all the difference, you know."

Lottie stared at her in dismay.

"Anyway." Rhonda hung up the towel. "I didn't come here to call you on the carpet. I came to talk to you about my area of expertise. I have collected some wonderful compositions written exclusively for the left hand. Most of them are easily as difficult and complex as any-thing written for both hands. I believe I'm in a position to do you some good, and I won't let you dismiss that."

Lottie drew a deep breath. "The truth is, I don't want to learn them. My style—my art, if you will—involves both hands."

"That's what every pianist thinks until they get hurt. How else do you think this repertoire came to be? A proficient, sometimes brilliant, pianist loses the use of his right hand but doesn't want to stop performing."

"But my injury is temporary," Lottie said firmly. "My arm is going to heal."

"Are you sure?" Rhonda sounded interested. "Has the doctor given you a written guarantee on that?"

Lottie stared at her for a long moment. "No," she said finally.

"How long does he estimate your recovery will take?"

"Twelve weeks."

Rhonda nodded, her gaze thoughtful. "So, you'll only be able to play piano with your left hand for three solid months? Sounds dull."

Lottie couldn't suppress a smile. "You really care about this."

Rhonda's face transformed. "Yes, I do. Where is the book I gave you? Won't you look at it with me?"

Lottie let out a small sigh and led the way to the music room. "I guess I've got nothing to lose."

Two hours later she looked up from sight-reading a Scriabin nocturne for the left hand. "You're right," she said. "The music is wonderful."

Rhonda beamed with pleasure. "When played well, these pieces sound like they were written for both hands."

"Can you teach me how to play them well?"

Rhonda's round face turned pink with pleasure. "I'd love to try. When I was doing my research, I met a man who lost his right arm in World War II. He was a self-taught pianist, and he'd learned a few techniques that brought a lot of precision to his performance."

Lottie gave her guest a puzzled look. "There's one thing I don't understand. You've got the use of both your hands, so how did you get interested in this subject?"

Rhonda shrugged. "I don't have a personal reason. I had to do a report on a pianist named Paul Wittgenstein in a high school music class.

Wittgenstein was from a fabulously wealthy European family, and he was on his way to a career as a concert pianist before World War I. Wittgenstein's right hand was amputated during the war, but he did not want to give up playing. After the war he discovered the existing body of work for left hand alone, but it wasn't difficult enough, so he commissioned dozens of compositions for left hand alone. His determination impressed me, and my interest grew from there."

Lottie gazed at her fellow professor with new respect. "Thank you for being persistent about this."

"You're worth it."

Twenty-Five

Monday morning Sam called the auction company and requested the phone number for the Higginbottom family. "I found some mementos they might want back," he told the girl on the phone.

"Better act fast," she advised. "I believe the only surviving member of the family is moving to Florida soon."

"The moving truck comes tomorrow," Maria Higginbottom Wheeler confirmed when Sam reached her a few minutes later. "We're at the house today, getting ready for it. Can you stop by this afternoon around five?"

Sam found the little white frame house in Columbus Junction without any trouble. "Sorry about all the boxes," Maria said as she led the way to the living room. "Good thing we couldn't pack the couch. Have a seat."

He sat at the edge of the royal blue cushion and looked at the woman next to him. She was the opposite of Johnny for looks, a short, plump, square-jawed woman with thick brown hair. The Johnny he remembered was tall, blond, and skinny. Of course, memories could trick a person, especially over a span of forty years. "You're going to Florida?"

She nodded. "My husband doesn't like winter. Never has. Now that Mom and Dad are both gone, we're free to live wherever we want."

"I'm glad I caught you before you left." Sam held out the cigar box. "I found some of your mother's personal effects."

251

She took the box and held it a moment, testing its weight. "Where did you say you found it?"

"At the bottom of a crate of motor oil."

"That's a strange hiding place for my mother."

He gave her a half-smile. "It must be important."

Setting the box on her knees, Maria opened the lid and picked up the contents one by one, first the crucifix, next the medallion, then each photo.

Sam pointed to the picture of Johnny. "There's writing on the back of that one."

She flipped it over and stared at the words. "These things weren't Mother's." She looked up, her eyes bright with feeling. "They were Dad's."

"How do you know?"

She picked up the medallion by its safety pin. "Dad wore this pinned to the inside of his coat. I used to unpin it when I did his laundry after Mom passed. That's his handwriting on the photo, too."

"Who's Saint Monica?" he asked.

"She's the patron saint of abused wives and wayward children." She darted a glance in Sam's direction. "I guess I thought Dad was praying for me all those years. I married a real stinker the first time around."

Sam didn't know what to say. The cigar box seemed to have touched a nerve.

"I'm glad to know he was thinking of Johnny, too," she said softly. "He must have regretted the last fight they had." She looked up, as though she'd just remembered she had a visitor. "Look at me, running my mouth about someone you didn't even know."

"I knew your brother," he blurted.

She brightened. "You did?"

"I played in his band way back when I was a kid."

"Did you keep in touch?"

He shook his head. "He was really my older brother's friend."

Her face went slack. "Too bad. I wish there was some way to ship this stuff to him. He deserves to know Dad kept this stuff."

"I have an idea." For the life of him, Sam didn't know why he was being so helpful. "I know a guy who's trying to find the men from the Neverland Orchestra for a book he's writing. I can talk to him. See if he's found your brother."

"Yeah?" She gave him a tentative smile. "Listen, if I keep this stuff, I'm sure to lose it in the move. Would you mind having your friend mail it off if he finds my brother? I'll pay for postage." A new thought occurred to her. "You came to the auction with Lottie Braun, didn't you?"

He nodded.

"I've got something for her." She left the room and returned with an old letter. "I found this stuck behind a baseboard the last time I walked through the farmhouse. I gave Miss Braun the other letters from Johnny. I'd like her to have this one, too."

The next thing he knew Sam was back on the road with the letter and the box still in his possession. He had no blessed idea what had come over him in that house. Now he'd made a commitment he was honor-bound to keep.

Lottie gazed across the kitchen table at Sam. The cigar box lay open between them, its precious contents neatly arranged inside. She'd listened to his story and examined the Saint Monica medal, but she was having some trouble with his conclusion. "What do you mean we have to find Johnny?"

"To give him back his stuff. This box." Sam nodded at the windowsill. "His train. All of it. He needs to know his family loved him."

She frowned. "You hate Johnny."

"I did."

"What changed?"

A slow smile spread over his face. "I forgave him."

For the first time she noticed the peace in his eyes. "Ah, forgiveness." She smiled. "That's where all the power is."

"I know. I can't believe I didn't do it sooner."

"Why did you do it now, Sam?"

He sat back, his shoulders relaxed for the first time since he arrived. "A week ago, I got a phone call from Emmet Carlyle."

Lottie was dumbfounded. "You talked to Carlyle? Why didn't you tell me?"

"I wasn't ready," he said simply. "We had quite a conversation. He acknowledged the rotten things the guys did to me." A look of amazement crossed Sam's face. "Things I didn't think anyone else remembered. Then he apologized."

Lottie's heart melted for the wounded boy Sam had been at fourteen. "What did you do?"

"I forgave him on the spot." His face lit up with a wondering smile. "It felt like a weight dropped from my shoulders. All at once those memories didn't hurt anymore." He shrugged. "It was an easy decision to forgive all the other guys, too."

She studied his face for a moment. "You've been a Christian a long time. Why didn't you forgive those guys a long time ago?"

"I've been wondering the same thing," he said. "I can't believe how free I feel."

She smiled. "So, you want to find Johnny?"

"Will you help me?"

Her gaze fell to the contents of the box, proof that even a deeply flawed young man like Johnny was loved by someone. Lottie had no personal desire to see him again, but if Sam was determined to go on this errand of mercy, she would not let him go alone.

She looked up and smiled at her dearest friend. "I'm in."

"Thanks for meeting me," Sam told Cal Jefferson as the host seated them at Tavern on the Square. "Lottie will be along in a few minutes."

"This is a real surprise," Cal said. "I thought the Neverland project was dead."

Sam shrugged. "We changed our minds. Are you still interested in finding more of the band members?"

"Sure."

Sam passed a manila envelope across the table. "This should help."

Cal glanced at the old group photo and pushed it back to Sam. "Thanks anyway, but I already got one of these from Lottie."

"Not like this one." Sam flipped the picture over and showed him the addresses on the back. "My brother kept up with the guys for years. They sent each other Christmas cards, believe it or not."

The jazz professor's face took on new hope. "Wow. This will help a lot."

Sam wasn't listening. He was watching Lottie cross the dining room.

"Sorry I'm late," she said as the host held out her chair. "What did I miss?"

"I was just about to tell Cal about my talk with Carlyle." He turned to the jazz professor. "He called me up a week ago. He'd gotten your letter about the Neverland project, and wanted to know if you were on the up and up. Before that we hadn't spoken in forty years."

Cal's eyes grew round. "What did you tell him?"

"I said you were trustworthy and good at your job." Sam raised an eyebrow. "You are, aren't you?"

"I like to think I am." Cal shook his head. "Though you certainly couldn't tell it from the way I've handled this project."

Lottie smiled. "You've done fine. It just isn't as simple as you expected it to be."

Cal looked from one to the other. "I don't suppose you'd be willing to elaborate on that."

Sam looked at Lottie, who nodded. "Sure, Cal. We'll help you all we can."

"Great." The jazz professor pulled a little notebook out of his breast pocket. "Let's start at the beginning. Sam, why did your brother start the Neverland in the first place?"

Sam was surprised at how detached he felt as he told the Neverland's story. Before his talk with Carlyle, he could hardly think about the band without feeling his blood pressure rise. Now he felt a rising affection for the enterprising young musicians who had joined together to form a Big Band orchestra.

Walt, Johnny, and the rest were flesh-and-blood human beings, not the comic book villains he'd made them in his mind. They hadn't treated him well. That much was true. But that was a small detail compared to the experiences, abilities, and faults each man contributed to the group as a whole. Sam did his best to pay tribute to the whole productive mess that was the Neverland Orchestra.

For the most part Lottie listened quietly, adding one or two clarifying comments when she needed to. Cal had interviewed her months ago when the whole project began. This was Sam's turn to talk.

He didn't skimp on Lottie's part in the story. Her arrival had been providential, and her gift had given the band the box office draw they so badly needed. Sure, she'd been looked on as something of a novelty act, but only until she started to play. Once she got going, everyone within earshot knew little Charlotte Brown was the real deal.

When Sam finished talking, Cal sat back in his seat with a big smile. "I believe we have a book," he said. "You two have dropped it right in my lap."

"You're going to do a fantastic job." Lottie beamed at her coworker. "I'm excited to watch it all unfold."

Cal nodded. "I'll contact the men on this list immediately."

"Start with Carlyle. He can help pave the way with the other guys." Sam pointed at the photo. "Johnny's the only one I don't have information for, but somebody else probably does. When you find him, could you pass his address on to me?"

"Sure." Cal stuck the notebook back in his pocket. "By the way, Sam, do you still play the drums?"

The question caught him off-guard. "No," he said too quickly. "I gave that up years ago."

Across the table, Lottie looked thoughtful. "I'll bet you could take it up again if you wanted to."

He glanced away. The woman always saw too much.

Twenty-Six

The last few weeks of April scurried past. Lottie returned to work and was quickly absorbed in the end-of-year activities of a busy college. True to her word, Rhonda met with her regularly to coach her in music for left hand alone. As Lottie's proficiency grew so did her confidence, along with her respect for her fellow piano professor.

One afternoon Rhonda brought a left-hand-only composition of her own for Lottie to try. "It was part of my doctoral work," she said with a self-effacing shrug. "I thought you might be interested."

Lottie played the first page of the lively dance and stopped. "This is very good."

Rhonda blushed. "I've always liked the challenge of writing music. This was a lot of fun to create."

Lottie took the piece home to work on. "Who knows?" she told Rhonda. "Maybe someday I'll be able to perform it in public." But not without a great deal more practice.

Twice a week she drove all the way to Iowa City for physical therapy, and slowly—slowly—she began to see progress with her shoulder. It still ached so keenly it kept her awake at night, but her strength and range of motion were growing.

Sometimes Sam went along for the ride. On those days the hour and a half trip seemed like minutes. Now that he was ready to talk about the Neverland, they could discuss it for hours.

They talked about other things too, like Sam's mixed feelings about

Jason being gone, and Lottie's fears about her injured arm.

Once when the conversation turned to Sam's family, Lottie made a gentle observation. "Everyone knows you love your kids," she said. "But it seems to me you'd love them a little bit more if they moved home to Collison."

She expected him to share the joke, but he didn't laugh. "I could never love my kids better than I do right now," he said. "That would be like God loving me more or less based on whether I do the right thing." He shook his head. "Love shouldn't be conditional."

His answer surprised and warmed her.

Lottie talked on the phone with Carlyle. He was a retired cop and devoted family man, and his voice sounded just the same as she remembered.

She spoke with Bobby Richards, too. Bobby had settled in L.A. and continued to play his trombone in local bands until the rock and roll revolution made them obsolete. He now owned a night club and banquet facility. "I book a lot of wedding receptions," Bobby told her. "It's not exciting, but it pays the rent. If you're ever in the area, you should stop by."

"I'll be in L.A. at the end of June. I'd love to see the place."

"Sure thing." Bobby sounded pleased. "I'll get in touch with the guys who live in the area. Maybe they'll want to join us for a drink."

"I'll bring Sam Harms," she said, then made the convoluted explanation as to why she and Sam would be in California at the same time.

Johnny alone remained elusive. No matter how Cal tried, he could not find the right John Columbus in greater Los Angeles. None of the band members knew where he was. Someone finally remembered he'd gotten married in the '60s and moved out of the area, but he didn't know where Johnny had gone.

Patti and Mitch came home the first weekend in May. They stayed with Sam but drove over to visit Lottie on Saturday morning. They found her working in the garden patch behind the garage. "I planted some lettuce and carrots," she said. "Marmalade has been helping keep the rabbits out, so they might actually grow."

"You look so much better than you did a month ago," Patti said. "I was pretty worried."

Lottie hugged her favorite niece. "I couldn't have made it without your help. You were a lifesaver that weekend."

Mitchell put his arm around his wife's shoulders. "That's my girl," he said proudly. "She runs a tight ship."

"Where have you kids been hiding lately?" Ed Williams waved from across the fence.

Mitch and Patti exchanged an unreadable glance. "Working," Patti said. "That's what keeps a roof over our heads."

Ed laughed. "Let me know if you'd like a little change of pace, Mitch. I've still got an opening in my office, and roofs come cheaper around here."

Ed strolled back inside, and Mitchell turned to Lottie. "Is he always home on Saturday mornings?"

"Unless he and Martha drive over to see their grandkids."

The kids had things to do while they were in town, so they left Sarah with Lottie during nap time. When the child woke up, Lottie entertained her at the piano, playing little tunes and letting her mash the keys with her tiny fingers. "I think she's going to be musical," Lottie said when Sarah's parents came home. "She seems to have an aptitude for it."

Patti looked dubious. "One musical genius is enough for any family, don't you think?"

Sunday morning Lottie's heart was full as she sat between Sam and Mitchell at church. Patti and Sarah filled out the pew, and the child was as well-behaved as any just-turned-two-year-old could be. Lottie's heart swelled with gratitude at the little family that by God's grace now belonged to her.

She glanced at Sam and found him gazing at his granddaughter. He caught her eye and they shared a smile of mutual pride.

Sam could live for days on a moment of shared understanding like that one. Sometimes the feeling that ran between him and Lottie seemed so strong it was all he could do to keep his distance from her. Fear of failure kept him strong, though. He'd rather hold his peace and remain her friend than tell her he loved her and be banished forever.

He was thinking the situation through for the thousandth time while he worked at his workbench Sunday afternoon. The sun had dipped low in the sky, its rays stretching across the garage floor to where Sam stood, sanding a pine board to use in a bookcase.

Mitch and Patti should be nearly home by now. They'd left right after lunch to make the four-hour drive, though neither one looked happy to go. Something was wrong. Sam could feel it in his bones. He should mention it to Lottie when they went to Iowa City this week. She'd probably know more about it than he did.

"Hey, Sam." Cal Jefferson stood in the doorway. "Mind if I join you for a minute?"

"Sure." Sam set his project on the workbench. "What can I do for you?"

"I got a letter from your friend Carlyle yesterday." Cal pulled something out of his pocket. "He sent me this picture."

Sam examined the black and white photo under the workbench light. A skinny boy in a black suit and bow tie glared at the camera from behind a massive drum set. "That's me, all right," he said, handing it back. "I thought that scowl looked cool."

"Carlyle says you were pretty talented."

"That's nice of him."

Cal nodded at something on the other side of the workbench. "Are those your sticks?"

Sam turned, and felt a stab of irritation. "I meant to put those things away."

"So you do still play."

"Only for my own enjoyment."

"A lot of the guys have told me that." Cal pulled up the extra shop stool and sat down. "I've got an idea I want to try out on you." His face took on its customary intensity. "Just once I'd like to hear the Neverland Orchestra play. Do you think there's any chance we could make that happen?"

"We could never recreate the old sound. Not with the missing instruments and the fact that most of us haven't played in years."

"I'll bet there's something left, some echo of the way it used to be. I've been wondering how expensive it would be to bring all the band members to the college for a weekend. What do you think?"

Sam put down his sandpaper and stared at the jazz professor. "I think you're crazy. If I've learned one thing from being on the building committee, it's that money is tight at Collison College. There's no way they'll let you put a Neverland reunion in your budget."

Cal's smile faded. "I guess you're right."

"Instead of bringing the guys here, why don't you fly to L.A. at the end of June and meet them there? That's what Lottie and I are planning to do." He smiled at Cal's dumbstruck look. "You can ask all your questions and listen to them swap stories. It'll be a gold mine of information."

"Would you mind?" Cal said. "Teresa and I would love to be there, but not if we'd be intruding."

"You're the one who made this reunion possible. I think you've earned a place at the table."

"Are they bringing their instruments?"

"They probably would if you asked them to."

Cal was getting excited. "I'll give Bobby a call tomorrow and see if he can track down a piano and a drum set. Just make sure you pack those sticks."

Sam laughed. "I'm not going to play."

Cal flashed him a grin. "I think you'd better. Where would the band be without its ace drummer?"

To Lottie's amazement, Patti and Mitchell came home the following weekend, too. "Is everything all right?" she asked them. "This is two weeks in a row."

"Too much?" Patti asked with a laugh.

"Never," Lottie said. "I'm just concerned."

"Lay your fears to rest." Patti's smile was mysterious. "Things are better now than they've been in a long time."

After church on Sunday, Patti caught Lottie's arm. "Ed and Martha have invited us all to lunch. Is that okay?"

The suppressed excitement in her voice caught Lottie's attention. "Why?"

"Ed and Mitch have a little announcement to make." Patti broke into a big smile. "Mitch is joining his practice."

"Yahoo!" Lottie threw her arms around her niece's neck. "It's about time you guys came home." She pulled back as a thought occurred to her. "Are you really all right with this? Any regrets?"

"I couldn't be happier." Patti's voice was emphatic. "I'm thinking about re-opening the tailor's shop downtown."

Lottie shook her head. "I have a better idea. Come work for me."

"Are you serious?"

"The pay is good, and the hours can be flexible. Heaven knows I could use your help."

Patti's face lit up. "That sounds perfect."

"So, Patti is your new assistant?" Miranda held the receiver between her ear and her shoulder while she started dinner. "That's exciting."

"I'm over the moon about it," Lottie said. "The only person who's happier is Sam. He was lonely without either of his sons around."

Miranda ignored that last comment. Lottie didn't mean to touch a sore spot. "I need details," she said instead. "When are they moving?"

"They both have to give two weeks' notice before they quit, so they're moving the first of June."

"Have they found a place to live?" Miranda asked, thinking of her own struggle when she moved to Collison.

"You know how it is," Lottie said wryly. "Ed knows a real estate agent who just listed a little house south of town. He let Patti and Mitch look at it before it officially went on the market. So yeah, they have a place."

Miranda smiled. "Sounds like Collison, all right." She didn't mind it so much now that she was back in her own community. "This won't stop Mitch and Patti from coming to the wedding, will it?"

"No, we'll all be there," Lottie said happily. "How's the planning going?"

Miranda smiled. "We've got things pretty squared away."

Zac walked into the kitchen dressed for work and pointed at the phone. "Can you get off? I need to make a call."

"I have to go," she told Lottie. They said their good-byes and she turned to Zac. "What's going on?"

"I forgot I'm subbing for Ian's oldies show, and I'm late for work. I need to call the station."

"That reminds me," Miranda said, reaching for the pile of wedding invitations on the table. "Give Ian his wedding invitation."

Twenty-Seven

Mitchell and Patti moved into their bungalow on the first of June. Once the boxes were unpacked and the curtains hung, Patti plunged into her duties as Lottie's new assistant. The school year was over and Lottie had very few administrative needs, but Patti was determined to earn her paycheck. Consequently she set out to organize every last corner of Lottie's home and office.

Sarah came to work with her mama every day. The little girl kept Lottie entertained while Patti rearranged all the furniture. Lottie showed Sarah how to dig in the garden dirt and plant seeds, and let her make lots of noise on the piano.

To her surprise, Lottie missed running her own errands. "I'll take care of my dry cleaning from now on," she told Patti after the first week. "I feel silly having you do it."

Patti laughed out loud at that. "But this is how you always did things, Aunt Lottie. Are you telling me you've changed?"

Lottie gave her a lofty smile. "Why, yes. I believe I have."

"Speaking of the dry cleaner, I picked up that long black dress with all the beads."

"Good. I'm taking it to California."

Patti looked surprised. "Are you sure you want to do that? It's awfully formal."

Lottie raised her eyebrows. "There's nothing wrong with formal in my line of work. That's the dress I always perform in."

"But you're going to Los Angeles, where it's sunny and hot every day. Won't you be too warm?"

"So now you're my wardrobe consultant?"

Patti leaned over and kissed her cheek. "Only if you want me to be. Seriously, there's nothing wrong with owning more than one fancy dress. This house has gigantic closets. I wouldn't blame you if you filled them all with clothes."

The conversation stayed with Lottie all day long. At bedtime she took the black dress from the closet and pulled it over her head. Standing in front of the full-length mirror, she considered her reflection.

Patti was right. It was heavy and formal, but Lottie was used to it. She didn't want to go to the trouble of finding a new one.

She leaned toward the mirror. Something was different. The scooped neckline showed a fair amount of both shoulders, and they no longer matched. The line of her left shoulder sloped gently from neck to arm, but on the right the end of her collarbone stuck up from the injury, like a little ski jump under the skin. The way the dress was cut accentuated the difference.

Maybe it was time to go shopping.

The following Thursday Lottie's new assistant drove her to Cedar Rapids to shop for a California-worthy wardrobe. "It's no Michigan Avenue," Patti said as they walked into the double-decker mall. "You won't have much to choose from here."

Lottie gazed around the busy shopping center. "I'm sure we'll find something worth wearing."

They were both right. The selection of Patti-approved dresses was limited, but Lottie still managed to buy several lovely things. They left at noon with enough purchases to triple Lottie's current wardrobe. "That was fun," Patti said with a satisfied grin. "I like dressing you."

Lottie glanced at her watch. "Let's find some lunch and head for Iowa City. I need to be at physical therapy by two o'clock."

"How many more appointments do you have after this?" Patti asked as they drove south out of Cedar Rapids.

"I've got two next week and then I'm done."

"Did the therapy do its job? Are you all better?"

"Yes, I think so," Lottie said slowly. "I'm dying to play with both hands again."

Patti raised her eyebrows. "But…"

Her perception surprised Lottie. "I'm a little scared to find out what 'all better' really means. Will I be able to play like I used to, or will I fall a little bit short from now on?"

"You won't fall short," Patti said. "Not in any way that matters."

"I think we're finished here," the physical therapist said at the end of Lottie's appointment.

She smiled and reached for her bag. "I'll see you next week then."

He smiled and shook his head. "No, I mean you're all done. We've taken you as far as we possibly can."

Her mind went blank. "Now? How do you know?"

"We've been measuring your strength and range of motion." He held up his clipboard for her to see. "You're back in the normal range on both counts. Time to go home and get on with your life."

"That's it? I can do anything?"

The young man chuckled. "Stay off ladders. And I wouldn't recommend swinging on the monkey bars."

"But I still have some pain."

"And you probably always will." He held her gaze, his face serious. "People often develop a bit of arthritis after an injury like yours. It hurts, but it shouldn't stop you from being active." He gave her shoulder a gentle pat. "Go home, play the piano, and relax. You deserve it."

After the first shock of the news wore off, Lottie felt like she was walking on air. "They've discharged me," she said when Patti picked her up. "That was my last appointment."

"You're kidding. That's awesome! We should celebrate."

Lottie shook her head. "Take me home. I've got a piano to play."

Patti threw the car into gear and pulled away from the curb. "You're the boss."

Lottie spared a grateful thought to the police officers who didn't cross their path as they sped back to Collison. They covered the distance in record time. Patti helped carry the shopping bags to the house, then left for the day. "I know you want to be alone with your piano," she said with a smile.

Lottie didn't bother to deny it. As soon as she was alone, she hurried to the piano room. It lay hot and still in the late afternoon sunshine, so she flung open the french doors to catch the breeze before approaching her Steinway.

She seated herself, raised both hands, and froze. Her shoulder ached already, and she hadn't played a note.

She dropped her hands in her lap and frowned. Maybe she should start with her left hand alone. Then, when she worked her courage up, she'd add the right.

Rhonda had taught her to rest her right hand on the bench when she played with her left hand alone. She did that now and played a few measures of Scriabin's *Nocturne No. 9*. She'd practiced the nocturne constantly until it was secure in her memory. The ebb and flow of melody pleased her, as did the way Scriabin used the whole keyboard. She took her time, giving it all the attention it deserved, but deep down she felt like a coward.

This was silly. Her dearest wish had been granted. She'd been released to use her right hand. Anyone else would have gotten on with it already. What exactly was holding her back?

When the piece ended, Lottie dropped her hands in her lap and bowed her head. "Lord, what if I can't do this?" That was the crux of the matter. "What if it hurts too much, or I reinjure myself, or I just don't sound the same?" Her worst fears tumbled out into the stillness of the room. "Who am I if I can't play like I used to?" She fell silent, holding back tears.

The answer came as a still small voice, unexpected and exactly right. *You're my child.*

She looked up. "Your child?" Her voice rang out in the silent room.

My beloved child. The words sang in her mind. *I love you with an everlasting love, no matter what. Remember that.*

"I love you with an everlasting love," she whispered. Martha Williams was teaching that verse to her grandchildren. Now she understood why. The warmth of God's promise wrapped around her like a soft wool sweater.

This time when she placed her hands on the keys, the music seemed to flow from her fingertips of its own accord. Sacred music bubbled up from the depths of her memory: Bach's *Jesu, Joy of Man's Desiring*, followed by an arrangement of Handel's *Messiah* she'd learned at the conservatory.

It hurt to play. She could not deny that. She couldn't possibly use her right hand in Los Angeles next week. But the fear, which was so much worse than physical pain, had left her completely.

Sam heard the music as soon as he got out of the truck. It poured across the lawn through the open french doors, filling the air with joyful, crashing chords. "The Hallelujah Chorus." A funny choice for a warm June evening.

He crossed the lawn at a run.

Lottie sat at the piano, her back to the doors, her entire being focused on the keyboard which sang beneath her hands. Sam stood on the flagstones just outside and watched with rising excitement.

She stopped playing and turned around, her face alight with joy. "I knew you were there," she said.

He stepped over the threshold. "You got your arm back. How does it feel?"

"To tell you the truth, it aches like a son of a gun." Her radiant smile belied the words. "It's not healed yet. But that's okay."

He couldn't seem to stop grinning. "Hearing you play felt like rain after a drought."

She rose to meet him as he crossed the room. "That's pretty poetic for a plain speaker like you, Sam."

It seemed like the most natural thing in the world to slip his arm around her waist. "Lottie Braun, you'd bring out the poetry in a plywood board."

She raised her laughing gaze to his. "Plywood? That's more like it."

He could have stood there forever, drinking in the sight of her, but as she gazed at him with those warm blue eyes, he simply lost his head. With a sigh, he closed the space between them in a kiss so sweet it drew the breath from his body. Best of all, without hesitation she looped her arm around his neck and kissed him back.

When it ended, he said, "I have a confession to make."

She leaned back in his arms, her eyes alert. "Go on."

He took a deep breath and glanced away. "I love you, Lottie. I have for months." When he finally had the guts to look her in the eye, the relief he read there almost undid him.

"Oh, thank goodness," she said softly. "I thought I was the only one."

With a groan he gathered her close.

Much later, they were sitting together on the music room couch, he with his arm around her, she with her head on his shoulder. "We need to get married," he said.

"Married!" She leaned back to look at him. "I just found out you love me. Give me five minutes to get used to that."

He chuckled. "Do you need me to get down on one knee? I still can, you know."

"No." She brushed her fingers across his cheek. "I'll marry you, Sam. The sooner the better."

"How about tonight? I'll bet Bob Summers is still awake."

She smiled and snuggled closer to his chest. "What are you doing Sunday?"

Sunday morning Lottie sat behind Ed and Martha, with Patti and Sarah at her side. She wore one of her new dresses, an ice blue confection with a full skirt. Sam and Mitchell sat across the aisle, handsome in their dark suits.

After the offering, Reverend Summers stepped to pulpit and smiled out at the congregation. "In my years as your pastor, it has been my privilege to celebrate many important moments," he said. "Weddings, baptisms, and even funerals are all part of living as the body of Christ. Today, we have a unique opportunity to celebrate together. We have been asked to witness the bringing together in marriage of Samuel Harms and Lottie Braun." He turned his gaze on the two people in question. "Will the bride and groom please come forward?"

Twenty-Eight

On a warm Los Angeles evening, Sam and Lottie Harms disembarked from a limousine in front of an exclusive venue in the Hollywood hills. "Are you ready for this?" he murmured as they made their way to the entrance.

Lottie, looking splendid in a cream silk dress, nodded. "I've been ready for weeks."

He gave her a faintly worried frown. "Will your arm be all right?"

She squeezed his hand. "It certainly will."

They entered the mansion and were immediately greeted by Ernest Fleischmann, who bore Lottie off in the direction of his most valued guests.

Sam snagged a club soda off a passing tray and made himself at home in a corner of the room. "Better get used to this," he murmured to himself. "My wife is a celebrity."

Last night's party had been much more to his liking. In the banquet room of Bobby Richards' bar and grill, the surviving members of the Neverland Orchestra had gathered to reminisce about the old days. They'd brought photos, programs, train schedules, and other mementos to share, and the stories had continued in an unending stream on into the night. Cal and Teresa had spent the evening with their portable tape recorders, moving from table to table to catch every man's story.

Even Johnny showed up, at least in spirit.

At Jase and Miranda's wedding, they'd been introduced to Ian, a radio DJ with a local Swing program. On a whim Lottie asked him if he'd ever heard of the Neverland Orchestra.

To their amazement, his face lit with recognition. "My friend Johnny Higgins used to tell me about that band. They played the deep South in the 1940s."

"You know Johnny?" she asked.

"I did." Ian looked sad. "He died a few months ago of liver cancer, but his daughter lives here locally."

Sam and Lottie exchanged a questioning glance. "Would you take us to meet her?" Sam asked.

"Sure. Charlotte likes anyone who was a friend of her dad's."

"Charlotte," Lottie murmured, her face alive with pleasure. "What a lovely name."

Ian took them to meet Johnny's daughter the next day. Charlotte Higgins cried when they gave her the cigar box and the train and promised to call her Aunt Maria (whom she'd heard about but never met) as soon as possible.

Lottie pulled the yellowed envelope out of the box. "Your dad wrote this letter to my sister Helen, but it's never been opened."

"Do you want to read it?" Charlotte asked.

Lottie seemed taken aback. "I don't want to violate his privacy."

Johnny's daughter shrugged. "It's survived this long. Seems like someone should read it."

Reluctantly Lottie opened the envelope and unfolded the letter inside. "August 14, 1945," she began. "Dear Helen, I'm writing this letter to tell you I'm sorry. In the year since I last saw you, I've grown up a lot. I've come to understand that my actions toward you were unforgivable. I now know that you and I were never meant to be. I was wrong to ever force the issue.

"Please accept my sinsere apology. Give my best to Lottie and baby Billy.

"Yours respectfully,

"Johnny"

Lottie had tears in her eyes when she looked up from the page. "Thank you for this. You've just restored my faith in your dad."

Sam held his wife's hand all the way back to the hotel.

Charlotte drove to Los Angeles for the reunion and took her absent father's place on trumpet. That left an opening for conductor, which Cal willingly filled, directing the motley group in a decent rendition of "String of Pearls." Sam even did all right on drums, much to his wife's delight.

Lottie had been magnificent. Not the way she was tonight, all flash and elegance, but the way she was with family. She'd talked and laughed as loud as anyone, and when it was time to play music, she had unself-consciously done the best she could. As usual, she sounded better than any of them, even with only one reliable arm.

He was so proud of her.

Lottie slipped her hand through his. "It's almost time."

He put his arm around her shoulders. "Nervous?"

She shook her head. "I'm ready."

Ernest Fleischmann called the room to order. "Good evening. To-night, I have a wonderful surprise for you. This year we have a legend among us, the undisputed queen of the piano, Miss Lottie Braun."

Flash bulbs went off around the room, leaving Sam with spots in front of his eyes. Lottie let go of his hand and moved to stand beside Ernest Fleischmann. "Hello, everyone," she said. "I am sorry to say I injured my arm a few months ago, falling off a ladder. Tonight, I can only play for you with one hand."

Polite laughter rippled through the crowd.

Lottie gave them a gracious smile. "I will begin with Scriabin's *Nocturne for the Left Hand, opus 9, Number 2*, and conclude my performance with the premier of a composition by a gifted newcomer, Dr. Rhonda Kennedy."

She moved to the grand piano and seated herself before the keyboard. Then, placing her right hand on the bench, Lottie began to play.

Book Club
Discussion Questions

1. In Chapter 2 Lottie buys an old toy train. What is its significance? Have you ever bought something meaningful at a second-hand store or yard sale?

2. Why does Sam drive a "faded blue Plymouth Fury" named Bessie? Did you sympathize with his attachment to her? How did you feel when he finally gave her up?

3. Have you ever named your car? What did you name it and why?

4. Why does Lottie initially decide to accept the L.A. Philharmonic's invitation? How does Lottie's view of that goal change over the course of the story? In your opinion was getting the band back together a good idea?

5. By the last page of the book Lottie's right arm is still not back to full strength. Do you think it ever will be? How do you think her career will change as a result of this injury?

6. How would you describe the changes in Lottie over the course of the story?

7. Miranda has always had trouble fitting in with her parents' expectations. What is Sonia's role in helping her resolve that problem? Have you ever experienced a similar family issue?

8. Jason takes a leap of faith by moving to California. What kinds of challenges might he and Miranda face as they build a life together in San Francisco?

9. What motivates Patti and Mitchell to move home to Collison? Do you feel the same about your hometown? What are the pros and cons of staying where you were raised versus moving away?

10. Weddings play a big part in *Lottie's Freedom*. Whose wedding did you like best?

11. How did you feel when Lottie finally learned what happened to Johnny?

12. Which character is your favorite and why?

JANE M. TUCKER

Jane M. Tucker is a lifelong reader and writer who has a deep love for the art of storytelling. In fact, her favorite job at church is telling Bible stories to children. She's been a dedicated follower of Jesus since she was nine years old, and you can find strong Christian principles throughout her stories. Jane proudly hails from the great state of Kansas and her weekly blog, "Postcards from the Heartland," is about her life in the Midwest. Having lived in Wisconsin, Iowa, and on the Kansas/Missouri line, she has a deep love for the region. Her blog is filled with stories about her micro-travel adventures as she introduces her readers to places even she didn't know existed. Jane lives with her husband and three children in Overland Park, Kansas.

JaneMTucker.com
Facebook.com/JaneMTuckerAuthor
Twitter.com/JaneMTuckerAuth

MORE GREAT BOOKS FROM CROSSRIVERMEDIA.COM

LOTTIE'S GIFT
Jane M. Tucker

She's a little girl with a big gift. Lottie Braun has enjoyed a happy childhood in rural Iowa with her father and older sister. But the quiet, nearly idyllic life she enjoyed ends with tragedy and a secret tears the two sisters apart. Forty years later, Lotttie is a world-class pianist with a celebrated career and an empty personal life. One sleepless night, she allows herself to remember and discovers that memories are difficult to suppress. Will she ever find her way home?

LOTTIE'S HOPE
Jane M. Tucker

After forty years as a world class musician, Lottie has come home to Iowa, where an old home and a new job await. Then the trouble starts. At first she shrugs off the incidents as random petty crimes, but as they increase in intensity, she must face the fact that someone wants to hurt her. Can Lottie sort out her friends and her enemies before it's too late?

SWEPT INTO DESTINY
Catherine Ulrich Brakefield

As the battle between North and South rages, Maggie Gatlan is forced to make a difficult decision. She must choose between her love for the South and her growing feelings for the hardworking and handsome Union soldier Ben McConnell. Was Ben right? Had this Irish immigrant perceived the truth of what God had predestined for America?

POSTMARK FROM THE PAST
Vickie Phelps

In November 1989, Emily Patterson is enjoying a quiet life in west Texas, but emptiness nips at her heart. Then a red envelope appears in her mailbox with no return address and a postmark from 1968. It's a letter from Mark who declares his love for her, but who is Mark? Is someone playing a cruel joke? As Emily seeks to solve the mystery, can she risk her heart to find a miracle in the *Postmark from the Past*?

the Benefit Package

30 days of
God's goodness
from Psalm 103

CROSSRIVER

If you enjoyed this book, will you
consider sharing it with others?

- Please mention the book on Facebook, Twitter, Pinterest, or your blog.

- Recommend this book to your small group, book club, and workplace.

- Head over to Facebook.com/CrossRiverMedia, 'Like' the page and post a comment as to what you enjoyed the most.

- Pick up a copy for someone you know who would be challenged or encouraged by this message.

- Write a review on Amazon.com, BN.com, or Goodreads.com.

- To learn about our latest releases subscribe to our newsletter at www.CrossRiverMedia.com.

www.ingramcontent.com/pod-product-compliance
Lightning Source LLC
Chambersburg PA
CBHW070638260626
47161CB00007B/2755